Marina Anderson is the pseudonym of a British author. Her novels have sold half a million copies worldwide and she is a *Sunday Times* bestseller.

Also by Marina Anderson

Haven of Obedience

Dark Secret

Forbidden Desires

The Discipline

House of Decadence

Legacy of Desire

The Dining Club

Hotel *of* Seduction

MARINA ANDERSON

sphere

SPHERE

First published in Great Britain in 2015 by Sphere

1 3 5 7 9 10 8 6 4 2

A CIP catalogue record for this book
is available from the British Library.

ISBN 978-0-7515-5858-6

Typeset in Sabon by M Rules
Printed and bound in Great Britain by
Clays Ltd, St Ives plc

Papers used by Sphere are from well-managed forests
and other responsible sources.

MIX
Paper from
responsible sources
FSC
www.fsc.org   FSC® C104740

Sphere
An imprint of
Little, Brown Book Group
Carmelite House
50 Victoria Embankment
London EC4Y 0DZ

An Hachette UK Company
www.hachette.co.uk

www.littlebrown.co.uk

Hotel *of* Seduction

Part One

Chapter One

'Grace, she's flirting with Crofts,' whispered Fran, from her seat beside Grace at the back of the rehearsal room. 'Isn't she meant to be repelled by what he's just suggested?'

Grace, whose mind was miles away, quickly stopped checking her watch in the semi-darkness and brought her attention back to the scene in front of her. Fran was right. Emily Kelly, all tousled blonde hair and provocative curves, was most definitely flirting with the silver-haired actor sitting next to her, even though his words were meant to shock and repel her. 'Emily darling, gorgeous as John might be in real life, he is nearly three times your age and his character has just made an outrageous suggestion to you.'

'I know,' replied the young blonde sulkily.

'Well, do you think you could manage to look a little bit shocked? This is a very important moment in the play, and girlish giggles aren't quite how your character is meant to respond.'

'I was playing embarrassed,' explained Emily, pouting prettily. She clearly expected Grace to fall under her spell as easily as young men all over the country had fallen for her in her most recent TV series.

'Right, well, it's nearly four o'clock and I think it's time to call it a day,' said Grace, suppressing a sigh. 'We're all tired, and although I won't be here tomorrow, Fran is going to—'

'I won't be here either,' said Emily. 'I told you that I've got this voice-over to do and you said—'

'Yes, sorry, I forgot. That's fine, it means Fran can concentrate on working with Suzie and John, but by the time you're back on Friday do you think you could get over the embarrassment and—'

'I wasn't really embarrassed!' replied Emily. 'God, it would take more than that to embarrass me. I thought that my character would be embarrassed, because she wouldn't understand what he's suggesting? I mean, I realise she's clever and all that, but you know what the

Victorians were like about sex. They even covered up the legs of tables and things, didn't they?'

Grace counted to ten under her breath. 'Vivie is an intellectual, a Cambridge Maths graduate. Do you realise what an achievement that was for a woman in Victorian times? And now she's learnt that her mother was once a prostitute and owns a brothel with John's character, which paid for her education. What's more, he's just propositioned her. Trust me, she would definitely be shocked and repulsed.'

Emily sighed. 'I know all that, but it's difficult to realise what a big deal it was back then. They made sex so complicated!' With that she grabbed her bag from the corner of the room, waved and smiled at John and within seconds was out of the door.

'I did warn you,' said Fran as Grace sighed with frustration. 'John, fancy a coffee somewhere? You can flirt with me any time and Grace has to dash now.'

John, who was one of the most charming and accomplished actors Grace had ever worked with, smiled. 'That sounds like a good idea. Are you sure you can't join us, Grace?'

'Sorry, I've got a busy few days coming up, but I'd love to another time. I hope you and Suzie are coping all right with Emily. She'll get there in the end; I think she's probably a bit overawed. Theatre's so different from television, and you and Suzie—'

'Have been doing it since before she was born!' John said with a laugh. 'It will be fine, Grace. For me, simply being able to reprise the role of Crofts in *Mrs Warren's Profession* is fantastic. Shaw's often considered too wordy these days.'

'Isn't he lovely?' whispered Fran as Grace gathered up her things and passed her notes to her friend. 'That voice makes me go weak at the knees.'

'Really? Have fun then, and I'll see you on Friday morning.'

'Yep. What exactly is it you're doing this time with that rich lover of yours? Front of house at the boutique hotel you've been busy decorating?'

'You make it sound as though I've been stripping wallpaper and painting doors,' laughed Grace. 'The hotel is opening tomorrow, and I want to be there with David when it does.'

'He's back from Hong Kong then?'

Grace nodded, feeling a growing excitement at the prospect of finally seeing David after their three-month separation. She wondered what he had planned for them this evening, after so many weeks when her only satisfaction had been the phone sex they'd indulged in when their free time coincided. Her body ached with desire, a desire that only he could satisfy. He understood her needs even better than she did, having watched over her as she'd progressed through the challenges set for her at his secret club, The Dining Club.

She would never forget those months – months when he and his companions had tutored her body, teaching her more pathways to pleasure than she'd ever realised existed – but now their life together was moving forward and she was certain that once the small boutique hotel was open the two of them would become even closer emotionally, as well as providing lots of opportunities to experiment with their bodies even more ... He loved her, she knew that, but she sometimes found herself thinking of her old rival Amber, the woman who had been the centre of David's world for so many years, only to find herself displaced by Grace. In her quiet moments, Grace would recall Amber's parting words to her: *At the moment, you're a novelty, but one day you'll be in my position. No one can hold his interest for ever.* Now, with their new venture opening, Grace was determined to prove Amber wrong.

The small hotel, with its four suites, each one carefully themed and decorated by Grace, would be open once a month for four couples to rotate around each suite. They would be able to enjoy a three-day break living out their most private fantasies in an exclusive and secure environment, with everything they might need and more, and their anonymity ensured. Grace was sure that no one had ever offered anything like it before. She was also sure that these sensual mini-breaks were destined to be both highly successful from a business point of view and hugely exciting for her lover.

Fran sighed. 'You might as well leave now; you're already with him mentally if not physically. I wish I understood your passion for him. He's so not your type of man.'

Taking her denim jacket from the back of the hard wooden chair where she'd been sitting for the past three hours, Grace laughed. 'And how would you know what my type of man is?'

'Clearly I don't, but I know the type you used to fall for and they weren't at all like David. Anyway, you love him, and if you're happy I'm happy.'

'Talking of you being happy, are you still seeing Andrew?' asked Grace.

Grace had introduced Andrew to Fran after getting to

know him at The Dining Club last year. She sometimes wondered if it had been a wise move, given that Fran was still oblivious to Andrew's 'other' interests, but they seemed to be happy.

'On and off; more off than on right now. He's busy with his work, and he's been helping out with the renovation of the hotel, hasn't he?'

'Yes; lucky for me he's so fit. Make sure you keep him that way!'

'I will, given half a chance. He's busy again at the moment, so if John invites me out this evening I think I'll go. From what I've heard he's quite a lothario and you know what they say ...'

'What?' asked Grace, as she turned to leave.

'Older men make better lovers.'

'Yes, but older than what?'

Smiling to herself, Grace opened the door onto the London street, blinking in the bright sunlight. She would need to get a move on if she was going to be changed and ready to greet David when he arrived back. Luckily a cab dropped someone off right by her so she grabbed it, then settled back in her seat, letting her mind wander to their imminent reunion.

*

By the time they arrived at the four-storey building in West London – Grace's project for the last year – Grace realised that she was moist between her thighs. She and David hadn't been apart this long before, and her body craved the pleasure that only he had ever been able to give her. Paying the driver she hurried in through the smart black front door, which contrasted with the cream brickwork on each side. The mews consisted of a row of identical terraced houses, with black railings at the front and also beneath the windows on the first floor. There was a parking area for taxis on the far side of the narrow road, but no through traffic was allowed to disturb the peace. Putting her key in the lock of number 12 she thought how surprised the other residents would be if they knew what would soon be taking place behind its matching and tasteful façade.

Once inside the small cream and pale green entrance hall, her eyes took in the stunning displays of fresh cream roses and green day lilies set on either side of the small curved-back sofa that sat beside the winding staircase. To the right of the staircase an open door showed a glimpse of the only lounge, where two comfortable sofas and four armchairs were positioned around a low carved table with a recessed centre that held ornaments

David had collected on his travels and a crystal vase containing a single red rose. Over the fireplace an ornate mirror with gilt edging reflected the light back from the entrance hall, making the room look larger than it actually was. The overall feel was comfortable and safe, exactly the look Grace had wanted. It would make people's first visit all the more of a surprise.

'Excited?' asked a male voice, and she jumped with surprise.

'Andrew! I thought you'd have gone home by now.'

'I wanted to wait until you were back. It's looking fantastic. You must be very pleased.'

'I am,' she admitted. 'I hope David likes it too.'

'He'll love it. Do you know any of the guests?' Andrew asked. The first eight would be arriving in the morning.

'Only Lucien, and I don't really know him. I mean ...' Grace felt herself beginning to blush. 'He was there, that last day at The Dining Club, but I can't remember what he looked like.'

'Don't worry, Grace, this is a completely new venture. You're very different from when you arrived at the Club – you've moved on.'

She nodded. 'You're right. It was an amazing

experience, but I'm ready to move forward and I've loved getting the look of each of the four suites right. Some of them were quite a challenge, but I'm pleased with them all.'

'And will that give you the answers you're looking for?' he asked quietly.

Grace began to untie her long, dark hair, which she'd scraped back off her face for the rehearsal, shaking her head until it fell into waves that ended halfway down her back. 'What answers do you think I'm looking for?

'You're wondering if David can be the kind of man you want him to be; if he'll be able to offer you love and support as well as brilliant sex.'

Grace's body became very still, and she gazed into the mirror where she could see Andrew's expression reflected back at her. 'I think it's time you left,' she said quietly. 'David asked if you could be here around ten thirty tomorrow morning, so that you can help settle the guests in.'

'Still avoiding awkward truths, Grace? Right, tell David I'll be here, and have a great reunion tonight.'

After Andrew left, Grace ran up the stairs to the bedroom on the top floor, the one that was for her and David, and stripping off her jeans and jumper turned on the shower. She knew exactly what she was going to be wearing when David returned.

As his chauffeur drove the metallic-grey Mercedes-Benz from the airport towards the hotel, David put away his papers and looked out of the window, allowing his mind to turn from business to pleasure. He had every confidence in Grace's ability to transform the house he'd bought into a hidden hotel, where guests could indulge in three-day fantasy breaks, and was looking forward to seeing how she'd incorporated the chosen fantasies into the décor of the various suites. More than that, though, he was simply looking forward to seeing Grace.

He was surprised by how much he'd missed her while he'd been away. In the past he'd found it easy to compartmentalise his life. When he was working abroad, he'd always left the club and all personal relationships behind him with relative ease. The long hours spent in conference rooms helped, and without deep emotional ties to anyone there had always been sexual opportunities if he felt the need.

This time it had been different. If he was honest with himself, he'd missed Grace far more than he'd anticipated. He'd missed the soft look in her eyes after they made love, the way she looked naked as she waited for him to touch her, and the expression in her eyes when she was being pleasured. He realised that he had allowed her to get closer to him than any other woman, but he didn't like it. It made him vulnerable, and that was something he couldn't cope with. He knew, from watching his warring parents, that if you allowed a woman into your heart you could be badly hurt. They made you an emotional hostage, and before you knew it you were their prisoner. It had happened to his father, but it wasn't going to happen to him. All the same, his heart rate quickened as the car pulled up outside the front door of number 12. 'I'll park round the back, sir. Will you be wanting me tomorrow?' his driver asked, getting David's suitcases out of the boot.

'No thanks, I'll be driving myself for the next three days. Someone will phone you when you're wanted.'

Although he had a key to the front door, he decided not to use it, wanting, needing, to see Grace's expression when she saw him again, and to his surprise he felt himself harden in anticipation of what was to come. Taking a deep breath he reached out and pressed the bell.

Chapter Two

Grace was checking herself in the long bedroom mirror when she heard the bell ring. Her heart seemed to jump into her throat, making it difficult for her to breathe. It had to be David, even though she'd expected him to let himself in, and she hurried down the four flights of stairs. When she opened the front door he was standing back slightly, his cases by his side, the light tan he'd acquired while away only emphasising the brilliant blue of his eyes. Grace swallowed hard. 'Welcome home,' she said with a smile, knowing he wouldn't want any extreme expression of emotion from her.

His eyes moved slowly over her, and she could tell by the look on his face that the tight-fitting, coral-coloured lace dress with a keyhole cut-out that revealed just a hint of her breasts had been the right choice. 'I always think that homecomings are horribly awkward,' he said, picking up his cases and dropping them by the door. 'You look stunning,' he added, kissing her lightly before walking through into the reception area.

Grace wasn't sure how to react. Having longed for this moment for weeks and weeks, she didn't know what to say, and wondered what it was about him that could turn her into a tongue-tied schoolgirl when in reality she was a highly successful theatre director. She knew that Fran would be horrified, but despite everything that had happened at The Dining Club, and the fact that she'd banished Amber from David's life, she still didn't feel entirely secure in their relationship.

'It's all finished, then?' he asked, glancing through the lounge door.

'Yes. Do you want to look round?'

'I think we should have some champagne first,' he replied, slipping an arm round her waist.

'I've got some on ice.'

'Then let's take it up to our room. I assume we do have a room of our own somewhere in this hotel?'

She knew he was teasing her, and began to shake with increasing desire at the prospect of them going to their bedroom. 'Yes, but it's at the top of the house.'

His eyes swept over her. 'I don't know if I can wait that long.'

Quickly she went into the kitchen, opened the champagne, collected two glasses and brought it all out to him. Gently he took the glasses away from her and put them on the ground. 'We won't be needing those,' he murmured, his right hand sweeping her long dark hair behind her left ear so that he could kiss the side of her neck. Shivers ran down her spine, and then she felt him take the champagne bottle away from her too before he began kissing her throat and the soft skin in the gap at the front of the dress.

Swiftly his hands found the concealed zip at the side of the dress, and she could hear his rapid breathing as he peeled it down her body and then lifted her out of it, so that she was totally naked beneath his hands. Next he laid her down halfway up the first flight of stairs, her legs draping downwards on the deep piled carpet. 'Did you miss me?' he asked quietly, his eyes fixed on hers.

'You know I did.' Her voice trembled with anticipation.

'And did you miss this?' he murmured, before lowering his head to her aching breasts and licking her rapidly stiffening nipples.

Grace moaned with pleasure, but immediately he stopped. 'You didn't answer,' he said softly. 'You have to answer.'

'Yes, I missed that,' she gasped, her hips moving upwards as the ache between her thighs increased.

'Keep still, my darling. We mustn't rush.'

Grace wanted to rush, longing for the sweet release of pleasure, but she knew better than to try to control their lovemaking. David was taking off his own clothes now, but he still managed to keep her body aroused by letting his clothes brush against her naked flesh as he removed them, and then his fingers encased both her breasts and he gently squeezed and released the swelling globes as she moaned with a mixture of desire and delight.

'Close your eyes,' he whispered, and when she obeyed she felt his hands move beneath her thighs as he lifted the lower part of her body up and then he began to pour the champagne over her belly, making her jerk when the liquid splashed on her warm flesh. As it ran down into her pubic hair and between her thighs he licked it, and lapped at drops in her belly button while she twisted and groaned at the blissful sensations.

By the time his head moved between her thighs she was almost out of her mind with excitement, so that when he finally licked and sucked at the area around her clitoris she screamed aloud. 'Yes! Please, please don't stop. I'm coming!'

'Very soon, my darling,' he assured her, lifting his head so that the wonderful build-up was stopped in its tracks. Then he raised her arms above her head, poured some more champagne into her armpits and drank that. The delicious sensations drove her out of her mind, increasing the heavy feeling between her thighs without satisfying it.

'Open your eyes, I want to look into them when you come,' he said softly.

Gasping for breath, she did as he'd asked, and the expression in his eyes was more tender than anything she'd seen there before. Slowly, very slowly, he moved a finger around the swollen bud, lightly pressing on the side of the stem until her head moved from side to side with excitement.

'Keep looking at me,' he reminded her, 'you must be looking at me when you come.'

She wanted to ask him to hurry, but she knew better. Obediently she made herself keep her head still, gazing into his eyes as his knowing fingers played between her thighs until finally he allowed them to skim lightly over the opening to her urethra and Grace screamed with ecstasy as the hot rush of release flooded through her and all the time her body was in spasm their eyes were locked onto each other's.

Only when the very last tremors had died away did he enter her. Positioning his arms above hers he thrust upwards, and the angle of their bodies on the stairs meant that he was able to penetrate more deeply than usual. She felt herself tightening around him and when he groaned deeply as his own pleasure spilled, her internal muscles contracted with a second orgasm and she milked him while he shuddered above her.

When it was over, he remained on top of her, and the weight of his body was wonderfully reassuring. 'God, I missed you,' he murmured almost to himself and for that brief moment, Grace was completely happy.

After they'd showered they sat side by side on the sofa in the hotel's lounge, David's arm draped along the back so that his fingers could play idly with Grace's hair. He listened intently as she outlined what she'd done while he was away, and some of the closeness that she'd felt while they were making love began to slip away, as so often happened with David. Although she could feel his fingers in her hair, she knew that his mind was no longer on the two of them. It was on the excitement that the coming days would bring.

'Do we know everyone who's booked this month's three-day break?' he asked.

'We know one out of each pair, from the Club, just to be sure that they know what they've signed up for. Andrew's been in charge of the bookings.'

'And every suite is booked?'

'Yes, we could have double booked them, if we were in this for money alone.'

'Interesting,' murmured David, running the fingers of one hand gently over the back of her scalp in a soft, sensuous massaging movement. 'How many additional people are we going to provide in order to make these fantasy breaks work? I assume most of the guests will want a few extra characters, as it were.'

'We have two extra people for each suite, to be used as required by the guest who's booked the break. Obviously they will be dressed appropriately and can be summoned by a bell in the staff living room. Each bell

21

is marked with the theme so there won't be any mistakes. In addition we have four spare staff, who can also be used if advance notice is given.'

David looked doubtful. 'Sometimes it's difficult to tell what route a fantasy is going to take, don't you think? Why the advance notice?'

'I didn't think you'd want to be paying for people to sit around doing nothing for three days.'

His fingers stopped moving in her hair. 'Did you truly imagine I'd be concerned about money?' he asked incredulously. 'We're setting up a hotel to cater for people's ultimate fantasies and you thought the cost would matter to me? Our clients will expect the very best, and that's what they must get. They want to be able to live out their most extreme fantasies in every way imaginable. It's the most exciting venture possible for those who want to indulge in total abandonment to their deepest, darkest desires yet you're willing to risk us failing because of cost? Amber would never have made such a basic mistake.'

'I hadn't thought of it like that,' Grace began, shocked to hear him mention Amber.

'You hadn't thought, full stop,' he said sharply. 'Grace, this is a wonderful idea, your own concept and a brilliant one, but it's not one of your fringe productions where you have to come in under budget! I told you that you could spend as much as you needed to get everything right, and I was happy to leave it all to you. I hope I'm not going to be disappointed.'

It was the end of a long and exhausting day for Grace, and she was shaken to the core by David's words and the mention of Amber. He didn't sound like her lover, a man who'd just brought her to the pinnacle of sexual pleasure, and because she was hurt she spoke without thinking

'Don't talk to me like that!' she retorted. 'You haven't even looked round yet. You don't know what the suites are like, or who will be helping out. I admit I'm not used to the fact that money is meaningless to you, but even if everything else is perfect, and I think it is, no doubt you will still keep reminding me of my mistake for the next three days. It's probably your way of controlling people at work, but I don't work for you. My work and this hotel are two totally separate things. How can we be so close one minute and then you talk to me as though you're deliberately trying to put a distance between us?'

She'd never spoken to him like that before, and as

soon as the words were out she regretted them, waiting with trepidation for his response. Slowly he stood up and held out a hand to her. 'Right, time for you to show me around, I think,' he said calmly. 'I'm looking forward to this. You'll have to remind me of the themes, I'm afraid. I know we've talked about it over the phone, but I'm afraid I can't remember them all.'

Grace was confused. It was as though she hadn't said anything, but she was eager to show him the rooms so she took his hand and together they began to climb the stairs. 'I think of this as the pathway to pleasure,' she said with a smile, and turning he smiled back at her.

'Perhaps not at first, not for everyone, but eventually for most who walk up these stairs yes, a very apt description, my darling.'

Grace led him up to the first floor, relieved that he clearly hadn't objected to her outburst. However, she was greatly mistaken.

'I've put the Country Retreat Suite on the first floor, because in some ways it's the least extreme,' she explained, opening the door to show the rooms to him. David glanced around then walked over to the large, smooth mahogany rocking horse that filled the bay window of the suite's lounge. He ran his hands over it, and nodded approvingly. 'I like the addition to the saddle. That should provide a lot of pleasure and excitement.'

'If the weather's good then people on this break can use the garden, too. We do have a lot of tall trees around the perimeter, but it's still possible for it to be overlooked from the top floors of the adjoining houses, which will add a frisson of danger to any pleasuring that happens outside,' said Grace.

'Excellent; let's move on.'

Moving upwards through the house, Grace showed him the Victorian Suite, the Pleasure Suite and the Ultimate Fantasy Suite. He lingered longest in the Ultimate Fantasy Suite. 'Presumably the client chooses their ultimate fantasy,' he remarked, his eyes lingering on the sheer net curtains suspended from a circle in the ceiling above the bed and then drawn out to each of the four tall, carved columns at the corners.

'Yes, which is why it was difficult to decide on the décor, but I decided—'

'It's excellent, you've done a wonderful job,' he assured her, putting an arm round her shoulders. 'I can't wait for tomorrow. You and I will be joining Lucien and his partner. Do you remember Lucien?'

Grace felt herself blushing. 'Not very well. That last evening at The Dining Club is all a bit of a blur.'

He laughed. 'I'm not surprised! However, Lucien remembers you very well and he's asked that we join him each time he books a break here.'

'He's booked them all,' said Grace. 'Andrew told me. He said that Lucien told him he had someone interesting who would be the perfect partner.'

'Did he now? That sounds promising,' he remarked, his blue eyes glittering with excitement.

'There are only our rooms left,' said Grace as they left the Ultimate Fantasy Suite. 'They're not themed. Of course, we could always use one of the other suites if you wanted to, as we'll only have guests for three days each month,' she added teasingly.

'I think they're best kept for special occasions. No risk of boredom then,' said David, turning and starting to go back down the stairs.

'Don't you want to see them?' asked Grace.

'Not really; after all, we won't be using them much. I shan't be sleeping here except during the fantasy breaks.'

'Where are we going tonight?'

Holding her face between his hands he started to kiss her deeply, his tongue probing her mouth while his hands roamed through her long, dark hair. He pulled her close to him and slid a thigh between her legs. Her excitement mounting, she rubbed herself against him, uttering tiny moans of pleasure. His breathing was rapid now as his hands moved lower to cup her buttocks and pull her even more tightly against him. Feeling the first flicker of an orgasm deep within her she gave a soft moan of delight, but suddenly he put his hands on her waist and moved her away from him. 'I think I'd better be getting home. We'll both need all our energy tomorrow, I'm sure,' he said, watching her face intently.

'But I was about to come!' she retorted. 'Why did you ...?'

'I'm sorry,' he said, but he didn't sound sorry. Grace stared at him in disbelief. 'I'm very sorry,' he repeated. 'No doubt you'll keep reminding me of my mistake for the next three days.'

She recognised the words immediately, her own words said in anger earlier in the evening, and she realised that this was payback time. She'd been wrong in thinking she hadn't annoyed him, and now she was paying the price. 'David, this isn't how it's meant to be,' she said softly. 'Just because I lost my temper downstairs, it doesn't mean that—'

'I don't know what you're talking about, darling. I'm sure you're going to be very busy tomorrow, so no doubt you'll want to sleep here. I'm going to meet with Andrew in the morning so that he can fill me in on the new employees; I'll be here around ten thirty. That way you and I can meet and greet the guests together. You've done an amazing job, Grace, everything is absolutely perfect and I can't wait for us to join Lucien and his guest tomorrow. Make sure you get a good night's sleep,' he added, and bending down he kissed her gently on the forehead and then without a backward glance went down the stairs while she remained standing on the landing, frustrated, hurt and alone. At that moment, she wished she'd never fallen in love with him.

Driving back to his Grade II listed house on the outskirts of London, David's fingers gripped the steering wheel tightly as he concentrated on keeping his breathing slow and steady. He was furious, not with Grace but with himself. He'd been looking forward to spending the pre-opening night at the hotel with her, but his

Pavlovian response to her perfectly reasonable display of annoyance towards him had ruined it for them both. In his head she'd become his mother berating his father for some imagined slight, and immediately he'd reminded himself that this was why he didn't want to commit to a lifetime with one woman.

Grace's words had also hurt, because they were the truth, and hearing her say them had made him feel ashamed. Feeling ashamed wasn't something he was comfortable with either, so the combination of emotions had been fatal, meaning he was driving through London late at night back to a lonely bed, leaving Grace alone in the hotel. Now their special night of passion, so long-anticipated by him, would never happen. Tomorrow the hotel would open, and everything would change.

Before he finally fell asleep that night he wondered if he was capable of changing. He had no doubt that if he didn't change he would eventually lose Grace, quite probably to Andrew or Lucien. She'd learnt so much about her own sexuality at The Dining Club that she needed him, or someone like him, to keep her sexually satisfied, but she also needed to feel loved in other ways. David had kept his deepest emotions locked away for all of his adult life, and he didn't know if he was even able to be the kind of man she both needed and deserved. The only thing he was certain of was that by the time they had finished exploring the delights of the Hotel of Seduction they would both know the answer.

Chapter Three

'Excited?' asked Andrew as Grace entered the staff room the next morning. 'At least the sun's shining, which will make the Country Break more realistic. Mind you, every time I go and stay at someone's country house it chucks it down with rain.'

Grace smiled. 'I'm excited but nervous. There's so much to think about, and so many different people to keep happy. Isn't David here yet?'

'He phoned me to say he'd be a bit late. He wanted to drop by the Club on his way and check Louise is managing it all right without him.'

'And is she?' Grace asked.

'Fine, as far as I can see; not like when Amber was

there, of course, but well enough. I think the Club has lost some of its edge, though. It's probably going to be more of a training ground for this place, once you get it off the ground. Nothing stays the same for ever, does it?'

'No, but does David mind?'

'You worry about your hotel, and let him take care of the Club. You know how easily he gets bored; he's probably pleased things are changing. So, shall we run through the guest list?'

'OK, well, Lucien is bringing a partner; I don't think he's been going out with her all that long so I hope she's all right with it. He's chosen the Victorian Suite for their first stay. David and I will be there all the time, as Lucien requested that. We'll need the Victorian maid, too. Who's that going to be?'

'Tilly – a broadminded friend of mine. She's just back from six months as a chalet girl and is waiting to take up her place at Oxford to read History, so she'll be perfect. If you need another man, you want Grant. He goes to the same gym as me and he's a great guy, no worries there either. I'll keep him on standby.'

'Perfect. What about the other guests?' asked Grace.

'We've got a newly engaged couple in the Ultimate Fantasy Suite – the woman's a member of The Dining

Club, so she gets to choose the fantasy. The complete list of visitors is in the book at reception.'

'Okay, and are you sure the staff know exactly what they have to do? Nothing ruins an erotic fantasy more than someone stepping out of character,' warned Grace.

'Relax,' Andrew smiled, 'we've been over and over this. There's always Felicity, too, she's responsible for their behaviour, isn't she?'

'Yes, she used to work for a casting director, so she's brilliant. David remembered her from the Club years ago.'

At that moment the bell in the lobby rang. 'You'd better go and greet your first guests,' said Andrew. 'This is going to be a huge success, Grace. Believe in yourself; think of it as a production you're putting on.' He gave her a warm hug, and as he held her tight and kissed the top of her head, she began to relax, wishing for a brief moment that she'd been able to fall in love with him as he'd wanted, rather than with the complex David.

'Hopefully without any critical reviews,' she replied, drawing away, then smoothing down the soft folds of the pleated skirt of her peach-coloured maxi dress she went to greet the first guests.

'Darling, it's Lucien,' said David. 'We arrived together! I'm sure you remember him.'

Hoping she wasn't blushing at the memory, Grace smiled warmly at David's business partner. His dark brown hair was still quite long, he was lean and toned and his deep brown eyes were intelligent and observant.

'Lovely to see you again, Grace,' he said, kissing her on both cheeks. 'I'd like you to meet my girlfriend, Emily Kelly. Emily, this is our hostess, Grace.'

The two women started at each other in astonishment and, in Emily's case, horror. Flushing deeply, the young actress held out her hand while an equally discomfited Grace managed a brief smile. 'Let's show you to your suite,' she said, moving swiftly towards the stairs, while David gave instructions for their cases to be brought up.

Holding the door open for the two visitors to enter their suite, Grace's eyes met Emily's. 'I'm sorry,' whispered Emily. 'He told me I had to make up an excuse or he'd bring someone else and I—'

'Here we are,' said Grace brightly. 'I hope you like the rooms.'

'And I hope you enjoy surrendering to me for the next few days,' Lucien said to Emily, who looked confused by his words. 'My dear girl, this is a step back in time, and in Victorian days women had no rights at all, as I'm sure you know. They belonged to their husbands, and for the purpose of this little fantasy, I'm your husband.'

'I don't think I—'

Lucien put a hand under Emily's chin and turned her pretty face towards him. 'You don't need to think, Emily. Women's brains aren't meant to be used for thinking too deeply, it can make them nervous and unwell.'

As Emily continued to look confused, Grace felt a flicker of excitement at the thought of what lay ahead. 'Ring when you want us to join you,' she said quietly to Lucien. 'You'll find all the clothes you need in the wardrobe, and once you've changed a maid will come and take away what you're wearing now until you're ready to leave the hotel.'

'Wow! It's an amazing room!' exclaimed Emily as she gazed around, looking at the rich, dark colours of the red and green patterned carpet, slightly faded as though with years of wear. The walls were covered in water-silk paper, featuring large, overblown flower heads against a pale background. The furniture was crowded, three plump armchairs with button backs, two pouffes, and an ottoman at the foot of the bed, on which was seated a china doll in Victorian clothing. An ornate, cast-iron fireplace was filled by a large vase of dried flowers, while muslin curtains covered the windows, allowing a little sunlight into the room.

The bed was high, its faded cream damask throw covered with large, heavily embroidered cushions, while the over-sized headboard was ornately carved, with matching marble-topped tables on either side.

'The bathroom is through that door on the right,' explained Grace, 'and the study is on the left.'

'I imagine we'll be in the bedroom most of the time,' Lucien replied, 'and as I don't want to waste a moment of our stay, please join us as soon as you can.'

'We will,' David assured him, and Grace could hear the excitement in his voice.

Once they were back in their own room, Grace caught hold of David's arm. 'Lucien's girlfriend is in my production!' she exclaimed. 'She told me she needed time off to do a voice-over! How on earth am I going to face her at rehearsals on Friday? This is a disaster. If she talks I'll lose all respect at work. What can I do? It's the most embarrassing thing that could have happened to me!'

'Far more embarrassing for her, I imagine,' said David. 'In any case, if she's going to be coming here for three-day breaks with Lucien for the next three months then she isn't going to have time to appear in your play, is she?'

'But suppose she tells people?' Grace was close to tears. 'It's just unbelievable.'

'Grace,' said David sharply, 'I realise it's been a shock for you, but could you please concentrate on your project? I don't imagine Emily will be any more anxious for this to become public knowledge than you are. Right now the Victorian Fantasy is about to begin, and I for one can't wait.'

Taking a deep breath, Grace nodded. He was right. She would have to talk to Emily later, but she wished with all her heart that it had never happened.

Waiting outside the door of the Victorian Fantasy Suite, Grace knew that she'd been right when she'd thought of the concept. Simply changing the style of clothes she was wearing had transformed the way she felt, taking her away from her other life, and she hoped it would have done the same for Emily. David's white shirt with an inset bib front and high stand-up collar, teamed with tight-fitting black trousers, made him look more aloof and unapproachable than normal, while her long cream dress with three-quarter-length trumpet sleeves, tightly fitted bodice and wide skirt made her feel more feminine but also more restricted than normal, as though she were a prisoner in her own clothes.

David ran his fingers appreciatively over her bare shoulders, letting them linger in the dips each side of her neck for a moment. 'You're a very clever young woman,' he murmured. 'Now, let the games begin.' And with that he tapped on the door.

The Lucien who let them in looked very different from the Lucien David had greeted downstairs. Dressed in a white ruffled shirt teamed with a blue cravat and a three-quarter-length black jacket nipped in at the waist, he could have stepped straight out of a period play, but the expression in his eyes wasn't one that Grace would have wanted to see in the eyes of any of her actors.

'Emily is being difficult,' he said. 'I don't think she understands that life is different now we're in these rooms. Surely an actress should grasp the concept easily enough. Not that her reticence will spoil things. Quite the contrary, I suspect.'

'I'm sure we can help,' said David smoothly. 'Grace,

it's your duty to make things clear to her. You are, after all, a little older and I imagine a great deal wiser sexually. You certainly understand the importance in Victorian times of a woman being totally obedient to her partner's wishes.'

As Grace entered the room she was keenly aware that this wasn't only a game. She'd always known that. Like The Dining Club, each of these fantasies was a test, and if a player failed then no doubt the relationship between the two people involved would also fail. What she hadn't realised until that moment was the importance of her role. Unless she was able to make things run smoothly, as Amber had done at the Club, her relationship with David was destined to fail too. There was no room for compassion in the games, she saw now; the stakes were too high for that.

Emily was lying in the middle of the large bed, wearing a cream bodice with blue laces, which had clearly been pulled very tight as the tops of her full breasts were almost spilling out of it. Matching cream and blue pantaloons covered the lower half of her body, but it was plain from the sullen look on her face that she wasn't happy.

'I can't breathe in this!' she moaned as Grace

approached the bed. 'If I've got to dress up, why can't I have a dress like yours? I thought this holiday was going to be fun. Lucien said it would be adventurous and sexy. I don't feel very sexy right now. I thought this weekend would be more like the swinger's parties he takes me to. They're much more fun than this.'

'It will be,' Grace promised her, 'but you have to do as you're told. In Victorian times women belonged entirely to their husbands or the man of the house where they lived. They had no rights at all, and they certainly didn't throw tantrums.'

Emily blew some stray strands of her long, blonde hair off her face. 'I'm hot!' she complained. 'Hot and really uncomfortable. What am I supposed to do in an outfit like this?'

'You won't have to do anything except obey me,' said Lucien softly. 'You have no idea how long I've been looking forward to this, Emily. Now, I think it's time for the holiday to begin in earnest. David and I are going to help you relax a little, while Grace watches. If you find things difficult at any time, she'll help you, won't she, David?'

David looked across at Grace, who was sitting on the side of the bed. He nodded. 'Of course; Grace understands that she has to do whatever I want her to do, don't you, my darling?'

Grace swallowed hard but nodded, feeling the sexual tension that filled the room. Having devised this fantasy, she knew she must play it through to the end.

'Emily, lie flat and Grace, put a cushion beneath her hips,' said Lucien, 'then lie down next to her.'

'I don't want to lie down,' said the young blonde. 'I want—'

'Perhaps you want to go home, Emily?' suggested Lucien. 'You can if you wish; although I'd be sorry to see you leave before our time here has even begun. I thought you and I were a good match, but perhaps I was wrong.'

Emily looked confused. 'No, I don't want to go home but—'

'Then do as I say.'

Grace took hold of one of the feather-filled pillows and slid it beneath Emily's hips. 'Think of this as a play,' she whispered.

'No one asked you to speak, Grace,' said David. 'Apologise.'

Grace lowered her eyes. 'I'm sorry.'

'Lucien and I are going to make Emily feel better

now,' he said softly. 'No matter what happens, you are to lie beside her, and do not under any circumstances move or interfere. Do you understand?'

'Yes,' she said quietly, feeling her excitement rising, an excitement tinged with fear, the kind of dark excitement that David had taught her to enjoy and which brought her such overwhelming pleasure.

She saw Lucien sit on the bed by Emily's legs, while David stood by her head, his fingers playing idly with her hair. All at once Emily gave a muffled cry of protest. 'Don't do that! Not with other people in the room.'

'It's what I want to do. You know you like this,' Lucien replied.

'Your pantaloons are open at the gusset, just as they would have been in those days,' said David in a conversational tone. 'Lucien is merely taking advantage of that.'

As Emily's breathing began to quicken, so did Grace's. She could imagine how Emily's body felt at that moment, and knew very well that the other young woman would be mortified to have strangers witnessing her arousal. Tiny cries of pleasure escaped from Emily's mouth, and Grace could feel the mattress trembling beneath them.

An ache started deep in her belly, but she remained motionless, knowing that David would be watching her closely for any sign that she was disobeying him.

'If you were a well-brought-up young lady, you wouldn't be enjoying this,' Lucien told the whimpering Emily. 'Decent women didn't enjoy sex in Victorian times, so I'll be very displeased if you come.'

Grace saw him bend lower over Emily's body and guessed that he was going to use his tongue on her. Emily began to moan, her hips jerking upwards to try to hurry her moment of pleasure despite what Lucien had said. And Grace felt her own hips start to move.

'Grace, you are not to move,' David said sharply, and she tried to subdue her overexcited body.

All at once Emily's body twisted upwards and she cried out as Lucien's tongue, moving between the opening in the lower part of her costume, finally brought her to a climax. 'Yes, oh yes!' she screamed, and Grace broke out in a sweat as she forced herself to lie perfectly still despite her own rising excitement.

'Now you can pleasure her, Grace,' said David. 'Lucien and I will watch, but remember the pleasure must all be hers.'

As Grace got off the bed and walked slowly round to

the other side, she could feel Lucien's eyes on her. 'She's so beautiful, David,' he murmured. 'Beautiful and incredibly well trained. Tell me, Grace, don't you wish we were going to pleasure you? Wouldn't you like to feel my tongue between your thighs right now?'

Grace looked at David. 'You may answer,' he said and she could see how much he was aroused too.

'Yes, I would,' she said to Lucien, 'but it's not what's required of me.'

'No,' he said regretfully, 'such a shame, but your turn will come.' And he slid an arm round her waist for a few seconds as she walked past him.

'I don't want to come again yet, I'm not ready,' protested Emily when Grace took Lucien's place on her side of the bed.

'I want to watch Grace pleasuring you, so that's what will happen,' said Lucien. 'Or would you rather it was David?'

Grace waited, and saw Emily's big blue eyes assess the expression on David's face. 'No, I'd rather it was Grace,' she said hastily.

Grace pushed Emily's legs upwards until her knees were pointing to the ceiling, which opened her up more. Then she pressed the fingers of each hand into the creases at the tops of Emily's thighs until she heard the younger woman's soft moan of rising desire. Slowly, very slowly, she lowered her head and then ran her tongue lightly up and down Emily's inner channels until the blonde was soaking wet. Only then did she draw the small, tight clitoris into her mouth and suck lightly on it for a few seconds. Then, as Emily cried out with delight, she released it and skimmed her tongue down one side of the tiny clitoral stem.

Emily's entire lower body contracted and her head thrashed from side to side as the pleasure flooded through her once more.

'Well done, Grace,' said Lucien admiringly. 'It seems she was ready to climax again after all.'

Straightening up, Grace pushed her long, dark hair behind her ears and waited for further instructions.

'I think Emily needs a rest now,' Lucien went on regretfully, eyeing the motionless blonde. 'Perhaps it's time we turned our attention to you, Grace, if David agrees?'

'I don't want Grace to reach the peak of pleasure yet,' replied David, 'but it's certainly time she had some attention. Remember, Grace, feel free to respond but on no account are you to climax. After all, this is Emily's holiday, not yours.'

Already aroused by watching the men pleasuring Emily, Grace's heart sank at David's words. She felt so close to coming herself that she knew it would take all the skills she'd learnt to stop herself from reaching a climax. She also realised that this was her first test in her new role as David's partner. She was no longer the young woman he'd taken such delight in helping discover the many complex paths to ultimate pleasure, instead she must become the woman whose sexual skills the more innocent Emily would struggle to emulate.

Lucien was watching her closely. 'I think you've disappointed her!' he said to David with a smile.

David didn't smile back. 'Nonsense, she understands very well what her role is here, don't you, Grace?

'Of course,' she replied calmly.

'Excellent,' said Lucien. 'Then let us help you undress. I don't think we need the ladies' maid today.' Very slowly and sensuously he unfastened the shaped bodice of her dress, allowing her to breathe more easily. Next he slipped off the camisole before finally unfastening the tightly laced corset so that her softly rounded breasts were freed.

As David slid the dress down over her hips to the floor she felt his fingers stray through the opening of the linen, knee-length pantaloons, brushing lightly against her damp pubic hair for a few seconds. She drew in her breath, and with a laugh Lucien lowered his head, then ran his tongue around her areola, causing her nipples to stiffen.

'Do you want her completely naked?' asked David, his eyes on Grace's flushed face.

'I think so; it will make what I want to do easier. The pantaloons are arousing, but they might get in the way.'

Grace swallowed hard as David removed them, still watching her closely. 'Remember, you have to set Emily a good example,' he murmured as she lay back down on the high bed, waiting for whatever was to come.

'Emily, you must stand next to her and watch this,' said Lucien. As he pushed a cushion beneath Grace's hips she saw Emily standing wide-eyed and anxious-looking beside her.

'In Victorian times, woman weren't thought to have sexual desires, but they did suffer from what was diagnosed as hysteria,' continued Lucien, his fingers gently parting Grace's outer sex lips as he was talking. 'No doubt it was sexual frustration, which explains why massaging the vulva was often an excellent cure – undertaken by the family doctor, of all people. However,

David tells me that Grace is very responsive to having her G-spot massaged, so that's what I intend to do now. You'll enjoy that, Grace, won't you?'

Grace's heart sank, because both she and David knew exactly how much pleasure it gave her. 'Yes,' she said quietly.

'Of course,' continued Lucien, 'Victorian women weren't thought to be capable of climaxing, so any reaction was considered a medical response. We know differently now, though, and as Grace isn't allowed to climax she will have to supress her very natural response. Watch her closely, as we will be doing the same to you tomorrow.'

'I don't want—' began Emily.

'I'm afraid, Emily, that in the Victorian Suite, the men are in charge,' said David. 'Don't worry; Grace will show you how it's done and Lucien and I will be here to help you tomorrow. It will be fun for us all.'

Grace could tell by his tone of voice just how aroused David was, but she didn't know if he was aroused by the prospect of what lay ahead for her or by the thought of it all happening to Emily the next day.

Bending down, he moved her long, dark hair to one side and put his mouth close to her ear. 'Don't let me down, Gracie. Remember all you've learnt in the past year. I know you'll want to come, but I also know you won't disappoint me, however great the pleasure feels,' he whispered.

She tried to blot out his words, because even hearing him talk about it increased her arousal, as she had no doubt he'd known it would. Then, with David looking down on her and Emily watching, Lucien gently inserted a lubricated finger inside her, rubbing the pad of his finger back and forth over the incredibly sensitive nerve endings that lay beneath the skin covering the ridge of her pubic bone. His finger was long and, despite her best efforts, the moment he located the right area she gave a small gasp of pleasure.

'David was right; you like this, Grace, don't you?' His voice was quiet and gentle.

'Yes,' she admitted, trying to slow down her breathing.

'Let's add another finger and see if we can increase your pleasure,' he murmured. Within a few seconds he began pressing lightly against her cervix, his touch knowing and tender. For a brief moment she felt a slight cramping, but that quickly passed and the pleasure began to build and build. She heard herself moaning as he moved back to her G-spot, continuing the gentle massaging movement that made her feel hot and swollen inside, and her excitement built remorselessly towards a climax. Her head turned from side to side on the bed and she felt the muscles of her belly start to tighten. The pink flush of an impending orgasm swept over her upper chest and her hips began to twitch.

'See how close she is to coming, Emily?' asked Lucien. 'She won't, though, because she knows it's forbidden, and she's an expert at self-control. By the time we leave here, you'll have learnt to control your body almost as well as Grace controls hers. This makes the moment when you are allowed to come all the sweeter, although regrettably that won't happen today for you, will it, Grace?'

She couldn't speak as she fought down the hot waves of almost unbearable pleasure threatening to overwhelm her.

'Answer him, Grace,' ordered David.

'Yes,' she gasped, then groaned as Lucien's fingers continued to massage her G-spot until she cried out with ecstasy.

'Grace!' said David, and she could hear the note of warning in his voice.

Opening her mouth a little she forced herself to breathe slowly and steadily, desperately struggling to remove her mind from what was being done to her. For one brief moment she thought it wasn't going to work, but then the intense build-up of pleasure began to ease, the tightness in her belly lessened and she knew that she was safe.

Lucien tried his hardest to rekindle the sensations, but the moment had passed and eventually he gently withdrew his fingers and lightly stroked the soft flesh of her inner thighs. 'Incredible!' he said admiringly. 'David is a very lucky man. Now I want to spend some time alone with Emily, so ...'

'We'll go,' said David. 'I hope that was helpful, Emily,' he added, and as Grace began to dress herself she saw him smile at the young, blonde actress who was clearly highly aroused by the scene she'd just witnessed. She didn't answer, merely looked back at him, her eyes holding a mute appeal that Grace could tell he found highly arousing.

Leaving the lovers alone in the Victorian Suite, David cupped Grace's head in his hands and kissed her passionately. 'I must have you now,' he said urgently. 'You were amazing. Let's go up to our private rooms.'

*

Later, as they lay together in their bed, after he'd made love to her for almost longer than she could cope with, bringing her to climax after climax before finally entering her, she rested her head against his chest and he ran his fingers through her hair. She knew that she should be feeling as contented as David clearly felt, but she wasn't. She wasn't because she had recognised the look on David's face when he'd spoken to Emily. It was the same look that he'd had on his face in their early days together when she'd started visiting The Dining Club. She had replaced Amber's position in David's sexual life, but with a faint stirring of fear she wondered if the younger and untutored Emily would one day replace her in his affections. Were his deepest feelings only ever aroused by the seduction of innocence?

'What are you thinking?' asked David.

'That I need to get dressed, go downstairs and make sure all our guests are satisfied, not just Lucien.'

'If they're half as satisfied as I am, they're very lucky,' he replied with the half-smile that she always found incredibly endearing. 'You're right, though. Time to get back to work. I have to admit that your idea of a sexually themed boutique hotel is exceeding my expectations. You're a genius, darling.'

Half an hour later, discussing menus with the chef and checking with the rest of the staff to make sure all the guests were happy so far, Grace realised that as nice as David's praise had been, and as wonderful as their lovemaking had been, one small worry remained at the back of her mind: Emily.

Part Two

Part Two

Chapter One

Grace was feeling good. Everything seemed to be going well with the hotel, the suites were proving just as exciting as she'd hoped, and she and David were making up for lost time, reminding themselves what they found so irresistible about each other. She would just have to push her worries about Emily to the back of her mind.

After a lazy afternoon spent in bed with David, Grace finally headed back to her office. She found Andrew standing by her desk. 'We've got a problem,' he said.

'What kind of a problem?'

'The guests in the Ultimate Fantasy Suite want to leave. At least, one of them wants to leave. What do we do about that?'

Grace thought for a moment. 'That's the one booked by a woman from the Club, isn't it? She knew what she was booking.'

Andrew nodded. 'It is, but it seems that her fantasy of a Roman orgy wasn't to her guest's liking. I assume we refund their money?'

Grace hesitated. 'I'm not sure.'

'Not sure about what?' asked David, coming into the office. Grace explained the situation to him and he frowned. 'That's Daisy and her new fiancée, isn't it?' Andrew nodded. 'For heaven's sake, if he's visited The Club then he must—'

'She tells me that she's never taken him to the Club, but she must have thought he'd enjoy himself.'

'We'll have to give them a refund,' said Grace firmly. 'The whole point of this is that people enjoy themselves.'

'Try telling that to Emily earlier,' murmured David.

Grace ignored him. 'Give the refund, Andrew.'

'I don't want to undermine you, Grace, but I seem to remember that the financial side of this hotel is my affair,' David countered.

'Yes, of course, when it comes to the money spent on everything, but I've arranged the themes and—'

'And failed to consider all possible consequences,' he pointed out.

Grace felt herself flushing with anger, and saw Andrew walk quickly out of the office. 'That's most unfair. You assured me that by using people who belonged to The Dining Club we wouldn't get any problems like this.'

'I never said any such thing,' retorted David. 'No one is ill, there's no unforeseen emergency that's arisen, so they should still pay.'

'It's not Daisy's fault if he didn't enjoy something she thought he would!' protested Grace. 'I don't want this hotel to get a bad reputation the moment it's opened and if her disgruntled fiancée decides to talk—'

'That,' said David crisply, 'is something that most definitely won't happen. Now leave this to me and I'll get them out of here quickly and quietly. Who was the very large chap I saw hanging about in the staff room?'

'Phil, he used to be a bouncer.'

'Excellent. Send him out into the lobby while I go and speak to Daisy and leave the rest to me. Then can you send Phil out and do whatever you need to do. Lucien wants me in the Victorian Suite this evening, so if no one else wants you that gives you a few hours off.'

Grace didn't like the sound of that. 'Why aren't I needed? What's going to happen?'

Already halfway out of the door, David turned to look back at her. 'I have no idea, but I find jealousy a most unattractive trait, Gracie, as I'm sure you know.'

She did know, he didn't seem to have a jealous bone in his body, but she found that extremely unnatural. There were times now when she felt so close to him that her worries about their relationship from the early days seemed ridiculous. Then, at moments like this, they returned. If he truly loved her in the way that she loved him, why couldn't he understand how incidents like this made her feel? They'd been so close alone together after leaving Lucien and Emily but now it was as though that time counted for nothing.

With a sigh she went into the staff room to find out how things had gone for all the other guests, and what they needed for the evening.

With a mortified and apologetic Daisy finally on her way back home, the unfortunate soon-to-be-ex fiancée by her side, David wanted some time to himself. The office was empty so he went in there, locking the door behind him.

He knew that really he should have let Grace deal with the Daisy problem, even though he disagreed with her reasoning, but he was so used to having the final say in all his business affairs that it had been impossible for him to let her do what he considered the wrong thing. It would have set a dangerous precedent.

But it had been exciting watching Grace demonstrating her sexual control to the relatively innocent Emily, and had made him remember the early days with her when she had been even more naïve than the young actress. At the beginning, and he knew this very well, she'd only done everything out of love for him. Emily didn't love Lucien, he was sure of that, but she probably thought he could help her get on in her career, using contacts and money. Not that Lucien would mind. David suspected that Lucien was only here in some vain attempt to win Grace from him. He knew how much Lucien enjoyed Grace. By asking only David to join them tonight, Lucien knew that Grace would feel threatened and jealous, and he also knew how much David hated his girlfriends to become possessive.

It was a clever move, which David couldn't help but admire, but it wouldn't work. After his remark earlier,

Grace would almost certainly keep any jealousy hidden from him, and if he was honest the thought of a three-some with Emily and Lucien was very arousing. He wondered what Lucien had planned and whether Grace would ask him anything about it all when he returned to their bedroom later that night.

It was 8 p.m. and Emily, dressed in a white cotton Victorian-style nightdress, with pin-tuck pleats, mother-of-pearl buttons and a heavily embroidered front panel, stood looking out of the window of their suite into the garden below. She could see two men and two women at the far end, partly hidden by some tall shrubs, and wondered what they were doing.

'Are they guests?' she asked Lucien, pointing them out to him.

'I imagine so. I expect they're having the Country House break. We'll try that some time, but not yet. You're so well suited to this Victorian theme, Emily, although tomorrow we must get a maid to put your hair up during the day.'

'A maid?'

'Yes, you'll meet your maid when she comes to help you dress in the morning.'

Emily decided not to ask any more questions. So far the day hadn't been anything like she'd expected, and it was clear from what Lucien had asked her to wear now that the evening wasn't going to be a normal one either. He wasn't like any man she'd been with before, far more sophisticated and a great deal richer, for a start. She'd always thought of herself as being sexually experienced, but she was beginning to realise that Lucien's sexuality was far more complex than she'd imagined possible, despite their previous experiences.

After the hideously embarrassing moment when she'd come face to face with Grace for the first time, the whole day had been beyond her wildest imaginings, and although she would never have admitted it to her lover, she'd found it overwhelming and was extremely nervous about what was coming next. Having been attracted to Lucien because she found him good-looking and different from previous boyfriends, she was starting to wonder if she'd made a mistake. She hoped not. Having a rich lover had never hurt any young, aspiring actress as far as she knew, but the side of him that was being revealed to her now was something she'd never anticipated.

'What are you thinking about?' he asked, slipping an arm round her waist.

'Sex,' she replied truthfully.

'Interesting,' said Lucien softly, lifting her right arm and kissing the inside of her wrist. 'David will be here in a moment, and I think he'll be interested to hear that too. Do you like him?'

'I'm not sure. I don't really know him. He's Grace's boyfriend, isn't he? I know Fran doesn't like him, but that's because he represents everything Fran disapproves of.'

Lucien nodded. 'You mean because he's a rich businessman?'

'I suppose so. He's very good-looking.' Then, feeling reckless, she added, 'This is more your sort of thing, isn't it? This weekend? It could have been designed for you!'

'What do you mean?'

'Group sex, sex games, that sort of thing.'

Lucien looked thoughtful. 'This is more complicated than that, Emily.'

She shrugged. 'If you say so.'

'Spoken like a good Victorian wife.'

She was about to point out that she wasn't his wife

when there was a light tap on the door and David came in. Immediately his intensely blue eyes locked onto hers, and she felt her heart begin to beat faster, although she didn't know if it was due to nerves or excitement.

'I see she's ready for the evening's entertainment,' he said to Lucien.

'I'm afraid she needs calming down a little,' replied Lucien, sounding anything but regretful. 'She's just told me that she's thinking about sex, and as all Victorian people knew, for a woman to become interested in sex was physically debilitating.'

A frown furrowed Emily's smooth brow. 'What are you talking about?'

'It's time for the chastity belt,' explained Lucien. 'Lift your nightdress up to your waist, Emily, so that David can help me with it.'

'I don't think—'

'You're not required to think, Emily,' said David sharply. 'I hope Lucien hasn't made a mistake about you. He seemed certain that you were the type of guest who would appreciate everything that's on offer here.'

The atmosphere in the room had changed since David's arrival, and Emily was suddenly filled with nervous excitement. She could feel her nipples hardening, brushing against the cotton of her nightdress. 'I'm sorry, I didn't realise,' she said hastily, for some reason wanting to please David. Quickly she bunched the lower half of the nightdress up round her waist and then stood waiting passively for whatever was to come.

After three years at a leading drama school and two years as an actress she didn't have any hang-ups about exposing her body, especially as her feminine curves were greatly admired.

David went across to the drawer of the dressing table and she tried to make out what he was bringing back. 'It's a chastity belt,' he explained, unfastening the small lock on one side that allowed the leather front and back to be opened out flat. With gentle fingers he pulled the velvet-lined centre piece up tight against her sex lips before replacing the tiny padlock on the right-hand side. The whole belt was relatively small, ending at the top of her pubic hair, and she realised that there were holes at the front and back.

'There, that's not uncomfortable, is it?' David asked.

Emily shook her head, deciding not to mention that on the contrary the pressure from the leather between her thighs was already arousing her.

'Good, then we'll test how well it works,' said Lucien. 'Lie on the bed, Emily, and then we can begin.'

Emily lay down on top of the heavy bedcover and waited as the two men sat on opposite sides of the bed, both of them looking down at her but with different expressions in their eyes. Lucien looked excited, whereas to Emily's surprise the look in David's eyes was more one of keen interest.

'Just relax, Emily,' said Lucien. 'Tonight you'll get twice the pleasure you've ever had before.'

She lifted her head off the pile of cushions to see what they were going to do, but David stopped her. 'You must just lie there and try not to respond,' he explained. 'Lucien is worried you enjoy sex too much, which is why you're wearing the chastity belt. In Victorian times, only men really enjoyed sex, so naturally you accept what we do to you, but that's all. We explained this earlier today; hopefully you're better at controlling yourself now.'

Emily seriously doubted it. The pressure from the chastity belt was making her want to shift her hips restlessly around, deep within her there were darts of rising desire and neither man had touched her yet. Then she felt Lucien begin massaging her feet, his hands covered in an oil that filled the room with a heavy scent that was arousing in itself. As he pressed the pads at the base of each toe and then slowly worked his way up over her ankles and calves, a tiny moan of pleasure escaped from between her lips. Immediately David slid a hand into the front of the bodice of her nightdress, having unfastened the tiny buttons while she was distracted by Lucien, and he pinched her right nipple hard.

She gave a shocked cry of pain, but instead of releasing the nipple he merely eased the pressure for a few seconds and then slowly began to squeeze it harder again. This time the pain was different, warm and arousing, and Lucien's hands pushed the hem of her nightdress up further as he began to rub the oil over her inner thighs, below where the chastity belt ended, before moving higher, slowly rotating the heel of his hand over the base of her stomach.

Opening the top of her nightdress as much as possible, David forced her right breast out and lowering his head began to lick and suck at the already swollen globe, while Lucien continued to torment the frantic flesh of her belly with his deliciously cruel massage.

Emily's body felt as though it was on fire, and she knew that the tight leather between her thighs must be soaked with the juices of her arousal. She was determined not to allow herself to respond vocally, though, even when David brushed a strand of her sweat-soaked hair off her forehead and whispered, 'Why don't you let yourself come? You know you want to. Think how good it's going to feel.'

She stared up at him, and in his eyes she saw a mixture of excitement and admiration. When Lucien's fingers dug into the soft flesh just above the chastity belt, causing even more pressure to build between her thighs, it was this look that helped her subdue her climax further.

She wanted to please this blue-eyed man more than she wanted to please her lover, and swallowing hard she refused to let his words tip her over the edge.

'She's doing very well,' said Lucien, 'far better than I expected. Perhaps we could take off the chastity belt now. I want to be inside her when she does come.'

'Of course, it's your game,' said David, 'but first I must congratulate her.' And with that he cupped her tight, needy right breast in one hand and then with the lightest of touches let the lace on the cuff of his other hand brush with incredible delicacy over her red, swollen nipple.

The contrast of the almost tender touch combined with her body's desperate need for release proved fatal, and with a cry of despair Emily felt an orgasm sweep through her, her whole body shuddering in ecstasy.

Lucien quickly removed the chastity belt and thrust himself into her, but although his powerful thrusts and the pressure of his pubic bone against her clitoris enabled her to climax once more, it wasn't as intense as her first orgasm had been, and after her second one she lay motionless, her body finally sated.

'Sorry, that was my fault,' said David. 'My cuff brushed against her as I was withdrawing my hand.'

Lying still, with her eyes closed as the two men discussed the evening, Emily knew that he was lying. He had deliberately triggered her orgasm, and for some reason that made her feel very happy.

Grace had only just got into bed when David came into their bedroom, and she knew by the expression on his face that he'd enjoyed his evening. She was almost overwhelmed with jealousy, her mind conjuring up various scenarios that the three of them might have played out in the Victorian Suite, but she knew that she mustn't let him know she was jealous, or it would ruin the whole concept of the hotel, a concept that had been hers in the first place.

'I must get out of these Victorian clothes and have a shower,' he said. 'I was afraid you might be asleep.'

'No, there was a lot to arrange for tomorrow for all the guests, and some of them had decided to use the lounge tonight.'

'Rather than continue with their fantasy break?'

Grace nodded. 'I hadn't expected that either, but it was a nice atmosphere in there.'

'I'm not sure it's a good idea for the guests to meet. Personally, I'd want privacy.'

'If they wanted privacy,' said Grace, 'then they wouldn't have gone into the lounge so that's clearly not a problem for everyone. It was the Country Suite people and a nice couple from the Pleasure Suite. I think that Andrew had made their day very memorable!'

'An unqualified success for them, then. I won't be long in the shower,' responded David, but he didn't sound as delighted as Grace had hoped. While she waited for him to finish, she tried not to think about what he might be going to tell her. She knew him too well to think that he wouldn't be totally honest, but she wasn't certain that she was going to cope with it in the way he'd expect.

When she'd first come up with the idea of a small, exclusive hotel where couples could play out their fantasies in an authentic setting, she'd been excited by the prospect of setting it all up and had also felt that it was a way of keeping David's interest. Although he'd told her that he loved her, she was well aware that love was never necessarily eternal, and in his case might well be very short-lived if he became bored or she started to be too needy.

She wondered why it was that at work she was always decisive, firm and unwilling to tolerate difficult people and yet she'd fallen in love with a man who required totally different qualities from the woman in his life. David loved her for being vulnerable and obedient to his will in the context of their sexual relationship, but now that their private life was overlapping into a professional relationship as well, it was more difficult for her to be what he wanted in private. To make matters worse, she knew that with the arrival of Emily, jealousy was starting to eat away at her.

'How was your evening?' she asked lightly, as he came into the bedroom, towelling his light brown hair.

'Fascinating!' he exclaimed. 'I think Emily is finally beginning to understand how young women in Victorian times lived and behaved, and that makes the games so much more fun.'

It's a pity she didn't manage that during rehearsals for the play,' retorted Grace.

'Perhaps this will help her acting then!' said David with a smile.

'I very much hope she's going to drop out of *Mrs Warren's Profession*. I couldn't possibly—'

'I know, you don't want to face her after this, but in all seriousness I doubt if you'll have to. Lucien has booked them in for each experience, so she'll need three weekdays off every month. Now, let's not talk about your play.' And sliding beneath the duvet he put his arms round her and moved her close to him.

She could feel his erection nudging against her hip, but knowing that this was the result of what had happened in the Victorian Suite rather than because he wanted her, she drew away.

'What's the matter?' he asked in surprise.

'I'm tired,' she lied.

Pushing her back against the pillows, David leant over her and looked directly into her large, brown eyes.

'No you're not. You're annoyed because I've been turned on by my evening with Lucien and Emily.'

Staring up at him, and seeing the once-familiar shuttered look in his eyes, Grace knew that she had to tell him the truth, and decided to do it in a way that would hopefully give him something to think about too. 'Yes, that's true,' she confessed, 'but I'm also upset that I wasn't invited to take part. I like Lucien, and I wanted to spend more time with the two of them. I was disappointed they only wanted you there. I suppose I felt frustrated.'

For one brief moment, before he turned his head away, she saw a flicker of surprise cross his face. 'Unfortunately we can't choose what the guests want to do,' he replied. 'You'll be pleased to hear that Lucien wants both of us there in the morning, and the lady's maid. Hopefully that will satisfy you.'

'I'm sure it will.'

'In the meantime, perhaps if you close your eyes you can pretend I'm Lucien,' he added.

'I don't want you to be Lucien, I wanted—'

'That's what you said, so let's do it Lucien's favourite way, shall we?' he said quietly, and Grace knew that while she'd banished the spectre of unwanted jealousy, she'd also annoyed him.

'I don't know what his favourite way is,' she protested.

'No, you don't. You know very little about him, but since he fascinates you so much, I'll show you,' he retorted, turning her on her face and pushing a pillow under her stomach.

He was genuinely annoyed now, and Grace felt herself tense as he slid a hand between her thighs, reaching under her to caress her vulva until her sex lips began to open and she started to become moist. Swiftly he pushed a second pillow beneath her stomach, running his fingers lightly around her clitoris but never quite letting her excitement build to a peak.

She felt him straddle the back of her thighs, and then his fingers were moving with tantalising slowness up and down her inner sex lips, constantly brushing very lightly over the swollen clitoris but only ever just enough to make the hot tingles start and then he would stop.

She was desperate for him to turn her over and enter her now, but she kept quiet, not daring to say a word. She could hear his rapid breathing, which only added to her excitement. Then, without warning, he withdrew his fingers and she felt his hands parting the cheeks of her bottom. 'No!' she protested, unable to contain her frustration.

'But this is what Lucien likes, my darling,' he said softly, and then she felt him spreading her own juices inside her rectum, moistening the wafer-thin skin there before abruptly lifting her by the hips and thrusting hard into her back passage. But before he began to move inside her, he let one hand slide beneath her again. Then, using his thumb and index finger, he imprisoned her swollen clitoris and squeezed it at the base while at the same time beginning to thrust in and out.

Her trapped clitoris began to feel hot and the heat spread upwards to her lower belly, making all the muscles twist and coil. At the same time the fullness in her rectum put pressure on the tingling nerve endings, and the stimulating mixture of pain and pleasure spread through her entire body until with a loud scream her body contracted violently. She could feel the muscles in her rectum tightening involuntarily around David as he thrust, while her orgasm engulfed her.

When the last tremors of pleasure had died away, Grace remained lying face down on the bed, exhausted, sated, but slightly uneasy about David's motivation.

David rolled off her back and moved away to his side of the bed. 'It seems you were right. You will like Lucien,' he said after a long silence. She didn't reply.

'You enjoyed it, and you can't pretend you didn't,' he continued, almost apologetically. 'Your body is made for sexual pleasure, Grace. That's one of the reasons I fell in love with you. You don't like being forced to face the truth about yourself. I thought I was giving you what you said you'd wanted this evening, that's all. You like a mixture of pain and pleasure. We both remember the days at the Club, where you made that discovery. Why try to deny it now?'

'I'm not denying it. Everything you say is true, but shouldn't you be truthful, too? Weren't you a little bit annoyed with me just now, even though I enjoyed it? How can we have a proper relationship if you can't be honest with me?'

There was a long, long silence before he spoke. 'For a brief moment I was angry and I'm sorry about that. I rarely lose control of myself, and I'm not proud of it. I didn't hurt you, did I?' he added anxiously. She shook her head. 'Let's get some sleep, then. I think that's what we both need after today.'

Slowly he turned his back on her but she curled herself

round him so that they were lying like spoons. 'I hope this hotel works out for us,' she whispered, more to herself than to him, and as he slowly relaxed back against her she felt a rush of relief before drifting off to sleep.

Chapter Two

At eight o'clock the next morning, while Emily was eating breakfast in bed brought up by Tilly, her personal maid – a red-haired young woman whose buxom figure was clearly in evidence despite the shapeless grey dress she was wearing – Lucien went into the garden and phoned Amber on his mobile.

'You took your time!' she said irritably. 'You were meant to call me last night.'

'I was busy last night. I'm having a holiday with Emily; you can hardly expect me to give up the pleasures of her delightful body just because you want an update on everything.'

'Spare me the details. How are things going?'

'The hotel's very good. I think Grace is going to make a success of it.'

'That's not what I'm interested in.'

'Really? You do surprise me,' said Lucien in an amused tone. 'It's a little early to judge, but one thing that I hadn't expected has happened. Emily has definitely taken a fancy to David, without any encouragement from me.'

'Well, I did expect that. Much more to the point, does David fancy her? I don't think she's quite the shrinking violet in the boudoir that Grace was in the beginning, but she won't be used to the kind of thing the hotel has to offer.'

Lucien hesitated. 'I think she interests him, because he's always interested in untutored sexuality. Emily is enthusiastic but naturally lacks control, so in that respect she's of interest to him.'

'What about Grace? Is he still as keen on her?'

'My dear Amber, of course he's still keen on her, as you choose to put it. He's plainly delighted by the hotel, too, which was a masterstroke on her part. As to whether or not she'll continue to hold his interest in bed, it's difficult for me to judge. He isn't a man who goes round talking about his feelings, as you well know.'

'You said you wanted Grace. You'll need to persuade her away from him more forcefully if he's not tiring of her. I thought that was our agreement.'

'At the moment I don't think it would be possible for me to take her away from him, much as I'd like to. She seems contented, or as contented as any woman could be who was in love with him. Give it time, Amber. This is only the first break here for us. It would be foolish of me to show my hand too soon. In any case, I'd rather wait and see what happens without me having to do too much.'

'She ruined my life!' shouted Amber. 'I've lost David, and my role at the Club, I want her to pay for that, and the worst thing that could happen to her is for her to lose David's love.'

'Or fall out of love with him herself.'

'That wouldn't hurt her as much as him leaving her, but I suppose it would have to do,' said Amber sulkily.

Looking across the lawn, Lucien saw David strolling towards him. 'I have to go now. I'll ring you as soon as I get home and tell you everything.. But don't expect any more phone calls from here. David will get suspicious.'

'He's always suspicious of everyone and everything,

that's why he's so successful,' snapped Amber, and then the line went dead.

'I didn't know they had mobile phones in Victorian times,' remarked David when he reached Lucien.

'That's why I came out here to use it. It's not a Victorian garden!'

David nodded. 'Good point. Business problems?'

Since Lucien was a partner in one of David's businesses, he could hardly lie. 'No, it was a personal call.'

'At eight in the morning? Emily isn't enough for you?' asked David with a smile.

'Would she be enough for you? Sorry, that's a stupid question, no one woman has ever proved to be enough for you! We must get back to the hotel. I'm looking forward to this morning. Incidentally, I like that maid of yours.'

'Tilly? Yes, she's excellent.'

Lucien realised that David had sidestepped his comment about no one woman being enough for him. 'You and Grace will both be joining us soon, won't you?'

David nodded. 'You'd better come back in now, or your young Victorian mistress might start to feel neglected.'

As they walked back to the house together, Lucien

could sense that David was suspicious after finding him making a phone call in the middle of the garden at eight in the morning. He wished that Amber had been willing to wait for news. He was sure that he could win Grace away from David, using Emily as bait, but it would take time. However, the rewards would be high both for him and for Amber.

From the moment Lucien had set eyes on Grace during her final trial at The Dining Club, he'd known that he wanted her, but he'd also known that taking any woman away from David could prove difficult and – if you were a business colleague – dangerous too.

'I can't breathe!' Emily cried, clinging on to the window ledge in the bedroom as Tilly pulled hard on the laces of her corset.

'It's because your waist is too large. We need to train it, madam,' replied Tilly.

'You're not going to train it in two days,' Emily protested. 'That's tight enough.'

'I'm sorry, miss, but the master said you were to be laced as tightly as possible. There! That's better,' she added, pulling hard with a hook so that Emily was forced to breathe in. 'See how lovely your morning dress looks now,' she added, fastening the buttons down the back of the pale blue bodice.

Emily looked at herself in the dressing-table mirror. 'It's so tight,' she complained. 'I didn't enjoy my bath either. The bath on legs was nice, but the jugs of water got cold too quickly.' The maid didn't reply. 'Have you tried it?' Emily persisted.

'No, miss. Do you need any help putting up your hair?'

'I suppose so.' Emily sat down on the dressing-table stool and stared at her reflection. Her skin was glowing, probably from lack of alcohol, she thought to herself, and it was true that the tight lacing of her undergarments had given her figure a wonderful hourglass shape, but she wasn't comfortable and she was feeling irritable. When Lucien had promised her a short holiday of unimaginable Victorian delights, she hadn't expected anything like this. On the other hand, she hadn't expected such an exciting time sexually either.

Lucien was the best lover she'd ever had, but then he was older than any of her other boyfriends, and far more sophisticated. What he'd kept well hidden was his liking for more unusual forms of sexual pleasure, and she was struggling a little with this. On the plus side she really liked David, whose habit of watching her closely all the time was a big turn-on for her. She just hoped that things weren't going to get too extreme today, because she wasn't the kind of person who liked to fail at anything.

'You look lovely, Emily!' exclaimed Lucien, entering the room. Tilly gave a quick curtsy and went to leave. 'No, you stay,' Lucien ordered her. 'We may need you later. Emily, David and Grace are going to be joining us soon. I'm hoping we'll all find the morning stimulating and exciting. A lot went on behind closed doors in Victorian times!'

Emily glanced at Tilly, whose face was impassive, and felt a creeping sense of unease. 'What if I don't find it exciting?' she asked Lucien.

'Then of course we'll leave at once.'

'Oh, I don't want to leave, but if I don't enjoy whatever entertainment has been laid on for us, can't we miss it out?'

Lucien shook his head. 'That's not how it works here. Naturally we can leave, but it's not a pick-and-mix holiday. You and I embrace everything that each suite has to offer, or we pack our bags and leave. I hope it doesn't come to that, though, and I know David would be disappointed as well.'

Just the mention of David's name sent a shiver down Emily's spine and, remembering the previous evening, she was immediately determined that no matter what happened, she wasn't going to ask to leave.

Chapter Three

Grace glanced at herself in the bedroom mirror. The low-cut, gold-coloured morning gown fitted her perfectly, emphasising her narrow waist and her curves, but she was grateful that she didn't live in an age when women spent their entire lives physically restricted and socially governed by rules about the way they dressed.

'Beautiful,' said David, coming up behind her and a hand on either side of her waist. 'Leave your hair loose, though, it could be useful to you.' Then he lifted her hair off her neck and kissed the soft skin beneath gently. She trembled slightly, and he laughed. 'So deliciously responsive; what a lucky man I am!'

'What will we be doing this morning?' she asked.

'I think it will be more fun if all three of you ladies get a surprise,' he responded.

'What do you mean, "all three"?'

'Tilly is needed as well. It should be a most interesting morning for everyone.'

'I'm not expected to pleasure Emily myself again, am I?' asked Grace.

'I told you, it's a surprise. Come along, it's time we joined them.'

'I can't do that, David. Suppose I ever have to direct her again? It would be impossible once we'd been that intimate. It would be bad enough after last time.'

'Work and private lives are two totally different things. Don't start being difficult, darling.'

Grace could see both their faces reflected in the mirror. David's eyes were bright, and she realised that this was a test for her as much as for Emily. He was trying to find out how far she was willing to go with something that might affect her career in order to keep his interest. Her mind raced. Emily was never going to be a famous stage actress, in fact she'd be lucky to remain famous at all for very long, whereas she desperately wanted David by her side for ever. It wasn't fair of him, but she knew that something in him always drove him on to test the people who cared for him to their limits. Sometimes she wondered if he ever scared himself, risking his happiness with his own behaviour, like a child testing the boundaries of its mother's love.

'Do you love me?' she asked, without turning round.

'You know I do, but I don't like being asked. Now, can we join the others? It will be fine, I promise you. You're not used to your new role yet, that's all.'

'By "new role", I assume you mean I'm no longer the one who's a novelty to you?'

His hands tightened on her waist. 'That's not what I meant at all. You never cease to surprise and delight me, but Emily has no understanding of this way of life and you do.'

His voice was soft and seductive, and she believed him, because as far as she knew he never lied, but his words brought the shadow of the discarded Amber back into her mind. 'All right,' she agreed, and heard his soft sigh of relief as they left their room.

Inside the Victorian Suite, Emily was sitting in the window seat looking moody but beautiful, Tilly was waiting with her hands folded in front of her and Lucien was sitting in one of the two large chairs reading the paper. When Grace and David arrived he jumped out of the chair, crossed the room and kissed the back of Grace's hand.

'Emily, our visitors have arrived!' he announced.

Glancing up, the pretty, blonde actress managed a brief smile but she still looked sulky. It was an expression Grace recognised from rehearsals. 'Emily is feeling a little out of sorts this morning,' continued Lucien. 'I'm hoping some company will cheer her up. Tilly, arrange some pillows on the chaise longue.'

As the maid did as she'd been asked, Grace greeted Emily with a kiss on the cheek. 'Did women kiss each other in Victorian times?' asked the blonde girl irritably.

Lucien smiled indulgently at her, but Grace could see that the smile didn't reach his eyes. 'I'm sure they did a great deal more than that during their "At Home" mornings. Tilly, remove all your mistress's clothes for us.'

Emily frowned. 'I've only just got dressed. The tight lacing nearly killed me!'

'Then be grateful it's coming off,' Lucien retorted. 'After that, Tilly, please help Grace remove her morning dress, but she should keep her undergarments on for the moment.'

Tilly obeyed, her face totally expressionless. Once Emily was undressed, Tilly turned her attention on Grace. Lucien pointed to the chaise longue. 'Lie down there, Emily. As you're so clearly bored this morning, we're all going to play a game. It's called Peaks and Troughs.'

'I've never heard of it,' Emily retorted, looking uncomfortable standing nude in front of them all.

'Well, I can assure you, you'll never forget it after this morning,' Lucien responded, before smiling at Grace who was now standing in her undergarments, the soft swell of the tops of her breasts just visible. 'David will explain the game to you, because he's played it before and knows all the rules,' Lucien continued, and as Emily turned her head to look at David, Grace waited nervously to hear what was going to be expected of her.

'Because mornings were the time when Victorian women would sometimes call on each other, you three ladies will be the only players, but Lucien and I will watch,' David explained. 'Emily, your body will be played, rather like a musical instrument. You'll experience wonderful peaks of pleasure but never the actual moment of release. When Grace and Tilly sense you're near to that, they'll reduce the intensity of their playing and let you calm down to a trough, before repeating the melody again. In my experience, half an hour is the optimum amount of time to allow for the game, so thirty minutes of peaks and troughs await you. After that, it's up to Lucien what happens.'

'I'll want to come before then!' exclaimed Emily, her eyes huge in her face.

'What you want isn't of interest to us,' said David. 'The game is all that matters. In fact, should you fail to control yourself for the full amount of time, then Lucien and I will have to think of a forfeit for you, and I can assure you that it won't be one you'll enjoy.'

Emily looked at him in amazement, clearly shocked by both his words and the tone of his voice.

Listening to him talking, Grace could feel herself becoming aroused. She knew how difficult this was going to be for Emily, and how great a struggle. She also knew that she and Tilly had to judge everything exactly right if the young blonde wasn't going to end up paying a forfeit that wouldn't give her any pleasure at all.

'Of course, should you fail,' continued David, 'then naturally Grace and Tilly will pay forfeits too, because part of the blame will lie with them. Now, is everything quite clear?'

Grace and Emily nodded, but Emily shook her head. 'I don't understand!' she exclaimed. 'Why can't we just have sex and enjoy ourselves?'

'Because this is how I like to enjoy myself,' said Lucien, 'and as you're my girlfriend I want you to learn to enjoy the same things that I do. I'm sure you will. Grace was like you once, weren't you, Grace? You quickly learnt to love games like this, though, and I know you'll help Emily on her voyage of discovery.'

Grace nodded, not wanting to say anything about her early days with David in the presence of Emily.

'Excellent, everything you two "visitors" may need is on the side table, and if you wish to remove more clothing, Grace, then you may but Tilly must remain fully clothed throughout. Let the game begin!'

Grace crossed to the side table and picked up a long, soft Victorian feather boa, plus a small vial of lubricating jelly. As she knelt at the foot of the chaise longue she could see that Emily was trembling, her eyes darting around the room. She felt a moment's pity for the girl, but had no intention of earning any forfeit herself, so concentrated on the task in hand.

'Open your legs, Emily, relax and let them just fall apart.'

Emily remained motionless, her naked legs close together. 'Tilly, part her legs for me,' said Grace and the maid obeyed. 'Relax, Emily,' murmured Grace. 'Remember, this is going to feel wonderful.'

The blonde girl didn't reply, but when Grace began to move the feather boa softly up along the curves of her inner thighs she heard Emily give a soft sigh of pleasure, and saw her legs relax, opening her up more to the caress of the feathers. David and Lucien were standing on either side of the girl, looking down on her naked body with keen interest.

As Emily's breathing quickened, Grace bent forward and drew the boa up across the younger woman's vulva, allowing it to linger there for just a few seconds before taking it back down the inside of her thighs. 'Keep stroking her with that,' she said to Tilly, 'but don't go any higher than I've just done.'

As the maid obeyed, Grace moved so that she could let her long, loose hair brush over the exposed rounded belly of the prone Emily, whose hips began to twitch restlessly.

'Does that feel good, Emily?' asked Lucien.

'Yes!' moaned the young actress. 'But I want to come.'

'Of course you do, you're reaching a peak, but remember the rules. No climax, only a trough must follow a peak.'

Next Grace brushed the palms of her hands delicately over Emily's hard, tight breasts, feeling the nipples stiffening against her touch, and now Emily's whole body shifted restlessly, and tiny guttural cries escaped from her mouth.

'She's very close, madam,' said Tilly warningly, and Grace hastily stopped stimulating Emily's breasts, trailed her hair down over the thin skin covering Emily's hip bones and then both she and Tilly stopped all stimulation.

Emily cried out with disappointment. 'I was so close!' she whimpered. 'I need to come. I'm aching between my thighs.'

'Be grateful you didn't,' said Lucien. 'It's very early for the game to end. David and I wouldn't have been at all happy.'

'You were careless there, Grace, take care,' said David, and at the sound of the excitement in his voice Grace's whole body went tight with desire. She could imagine only too well how Emily was feeling at this moment, and her own body was also highly aroused.

For several minutes she and Tilly left Emily alone, until her breathing was back to normal and the flush of arousal had vanished from her upper chest. Then as Tilly began to caress Emily's breasts with the boa, Grace dipped her index finger into the vial and moved it in circular motions around the blonde's vaginal lips. Despite the rules, Emily tried to move her body so that Grace's finger would move inside her.

For a long time Grace continued to play the frantic Emily, applying more pressure by massaging her outer sex lips, moving them slowly over the swollen clitoris beneath. Every time Emily's moans turned to little cries, Grace stopped, aware that was the clue to the fact that Emily was about to climax. Each time she stopped, Emily cried out in a mixture of frustration and relief and Grace guessed that the aroused and tormented girl didn't know if she wanted a climax more than she feared a forfeit.

Eventually, as Grace and Tilly continued to play with Emily's body in the same mixture of ways, stopping, waiting and then restarting every time she was about to come, Grace lost track of time and was relieved when Lucien said, 'Only five minutes more, ladies.'

'I think you should increase the stimulation now,' said David, and despite Emily's frantic protestations,

Grace knew that she had to obey. Dipping her finger back into the vial she moved the lubricated pad of her index finger slowly inside Emily's outer sex lips and very gently rolled it over the swollen, moist clitoris.

Forgetting everything else, Emily's body became frantic to climax and her legs opened wider as she writhed on the chaise longue while Tilly continued to caress her breasts with the feather boa.

'That's good, Grace,' said Lucien, 'and it's nearly thirty minutes, so just make sure you don't come, Emily. You've done very well, and you must be longing for this peak to be allowed to reach its climax.'

'Imagine how great the pleasure would be,' mused David. 'That hot rush of release flooding through her body. She must really need that now.'

Grace wanted to beg him to be quiet, not to make her task even more difficult, but she knew better than to say a word. Slowly she circled the girl's clitoris with steady rhythmical pressure and then, to Grace's dismay, without warning Emily's body arched off the bed and with a loud scream of ecstasy the hot, sweet flood of an orgasm overcame her and she wept with what Grace knew from past experience would be a mixture of blissful release and despair at her own failure.

'Such a shame,' said Lucien, sounding anything but regretful. 'You only had two more minutes to go before the game ended, my sweet. Rest now; I'll decide what your forfeit must be when you've recovered.'

'I don't think Grace needs time to recover,' said David. 'Stand up, Grace. Emily's failure was – as you know – your failure too, was it not?'

'Yes,' she admitted.

'Do you feel aroused by what's been happening?'

She was sure that he knew full well how unhappy she would be that this was happening in front of Emily. 'Yes,' she repeated softly.

'Then you can be pleasured once Emily feels strong enough to get up and watch. She can stand by Lucien.'

For a moment, Grace almost hated him, but due to her desire for sexual release and her instinctive longing to do as he wanted, understanding that this was how he could reassure himself that she loved him, she knew that she had to obey.

'I'm sure it won't take you many minutes,' he added, as Emily got up and Tilly helped her into a wrap before removing Grace's undergarments until she was standing naked in front of everyone. She lay down on the chaise longue, the scene of Emily's struggle to control her sexuality, and David crouched down next to her.

'Your nipples are already hard,' he murmured, running the back of his hand across both her breasts. 'That really turned you on, didn't it? You're so ready to come, but do you know what I'd like you to do? I'd like you to show Emily that it's possible for you to wait another fifteen minutes for total satisfaction.'

She looked at him in horror. 'I can't do that!' she whispered. 'You know I can't.'

'If you love me as much as you say you do, you can,' he said quietly. 'I'll let Lucien have the honour of testing you. Knowing your body so well it would be unfair on you if I did it.'

'You want me to fail,' she said accusingly, keeping her voice low.

'Of course I don't, but I miss seeing you struggle as you used to struggle. Watching you with Emily was incredibly exciting, but this will be even better.'

It was just as she'd feared. Grace knew that unless she could offer him the same level of excitement that she had done in their early days, and certainly as much as Emily, then she wasn't going to be able to keep his love.

'All right,' she agreed, and the look of love and admiration in his eyes was almost enough of a reward for what was to come. But as he stood up and Lucien knelt at the foot of the chaise longue, his fingers parting her sex lips, already moist with excitement, she wondered how she was ever going to manage.

At first he used his fingers on her, but she was able to control her mounting excitement by keeping her breathing slow and steady. Once he realised that, he used his tongue instead, licking and sucking at her swelling flesh while his fingers played across the base of her stomach, occasionally pressing down above her pubic bone.

Slowly she felt her orgasm building, starting as the merest flicker deep within her belly, but spreading quickly as his tongue swirled around the base of her clitoris before flicking inside her, drawing her juices out to make her so wet between her thighs that she was ashamed of her own need.

'Only three more minutes to go,' said David, and Lucien swiftly pushed his other hand under her body, lifting her vulva closer to his mouth as he very slowly inserted the tip of the middle finger of this hand into her rectum. Her tight rectal muscles made it almost painful, but then the nerve endings from her rectum sent shards of pleasure darting through her to join those deep inside her vagina. She felt her vaginal muscles tightening around Lucien's tongue and her whole body tensed.

Withdrawing his tongue, Lucien pressed the palm of his hand over the outside of her vulva, and he applied slowly increasing pressure that stimulated her already desperate clitoris until she couldn't control her excitement any longer and as she went into a spasm of overwhelming and blissful release she wanted to cry at her own failure.

Lucien continued to stimulate her until her body became still, and she closed her eyes in disappointment. Then she heard David's voice. 'You did it, Grace,' he said quietly. 'Lucien took two minutes too long. You were amazing.' And he kissed her gently on her sweat-streaked forehead.

Dazed and totally sated, she allowed herself to be dressed again by Tilly, and then leaving the maid to whatever forfeit Lucien chose for her, she and David left the Victorian Suite and returned to their rooms at the top of the hotel.

'Which suite has Lucien booked for next month?' asked David, as the two of them changed back into modern clothes.

'The Pleasure Suite,' Grace replied, piling her hair up into a French pleat.

'Interesting, is it for his pleasure or Emily's, I wonder?'

'The intention is that everyone gets pleasure from it.'

'Of course, but I'm sure Lucien intends to initiate Emily into some new form of pleasure.'

Grace glanced at him. 'You mean you hope he does.'

'Naturally. You know, Grace, watching you today I could hardly believe how far you've come since I first met you. You've chosen such clever themes, and I know that no matter what you may tell yourself, vanilla sex will never be enough for you now.'

Grace thought for a moment. 'Sometimes it is; sometimes it's what I want more than anything, because it's then that I feel closest to you.'

He raised an eyebrow. 'Really? I feel closest to you at moments like this morning, when I watch you struggling to subdue your desires in order not to fail at a game. It's incredibly erotic to watch. I wanted to take you there and then. I was so proud of how much you've learnt.'

'You're a good tutor,' she said quietly.

'You make that sound like a bad thing.'

'No, but I can never go back, can I?'

'Go back?'

'To the person I was before you took me to The Dining Club.'

Cupping her face in his hands, David kissed her gently. 'No, my darling, you can't, and if you're honest with yourself I don't think you'd want to either. You were made for this kind of life. You're everything I've ever wanted, and it makes you happy too, doesn't it? You enjoyed this morning as much as I did.'

Grace relaxed against him, savouring this rare moment of tender honesty between them. 'Of course I did, but have I really gained more than I've lost?'

'That rather depends on how much you value innocence,' he replied, 'and judging by your brilliant hotel, having your eyes opened to a new world of sophisticated sexuality is the best thing that's happened to you. Your body experiences pleasure like never before, and you've used your creative talents to set up a unique business that will make a lot of people very happy, and be a success.'

She knew that he was right, and suspected that her unexpected moment of doubt was more about the fact that she was no longer the young innocent in the games her lover enjoyed so much. Her hard-won victory over Amber nearly a year ago had seemed such a triumph at the time, but now she was beginning to realise it was possible that it hadn't been a victory so much as an opportunity for her relationship with David to progress.

The question she now had to face was whether or not he was ever going to be able to give her what she most wanted: commitment and unconditional love.

Chapter Four

Emily woke early as the sun streamed in through the light muslin curtains. Lucien was still asleep, and turning on her side she studied him closely. They'd met at a show business party, when the director of a short, independent film she was in was hoping to get his financial backing. He'd told Emily to pay him plenty of attention, but in fact Lucien had paid her attention from the moment he arrived.

He'd told her how much he'd enjoyed watching her in *Kesby Close*, the TV serial in which she'd made her name, and remained by her side the whole evening. When they'd left together she'd known they'd go back to his place, and was both excited and flattered. He was wealthy, sophisticated and interesting, and also considerably older than the other men she'd dated who'd all been in their early twenties, like her.

Lucien had turned out to be a considerate and highly inventive lover and although she wasn't in love with him, she liked him a lot and hoped that with his money and influence he might be good for her career, too. She had no illusions about the profession she was in, and was determined to get to the top one way or another. Her pretty face and very feminine figure wouldn't last for ever, but while they did she intended to make full use of them.

When Lucien started taking her to swingers' parties and dinners where sexual games were the after-dinner entertainment, she'd been in her element. Emily had never been shy, and had a high sex drive that Lucien and his friends were always able to satisfy.

When he'd told her about a new themed hotel catering for sexually sophisticated couples, she'd imagined them spending time together, and assumed that in the evenings it would be similar to the after-dinner games the two of them took part in. In the event it hadn't turned out to be like that at all, and she wasn't sure how much she was enjoying herself.

Lucien seemed different here. He was taking the Victorian theme far more seriously than she'd expected and this holiday break went further than anything she'd ever imagined. If she was honest, the best thing about it was David. He really turned her on, and his silent intensity was incredibly arousing. He wasn't like any man she'd met before, and the fact that he seemed relatively disinterested in her as a person only made him more intriguing. She was used to a very different response from the men she met.

On the other hand, she knew she couldn't go back to the play, so that was a job lost. Not that she'd been enjoying it much, but Grace had such a great reputation as a director that her agent would be furious if she pulled out, but pull out she must, especially as Lucien said he'd booked them in for further breaks here. She still found it difficult to believe that the Grace who ran the hotel was the same Grace who'd been directing her in *Mrs Warren's Profession*. She seemed totally different here, almost subservient to David at times, whereas she was always in absolute command in the theatre.

As Lucien turned towards her in his sleep she slid one hand down his body and felt his early-morning arousal. Lightly stroking his erection with her fingers she kissed him and snuggled close to his warm body. She loved half-awake morning sex. Lucien's eyes opened and she smiled happily at him. 'I hoped that might wake you!'

He frowned. 'What on earth do you think you're doing?'

Emily laughed. 'What does it feel as though I'm doing?'

To her dismay he got out of bed and pulled a robe on over his nightwear. 'There must be something wrong with you!' he exclaimed. 'Victorian wives don't behave like that. You must be sick.'

'But I'm not a Victorian wife!' exclaimed Emily. 'Surely I'm allowed—'

'Stop right there,' said Lucien sharply. 'You're in a Victorian play at the moment, aren't you?'

'I was!'

'And would you have come out of character and had a little chat with one of your fellow actors during a performance?'

'Of course not.'

'Then don't do it here. I'm sorry, Emily, but from the moment we arrived you became a Victorian woman, and as such your behaviour this morning is totally unacceptable. I'm afraid that I'll have to speak to David about it. I'm sure he'll help me think of a suitable punishment for you.'

There was no hint of amusement or playfulness in his dark brown eyes, and Emily began to feel nervous. 'I'm sorry, but all I wanted was for us to be the way we usually are for a moment. Is that so wrong?'

'Yes, and if you can't, or won't, understand that then I suggest we finish right now, pack our bags and I'll drop you off at your flat on my way home.'

'You mean, we'd split up over this?'

'Emily, the parties we've been to, the things we've done, they were nothing compared to what I really enjoy. You're made for sex, we both know that, but for me it has to be different sometimes, more extreme. I hoped you'd like it too, and if I made a mistake then I'm sorry.'

She lay on the bed, wishing that she wasn't already aroused, and began to wonder if she'd made a mistake too, misjudging both herself and Lucien. However, he'd now mentioned David, and although the thought of David made her nervous, it also excited her.

'I'm sorry, but you should have explained it more,' she said at last.

Lucien raised his eyebrows. 'So your mistake is actually my fault?'

'No, of course not,' she said hastily.

Lucien nodded approvingly. 'That's a good girl. As we're awake I'll get Tilly to come and help you wash and dress, while I dress and take a stroll round the grounds. You must stay in our rooms. Once David is free, we'll administer your punishment and then hopefully we can put the whole incident behind us.'

As she watched him go into the bathroom and waited for Tilly to arrive, Emily hoped she hadn't just made another mistake.

'Any problems this morning?' Grace asked Andrew at their start-of-the-day staff meeting.

'None at all. It's all going very well,' he assured her. 'You and David are wanted in the Victorian Suite this morning, of course, although at the moment Lucien isn't sure what he wants for this afternoon. All the guests know they have to leave at six.'

'Fine. So far it seems to be a success,' said Grace.

'You've done a brilliant job. Everyone has booked to

come again next month as well, and we've had a new booking for next time, which will fill the place left empty by the couple that left the first evening.'

'I'll celebrate tonight, when I can relax. Will you be around to have a drink with us?'

Andrew shook his head. 'Sorry, I thought I'd see if Fran's free to go out for a meal.'

Grace was surprised. The last time she'd seen Fran, her friend had suggested that her relationship with Andrew was more off than on. 'That's nice,' she murmured.

'Don't worry; she won't be visiting The Dining Club or this hotel. It's not her scene.'

'But it's yours!'

Andrew shrugged. 'I'm beginning to realise that other things matter too. Don't panic, I won't be leaving here, but my private life is changing. You were right not to choose me, Grace. You'd soon have grown tired of me.'

She smiled at him. 'Perhaps. I'll always think of you as "The Road Not Taken", which incidentally is my favourite poem.'

'Too sad for me,' he replied. 'So many choices, how can we ever be sure we've made the right one? Are you sure now, Grace?'

She hesitated. 'I'm sure at the moment,' she said quietly, and he nodded in understanding.

'Sure of what?' asked David, as he came into the staff room.

'That everything's under control,' said Grace quickly.

'Yes, it's going exceedingly well,' agreed David. 'Lucien wants us in their room at ten o'clock. I'll take a coffee upstairs, make a few business calls and then when you join me we can get changed and the fun will begin.'

'I hope it's fun for Emily,' said Grace.

'From what I've heard it will be fun for all of us,' he assured her and she felt the familiar tightening of her stomach that was half excitement and half nervous tension, well aware that David and Lucien's idea of fun would be testing for both her and the younger woman.

At ten o'clock there was a tap on the door of the Victorian Suite. 'That will be David and Grace,' said Lucien. 'Open the door please, Tilly.'

Emily was sitting in one of the armchairs wearing her robe over her corset and pantaloons. She swallowed nervously as the two visitors came in, knowing that some form of punishment now awaited her.

'I know this will shock you both,' said Lucien, 'but

I'm afraid Emily displayed highly unnatural behaviour for a Victorian woman this morning.' And he went on to describe exactly what Emily had done to him in the bed that morning.

Grace's face remained expressionless, but David eyed the young blonde with keen interest. 'Dear me, Emily, what were you thinking of?' he asked.

'I—'

'The question was rhetorical,' he continued. 'Lucien, what would you like us to do?'

'I think the birch will be the most suitable punishment. If she shows sufficient regret then nothing else will be necessary. If not, I found an interesting object in one of the bedside drawers that we can use. If we don't use it now, I'll use it later.'

Emily saw David nod in approval, and noted the look of sympathy on Grace's face, although her expression became neutral again when David turned to look at her.

'What do you think, Grace?' Lucien asked.

'It sounds very appropriate,' she replied.

'I don't want her to make a big fuss,' he continued, 'so I thought it would be a good idea if you were to experience the birch first. That way she'll understand how to conduct herself. I'm sure you're more than capable of remaining silent, which is what I expect from Emily.'

'Grace's self-control is legendary. She won't disappoint us,' David assured him.

Lucien smiled. 'Excellent. Tilly, please help Grace undress, then take a spare robe from the cupboard and put it on her, but back to front. Don't do up the buttons. This will mean she can be fastened face down to the bed with straps, the front of her body covered but leaving her back totally exposed.'

Emily watched in dismay as Tilly quickly helped Grace remove all her clothing, then pulled the robe on from the front, rather like a hospital gown, leaving the tender flesh of her back and buttocks free for Lucien to work on. Emily was amazed at how obedient Grace was, and how quietly she obeyed all his commands.

Swiftly the two men spread-eagled her, fastening her wrists and ankles to the sides of the bed, using black Velcro straps. Lucien then went to his wardrobe and Emily's eyes widened in shock as he withdrew a long, pliable birch rod.

'I think six strokes, slow but firm,' he murmured, and Emily noticed Grace's body tremble slightly at his words. 'Each strike will be in a different place, and providing Grace remains silent then that will be sufficient. Of course, if Grace should make any sound, then I would add one extra stroke for each sound she makes. It's unfortunate that she has to do this merely to show you how to behave, Emily, but I think that seeing what awaits you might help you, too.'

Emily wasn't stupid, and knew full well that seeing what she was going to have to go through would make it even worse for her, but she was learning fast and said nothing, merely nodding her head in agreement.

'Some women,' said David quietly, 'can take pleasure from this kind of thing, especially when the front of their body is being rubbed against the inside of their robe. Any response of a sexual nature would unfortunately only compound the error you made this morning, so be very careful that doesn't happen, Emily.'

She didn't think there was much chance of that, but again simply nodded, almost hypnotised by the sight of Grace's long dark hair spread out over her creamy flesh as she waited for the birch to fall.

David then guided Emily round to the side of the bed, holding her in front of him so that she could watch everything that happened to Grace and every response the other woman made. His hands were tight on her shoulders, and she could feel his body close behind her.

Lucien moved very quietly round to the other side of the bed, drew back his right arm and then flicked the birch with surprising force so that it fell across the left-hand side of Grace's back, just below her shoulder blades. Her whole body jerked with shock and Emily saw a thin red line appear on the creamy skin, but not a sound escaped Grace's lips.

Lucien paused. 'That's a good girl,' he said quietly. 'You really are adorable, Grace. So well trained and obedient, but also very receptive to pleasure-pain, I'm told. Is that true, I wonder?' Gently he slid his left hand between her naked, exposed thighs and his fingers moved upwards. 'Yes, it's true,' he said with a hint of satisfaction. 'Fortunately for you, there is no punishment for any pleasure you may gain, David must decide whether you're allowed that or not. No, all you need to do is remain silent.'

As he was speaking he was also raising his right arm again, so that the next blow fell while he was still speaking. This time Grace's body jerked even harder, and Emily heard the sound of the other woman's sharply indrawn breath. She began to shake with genuine fear at the prospect of this being done to her in a few more minutes, and then David's grip tightened on her shoulders.

'It doesn't really hurt,' he murmured. 'Watching it is much worse than experiencing it. You'll do well, Emily. Trust me, you may even enjoy it, as Grace is enjoying it, although you must remember to conceal that from Lucien.'

Swiftly Lucien finished off the strokes, and by the time Grace was being unfastened it was clear that she was highly aroused. As Tilly removed the gown, Emily noticed how stiff Grace's nipples were, and saw that her breasts were tight and hard, but she'd never uttered a sound.

Now David released Emily, so that Tilly could prepare her for her punishment, and she saw him pull the naked Grace hard against him, his hands fondling her until the sound of her rapid breathing seemed to fill the room. 'Let Emily hear you come,' he ordered her. Emily didn't want that to happen, didn't want to hear anything that might arouse her, as she knew she would struggle to remain silent during her punishment.

Despite this, as she was fastened face down to the bed, her back exposed as Grace's had been, she suddenly heard a gasp from Grace followed by a sharp cry of pleasure as she climaxed. Half-aroused and half-terrified, Emily waited for what was to come.

The first blow fell near her waist, and the hot, stinging sensation was like a minor burn. Emily nearly cried out with shock, but just managed to keep her mouth tightly closed so that only a tiny squeak escaped her lips, and she buried her face deep into the bed to try to muffle it.

As the first five blows fell, her body, like Grace's, jerked in response. Desperately she strained to remain silent, secretly striving to do as well as Grace and win David's admiration.

'That's very good,' said Lucien softly. 'David, is this arousing her?'

She wanted to beg David not to touch her, because she knew that despite the short but sharp moments of pain her flesh was responding in the same way as Grace's had, and the touch of his fingers would only arouse her more. She had to stay silent, though, even as she felt him sliding his hand, palm uppermost, beneath her, his fingers lightly caressing the small, swelling bud between her sex lips. As the sixth blow fell he swirled the pad of his finger around the sides of her clitoris and to her shame her whole body convulsed as an orgasm spread through her with such intensity that she could hardly bear it.

'It seems so,' he remarked, and she could hear the amusement in his voice.

'What a shame,' remarked Lucien, as he freed her from the bed. 'You were so good about not crying out, Emily, but it seems that you're even more wanton than I suspected. Well, we'll have to work our way through that on our own, I think. I'm sure David and Grace are needed elsewhere now, but we'll see them again next month in the Pleasure Suite.'

Lying motionless on the bed, Emily wasn't sure whether to feel excited at the prospect or not. Her body had never experienced anything like this before, but sated as she was, she was very much afraid that next time the Pleasure Suite might prove even more intense. All the same, she knew that she would agree to return to the hotel with Lucien. He and David had awakened something in her that she'd never experienced before; she only hoped she was able to cope with whatever lay ahead.

Shortly afterwards, at the top of the hotel, in the privacy of their own suite, David lay the naked Grace face down on the bed and then tenderly licked the red stripes on her back. She trembled with desire as his hands then raised her hips so that he could enter her from behind.

He moved slowly in and out, his fingers splayed each side of her waist, and she felt the warm glow of an impending climax growing deep inside her. 'I'm coming!' she cried, but immediately he stopped moving and she groaned with disappointment as the warmth slowly dissipated.

'Soon,' he promised her, as her body slackened slightly, and then he was moving inside her again, and once more she felt herself approaching the point of no return. This time she kept silent, but David knew her body too well for her to be able to deceive him and just as the intense pleasure was about to flood through her, he withdrew and she found herself flat on the bed again.

'Please, I want to come now!' she exclaimed.

She winced slightly as David turned her over. He looked down at her and smiled. 'I wish we were in the Victorian Suite. I'd enjoy punishing you for being so wanton,' he said softly.

She could feel sweat beading her top lip, and her body was frantic for release. 'We're not in the Victorian

Suite,' she gasped, as he caressed the insides of her thighs, 'and I want to come now.'

His blue eyes darkened for a moment, but then he lifted her hips so that she could wrap her legs round his waist and thrust into her, rotating his hips at first until she was nearly crying with frustration. Only when she gave a sob of frustration did he finally switch to the rhythm that he knew she liked best and almost immediately her body arched and twisted in a climax.

David's climax followed immediately, and for a few minutes they lay entwined on the bed, his arms wrapped round her, and for that moment she was truly happy.

'Enough?' he asked her, and she nodded, her body tired and sated after their time in the Victorian Suite followed by their lovemaking now. 'I'm sure you could manage more.'

Grace shook her head. 'I can't, and I need to get downstairs and—'

'I don't want you to think about work yet. I want to prove you wrong,' he replied, his hands wandering across her rounded breasts until she felt her nipples start to harden again. 'You see, I know you better than you know yourself.'

'David, I don't want to come again.'

'But I want you to,' he replied. 'I like watching you come.'

'This isn't a game,' she responded, but she could tell by the expression on his face that for him it was either a game or a test. He didn't reply, merely spread her long, dark hair out over the pillows, gently stroked her forehead, then slid down her body and pushed her thighs open before letting his tongue move up and down her inner sex lips.

Despite her exhaustion, Grace felt herself responding but she fought to subdue her excitement because she didn't want this to happen. She heard him laugh softly to himself, because he knew what she was trying to do, but when he pushed the protective hood back over her swollen clitoris she knew that he was going to get his way. He paused for a few seconds, and she trembled with despairing excitement as the first flickers of yet another orgasm increased in intensity. Then, when he finally drew the incredibly sensitive bud into his mouth and swirled his tongue over the surface she gave a scream of pleasure mixed with pain, the orgasm was so intense.

Only when her exhausted body stopped responding did he release her, before lying down next to her and nuzzling her neck. 'You see, I know you better than you know yourself. Wasn't that good in the end?'

'Yes,' she admitted.

'I love to watch you fighting against your own sexuality. When we were with Lucien and Emily just now, it reminded me of our early days,' he murmured, pulling her close to him.

Enfolded in his embrace, with the morning sun shining in on them through the bedroom window, Grace knew that she should have been happy. Unfortunately, after hearing his words, she understood that it was watching Emily's struggles that had brought about their lovemaking session. As a result she couldn't help wondering what lay ahead for them all the next month, and whether watching the relatively naïve Emily's struggles were slowly but inexorably going to draw David away from her.

Part Three

Chapter One

Grace had spent the day keeping herself busy, trying not to think about how Lucien had asked David and Tilly to join him and Emily in the suite, but not her.

When the three of them finally came downstairs, Grace could tell by Emily's flushed cheeks and inability to look her in the eye that David had been heavily involved in whatever had taken place.

Lucien smiled warmly at her. 'We've had the most fantastic time, Grace. This hotel is amazing and we can't wait for our break in the Pleasure Suite next month, can we, Emily?'

The blonde young actress, now dressed in a figure-hugging turquoise dress that complemented her bronzed arms and legs, smiled at Grace. 'I certainly can't,' she agreed, and then her eyes flicked to David who was standing just behind Grace. 'Thank you for your help,' she added. 'I don't think I would have enjoyed it the way I did this afternoon if you hadn't been there.'

David rested his hands on Grace's shoulders. 'It's all part of the service,' he said lightly. 'If you and Lucien are happy, then we're happy. Isn't that right, darling?'

'Absolutely,' Grace agreed, hoping that her smile looked genuine.

'Tilly is a gem too,' added Lucien. 'I'm only sorry you didn't fit into my little scenario this afternoon, Grace. Next time I'll make sure we see more of you.'

'God, I'm tired,' said David after Lucien and Emily left. 'I think I'll go back to my place tonight. I've got to leave for Germany at six in the morning, and presumably you'll have to be up early too.'

'Yes, I guess I'll have to phone around to find a replacement for Emily in the play, and that won't be easy at such short notice.'

'It's a pity really, now that she's such an expert on the role of women in Victorian society!' David said, laughing. 'If everyone's gone, let's have a drink before I go.'

Grace didn't want him to go. She'd hoped for an intimate night together, but was determined not to let him know. 'Sounds good to me,' she said brightly. 'You can tell me how the afternoon went if you like.'

'I think not,' he replied. 'After all, if Lucien had wanted you to know then he'd have invited you to join us. In any case, we need to talk about how things went for everyone, and discuss any small problems that need ironing out. I understand we were a man short for the Country Retreat Suite. You'll need to find someone suitable before next month.'

'Who told you that?' asked Grace.

'Who told me doesn't matter. The important thing is that we were a man short. I did mention that you needed more staff, even though it might involve paying them to sit around doing nothing for a lot of the time.'

'You were right,' agreed Grace. 'And I'll sort it out in the morning. For now, I think we should celebrate our success. There's champagne in the fridge.'

'Absolutely,' he agreed. 'I only wish I could spend the night here, so that we could carry on celebrating.'

'Not to worry, I'm quite tired too,' she lied, and was pleased to see a look of surprised disappointment cross his face. Clearly he'd hoped that she would feel disappointed, and although she wished he'd stop playing mind games with her, it was very satisfying when she was able to outplay him.

After their champagne, David looked at his watch. 'Perhaps I could stay over,' he said. 'If I get up at—'

Grace feigned a yawn. 'I'm sorry, but I need my sleep. I think your first idea was the best one, unfortunately.'

Putting an arm round her shoulders, he kissed the side of her neck. 'Are you sure?' he asked softly.

'Quite sure,' she said sleepily, getting to her feet. 'Have a safe flight, darling.'

As she closed the door of the hotel behind him, her pleasure at having outplayed him wasn't quite as great as her frustration at missing spending the night with him, but she knew that she'd done the right thing. David wouldn't risk doing anything like that again.

Lucien dropped Emily back at the flat she shared with three other young actresses and reluctantly took his leave of her. She'd been the perfect partner for what he'd wanted during their break, chiefly because she'd so clearly become desperate to please David. It didn't trouble him that she was more eager to get David's praise than his, because he wasn't in love with her. She was a very pretty young woman, she looked good on his arm and she amused him, but she was merely a pawn in the game he and Amber were playing. A game with high stakes. Grace was the prize he was after, and Amber wanted David back by her side.

Back at his small London town house he phoned Amber, who picked up on the first ring.

'How did it go?' she asked, the tension clear in her voice.

'Better than we could ever have hoped. I did as we'd agreed, and left Grace out of our final afternoon in the Victorian Suite. David certainly enjoyed himself, but more to the point Emily was extremely eager to please him, and by the look on Grace's face when we left, she wasn't happy to be left out of the fun and games.'

'Is David interested in Emily?'

Lucien thought for a moment. 'Not seriously interested, but you know how much he enjoys taking young women by the hand and leading them down his particular pathway to pleasure, especially when they resist at first.'

'And did Emily resist?' she asked eagerly.

'She certainly did. In the end she enjoyed herself, but

it was extremely arousing watching her struggle to cope with all the sensations and new experiences. I would have liked to have got more benefit from that myself, but in order for this to work, sacrifices have to be made!'

'This is no laughing matter, Lucien,' Amber said. 'I want Grace to know exactly how I felt when David left me.'

Lucien's voice hardened. 'It was no laughing matter for me. Emily is, after all, my girlfriend, not David's.'

'But it's Grace you want, so don't pretend otherwise. For the life of me I can't understand what you and David see in her.'

'No, you can't, and that's probably why you lost him,' Lucien retorted. 'I'm not interested in your moods, Amber. We both stand to profit if this works out, and at the moment it's all falling into place perfectly. I'll let you know if I make any more progress but for now I have to keep Emily happy or she might drop me, and then we'd have to find someone else and start all over again.'

'She won't drop you,' said Amber scornfully. 'You're rich, charming and influential. Actresses like her are ten a penny. She thinks you're her passport to fame and fortune.'

'Possibly, but there are plenty of other rich men who would be happy to take her out. I'm not quite in David's league yet, you know, and I'm not as interested in the Arts. I only work for him, and if he ever got wind of what I'm doing, he'd fire me.'

'You're a partner in his company,' Amber retorted.

'No, I'm a partner in one of his companies and on the board of two more. Believe me, Amber, I'm replaceable, so control yourself and be patient, difficult as I know that is for you.'

With that he ended the call, poured himself a whisky and then sat in the window seat of his study, nursing his glass and remembering how Grace had looked when David had teased an orgasm out of her just before he himself was about to use the birch on Emily. At that moment he had felt a moment of pure, unadulterated jealousy, before he'd managed to get himself under control and turn his attention back to the trembling, waiting Emily.

'One day,' he murmured to himself, 'one day, Grace, you will be mine.'

Chapter Two

'Your phone's switched off,' said Fran accusingly, as Grace hurried into the rehearsal room.

'Is it? Sorry, I must have turned it off by mistake. It was on earlier. Have you been trying to get me?'

'Emily's agent wanted to speak to you, but in the end she gave me the bombshell instead.'

Grace tried to look puzzled. 'What bombshell? Is Emily ill?'

'It seems she doesn't think she's right for the role and she's withdrawing. I suppose we'll have to put "artistic differences" as the reason in the announcement. What a crap thing to do to us at this late stage. We've only got another two weeks before we open. What the hell are we going to do?'

Grace's relief was so great that she had difficulty in hiding it. 'I've no idea,' she admitted. 'It's a big role, and you need a very specific type of actress. Getting the right person at the eleventh hour will be a nightmare, plus they'll have to be able to learn lines quickly as well.'

'You don't seem angry,' said Fran, puzzled by her friend's muted reaction. 'I'm livid. I don't think you should ever work with her again after this.'

'Believe me, I won't,' Grace assured her. 'Of course I'm angry, but I'm trying to think as well.'

'Morning, everyone,' said John, throwing his bag down with a thump. 'You two don't look very happy.'

'We're not,' said Fran, going on to explain why.

'I might be able to help,' John said when she'd finished. 'The girl who played Vivie opposite me last time has just heard that they've pulled the plug on a film she was due to start this week due to lack of funding. That means she's free, and if she's prepared to do it then there's no problem over learning lines. I'm sure she'll remember most of them. It was only two years ago.'

'Who is it?' asked Grace.

'Belinda Groves.'

'She's doing really well at the moment. Will she be

willing to do this? I don't think we're going to get a West End transfer afterwards.'

'No harm in asking her,' said John. 'I've got her number somewhere, but I don't know who her agent is.'

'Ring her,' said Fran. 'If she seems okay with it, she can give you her agent's number and Grace will call her.' John nodded, then went outside to try to get a better signal.

'I went out to dinner with John last night,' said Fran. 'I'm sick and tired of fitting in around Andrew's schedule. He's tied up one weekend in four and now three days a month helping you out at the hotel. When's he going to finish there? There can't be much for him to do now you've opened.'

'Some of our guests expect there to be a personal trainer on call, so he's still needed, plus he can turn his hand to anything,' added Grace truthfully.

'Well, I had a lovely evening with John, and we're out again tonight, so Andrew will have to wait. I'm not going to be like you were when you first met David: hanging around waiting for him and conforming to his every whim.'

'I wasn't like that!' protested Grace.

'You were, and for all I know you still are. John's

great. He's been in the business so long that he knows loads of inside gossip, and he's good in bed too.'

'You slept with him?' asked an astonished Grace.

'Why not?'

'I would have thought he was a tad old for your taste.'

'He's mature and he certainly knows a thing or two, so I'm quite happy, thank you.'

'You do know he's incapable of being faithful to any woman for longer than twenty-four hours, don't you?' asked Grace. 'When he was younger his reputation—'

'Keep out of my private life,' said Fran sharply. 'Yours seems to give you nothing but problems, from what I can see. I just want to enjoy myself and be with someone who makes me feel good. Andrew can do that, but he's hardly ever around. John is around right now, and he can do it too. Okay?'

'Sure, and I'm sorry,' said Grace hastily. 'I just thought you and Andrew were an item now.'

'So did I, but he's so busy these days it's utterly ridiculous. Now, can we try to sort out the play? I'm happy, Grace, and I've been happy to cover for you these past three days, but right now I'd like you to take over again. One of these days I'd like to have some time to get back

MARINA ANDERSON

to writing; my new play is coming along nicely, thank you for not asking.'

Grace felt very guilty. 'I'm really sorry. It's chaos at the moment, but I do appreciate all you're doing for me. I could never have got the hotel opened and this play on its feet without you.'

'No, you couldn't,' said Fran, but then she grinned. 'Look, we're friends and that's what friends do for each other, but right now I'm out of my depth and need your input. I enjoy directing, but I don't want it to become my full-time job, that's all I'm saying.'

Before Grace could reply, John came back into the room. 'Belinda would love to do it. She and I had great fun last time, and she says it won't take her more than a couple of days to brush up on the lines. Her agent is Miranda at Hutchins and Dawson, so I said you'd phone them later this morning, Grace, after Belinda's spoken to Miranda.'

Grace slumped into one of the hard chairs and sighed with relief. 'That's fantastic! Thanks so much, John. Shouldn't Suzie be here now? I thought we were concentrating on Mrs Warren's long speech today, Fran.'

'She had to see the dentist and said she'd be here as soon as possible, so I stupidly said that if John came in

138

he could do his main scene with Emily again, as she's been away doing her voice-over for three days, but now we don't have Emily and we don't have Suzie. Very soon we won't have a bloody play!'

'Of course we've got a play,' said Grace firmly. 'Fran, you can read Mrs Warren's lines until Suzie arrives, and we'll go through her first scene with Crofts, so that we don't waste John's time. When are the rest of the cast coming?'

'After lunch,' said Fran, picking up her copy of the play and moving to the end of the rehearsal room.

'Fine, so we can all settle down for a long day,' replied Grace. 'I'll phone Belinda's agent when we take a break for lunch. Now, let's get started.'

At seven thirty that evening, with Belinda's casting confirmed and a good day's rehearsing behind them all, Grace called a halt.

'Coming to the pub?' asked Fran.

'I'd like to, but I'm absolutely shattered,' confessed Grace. 'I'm sorry, Fran. Maybe tomorrow?'

'Sure. You do look tired. I should have asked you how the hotel opening went, but with all that trouble over Emily, I just forgot. Sorry.'

Grace smiled. 'Don't be daft. You must have been working flat out too, because everyone's really come on since I last saw them. I think you're good for John! The hotel opening went fine, but people can be quite demanding at times.'

'Rather you than me, but you're good with people, even David! See you tomorrow then.' And with that Fran left the rehearsal room with the others and a tired Grace picked up her things and wandered out into the busy London street.

She managed to get a taxi quickly, and had just arrived back at the hotel and kicked off her shoes when the hotel phone went. As most people had her mobile number she had no idea who it could be, but much as she wanted to ignore it she knew she couldn't in case it was a guest with a complaint, or someone wanting to book ahead.

'Grace, thank goodness I caught you,' said a familiar voice. 'For some reason I don't have your mobile number. I thought you might like a quiet dinner out tonight, after a long day spent rehearsing.'

'Lucien! I've only just got back,' she exclaimed.

'I know. I'm parked opposite, in one of the residents' bays, I fear. Well, would you like to eat out?'

Grace hesitated. 'I'm very tired. I won't be sparkling company.'

'You don't need to sparkle. With David away I thought you might not feel like cooking.'

She didn't know what to say. She was fairly certain David wouldn't be pleased, but on the other hand she had no idea how many women he would take out for dinner during his trip to Germany, and he often said how important freedom and personal space were in a relationship. A meal would be nice, and Lucien would be interesting company.

'Grace . . . ?' he asked.

'Sorry, I was thinking. Yes, I would like to eat out. I'm too tired to cook and I missed lunch as I had to make a phone call, so thank you very much. I need half an hour to shower and get changed, though.'

'I'll book a table for nine thirty and pick you up in thirty minutes, then. See you soon.'

As soon as he'd ended the call, Lucien phoned Amber. 'She's agreed,' he told her. 'She hesitated, but she's coming.'

'I didn't think she would. She must have changed since I last saw her. That's brilliant. Enjoy your meal, Lucien, or should I call you Iago?'

He laughed. 'I don't need to go to the lengths he used. Grace is already unsure and trying not to be jealous. My job will be easy.'

'Let me know how it goes,' said Amber eagerly.

'This evening is personal,' he replied. 'You'll have to trust me. After all, we both want the same outcome.'

'But—'

Lucien terminated the call. Amber wanted David back, but tonight was all about steering Grace towards him, and showing her that he was someone she could trust and confide in. He had no intention of giving Amber any details of that. He was more open than David in his personal life, but there were still things he liked to keep to himself, and his progress with Grace was definitely one of them.

Chapter Three

It was a long time since Grace had been out for a meal with any man apart from David, and she felt slightly nervous as she quickly showered, applied a little make-up and then put on her black Diane von Furstenberg wrap dress, its low-cut V-shape neckline contrasting with the long sleeves. She teamed the gold obi-style belt with a pair of gold, high-heeled strappy sandals, grabbed a small gold clutch bag and was out of the hotel with five minutes to spare.

Lucien's silver BMW convertible drew up beside her within seconds, and when she got in he leant over and kissed her chastely on the cheek. 'You look absolutely beautiful,' he said with a smile of appreciation. 'I don't recognise the perfume, though.'

'David has it made up for me in France,' replied Grace. 'So, where are we going?'

'Alain Ducasse, the French restaurant at The Dorchester. I've chosen it because we can have some privacy there.'

'Why, don't many people like it?' she asked with a laugh.

Lucien laughed too. 'Oh yes, but you'll see what I mean when we get there. Now, tell me about your day. I assume Emily has withdrawn from your play?'

'Fortunately, yes. I think we'd both have been very embarrassed if she'd continued in it,' replied Grace. 'As for the rest of the day, you'd find it very boring.'

'No, I'd like to hear about it,' he assured her, and listened keenly as she talked while he drove them towards Mayfair.

When they finally got to the restaurant, it was very crowded. 'Privacy?' queried Grace with a smile.

'Wait and see,' he replied, smiling back at her as he gave his name to the waiter. Within minutes they were being ushered across the restaurant floor and then the waiter drew back an oval curtain of flickering fibre-optic strands to reveal a private dining table, separated from the main restaurant by the curtain.

'It's called the Table Lumiére. It's a hidden gem for people who want to dine discreetly, away from other people's eyes for whatever reason,' Lucien explained.

Grace's eyes widened. 'What an amazing idea! How did you manage to get us seated here at such short notice?'

'David has it reserved on a regular basis for client dinners. Luckily for us, tonight was one of those reservations.'

'He's never brought me here,' said Grace.

'He had no reason to want to keep you hidden from prying eyes, whereas I felt sure you'd be more comfortable if you knew no one would see us.'

'You were right,' she admitted. 'I'm not sure that David would be very happy if he knew I'd come out to dinner with you.'

'But you still came,' he said softly.

'Yes. You're one of his closest friends, and we do know each other quite well! In any case, I have no idea who he takes out to dinner when he's abroad, but I'm quite sure he doesn't mope around alone in hotel rooms.'

'No,' said Lucien. 'He definitely doesn't do that.'

Grace didn't like his reply, but didn't rise to the bait.

She had no intention of using Lucien to pry into David's life, and quickly picked up a menu. 'This all looks delicious,' she said. 'It's going to be hard to choose.'

The evening passed very quickly. The food was excellent, the wine smooth and Lucien proved to be great company. Watching him talking about his love of horse riding, Grace realised that he was an extremely good-looking man. He was of a slighter build than David, and his dark brown hair flopped over his equally dark eyes at times. He smiled quickly and easily, and unlike David was clearly comfortable in his own skin.

After they'd finished the meal and were nibbling on the hand-made chocolates that had been served with their coffee, she asked Lucien a question that had been on her mind for a long time. 'How did you and David meet?'

'We first met at a squash club, about eight years ago. I was top of the rankings there, so naturally David kept practising until he was able to take over the top spot.'

'And you didn't mind?'

'He became a better player than me. In any case, I admire anyone who is willing to work hard to get what they want. He never socialised much at the club, though, but quite by chance we met up at a nightclub in London that specialised in the kind of sexual experiences we both found interesting. Later he offered me a place in one of his companies and we've remained friendly ever since.'

'He doesn't have many friends,' mused Grace.

'I don't think he'd consider me a close friend,' said Lucien. 'He isn't big on male bonding. Actually, he isn't big on any kind of bonding, although you've certainly found his Achilles heel.'

'Have I?' asked Grace.

'It seems that way. He's changed since he met you. He's less restless, and isn't forever searching for the next sexual thrill. Why, he even gave up Amber for you. That took everyone by surprise.'

'But he set up a situation where he risked having to do that,' said Grace quietly.

Lucien nodded. 'Indeed he did, but I doubt that he expected the outcome that he got.'

'I wonder if he misses her,' Grace mused.

'I'm sure he does, but he'll always find new ways of keeping himself sexually satisfied. And of course at the moment, he thinks he's in love with you.'

It took a few moments for Lucien's words to sink in, but then Grace looked at him in astonishment. 'What do you mean by that?'

'We have to be sensible, Grace. He's never fallen in love before and suddenly he finds you. You're everything he wants sexually, and to his surprise he also feels protective of you. It's a heady combination, and he's convinced himself that this is love.'

'It is love,' she retorted sharply.

Lucien shrugged. 'Perhaps; who knows what love really is? The problem for David is that he will never be satisfied. When he reached the top of the squash rankings, he took up golf. He had nothing left to prove to himself on the squash court. Now he has you, and you love him a lot, and do everything he wants in and out of bed, so what kind of a challenge are you offering him?'

'He has the hotel. Emily offers him a challenge, and so will other guests. He can combine the best of both worlds. He needs love, Lucien. I don't think he's ever experienced it before, even as a child.'

Lucien touched her hand across the table. 'I'm sorry, I shouldn't have said what I did. I suppose I'm envious of him, because if you were in love with me, I wouldn't expect you to keep proving yourself. Deep down, I'm not sure that David has tapped into a side of you that would otherwise have remained undiscovered. I suspect that you're doing things you're not totally comfortable with in order to keep him, and that's not the same thing.'

Grace shook her head. 'That's not true. I enjoy everything we do. Sometimes I feel it's wrong, that I shouldn't enjoy it, but I do. David has opened up a whole new world to me, and I don't know what I'd do without him now.'

'He isn't the only man who could satisfy that side of you,' said Lucien quietly. 'But most of them would be able to form a closer bond than David will ever be able to manage.'

Grace bit on her bottom lip. His words had made her feel immensely lonely and vulnerable, and she was close to tears at the thought that despite what she believed, Lucien could be right. 'I think I should be getting back,' she said. 'I've got another early start tomorrow, and David might phone me later.'

'If he does, will you tell him about our meal?'

'I don't know,' she said slowly.

Lucien remained quiet during the drive back to the hotel, but before Grace got out of the car he kissed her gently on both cheeks. 'Thank you for a lovely evening, Grace. Remember, if you ever feel you need to get out while David's away, just give me a call. My number must be in the hotel booking records. And take care of yourself. You don't seem to realise quite how special you are.'

Grace shook her head. 'Don't be silly, Lucien. I'm not that special, but thank you for a lovely evening.'

Once in bed, instead of falling asleep quickly, Grace found herself going over and over the evening's conversation. She wished that David would phone her to help her sudden attack of insecurity, but the phone remained resolutely silent.

At the same time, a very contented Lucien fell asleep almost immediately his head touched the pillow. He knew that he'd tapped into Grace's doubts without appearing disloyal to David. David, who had always pushed Lucien into second place since their first meeting and who didn't deserve to keep her.

David lay awake in the bedroom of his hotel suite and glanced at the bedside clock. For some reason he felt an almost overwhelming urge to phone Grace. He missed having her beside him, and needed to hear her voice.

The hotel's opening had been a huge success, and even now he could become aroused at the memories of some of the things that had taken place in the Victorian

Suite. Grace was clever, sexually exciting and probably the most genuine person he'd ever met. Yet despite that, he continued to keep her at a distance some of the time, unable to trust his instincts that were telling him it was safe to love her. She wouldn't change and she wouldn't try to change or control him, he was certain of that. All the same, he felt the need to test her, by returning to his own house when he knew she wanted him to stay, or holding back from saying things that he sensed she needed to hear from him.

He was about to call her when the phone rang, and he hoped that it was Grace. That way he would get his wish without her realising how much he'd wanted to hear her voice. But it wasn't Grace, it was his contact at the Alain Ducasse restaurant, and as was usual, he was calling David to tell him that the Table Lumiere had been used on one of the company nights, and who had used it.

'That's fine,' said David, trying not to let his disappointment at the identity of the caller show in his voice. 'Lucien often uses it, but thank you for telling me. Was he with a very pretty young blonde, by any chance?'

'No, sir, he was with an extremely attractive young woman with long dark hair. I've never seen her here before.'

David tensed. 'Did the waiter catch her name?'

'Our waiters are the souls of discretion, sir.'

'Yes, but they're not deaf. Did he?'

The man sighed, but David was a very important client. 'I believe her name was Grace, sir.'

David felt as though he'd been punched in the solar plexus, but he managed to thank the man before replacing the receiver. The palms of his hands were sweating and he felt sick. He knew Lucien very well, and was acutely aware of how much the other man resented him. They had many interests in common, but the only reason David had so much to do with him was that he believed in the saying that you should keep your friends close and your enemies closer. Clever, sophisticated and charming, Lucien was born to do well in life. His problem was that he didn't have the hunger that drove David on. In David's opinion he was lazy, and had almost certainly been spoilt as a child.

He wasn't surprised that Lucien had asked Grace out, but he was surprised that she'd accepted his invitation. He hadn't sensed any strong sexual attraction between the two of them, and he was sure he would have picked up on that.

He turned the news over and over in his mind, before

realising that thinking about it was pointless. He would wait until he returned to London and then see if Grace told him about the meal out. If she did, then it was of no importance. If she didn't, then he'd been on the verge of making a terrible mistake. For the first time in his life he realised that he was afraid.

Chapter Four

'It went even better than I'd hoped,' said Grace, standing at the crowded bar with Fran after the opening night of *Mrs Warren's Profession*.

'Belinda did brilliantly,' Fran agreed. 'She was better than Emily would ever have been.'

Grace nodded. 'The audience liked John too much, though. I might have to ask him to tone down the charm a little towards the end. It's fine at the start but—'

'Leave him alone,' said Fran. 'I know why you're picking on him, and it's not going to stop me going out with him, so you can save your breath. If Andrew wants me then he'll have to make more time for me. Unlike you I don't enjoy sitting around alone, especially at weekends. He didn't even come to watch tonight.'

'He's busy; the hotel has its second set of guests next week and there were things we needed to get done.'

Fran shrugged. 'It's his choice. Which reminds me, is David still abroad or wasn't he interested enough to come tonight?'

'He's due back at midnight,' said Grace defensively.

'Who is?' asked a familiar voice, and she spun round to find David standing behind her.

'When did you get here?' she asked in astonishment.

'Just in time to watch the play. It was wonderful. Are you sure there's no chance of a West End transfer?'

'Positive, but maybe we can do a revival if a theatre comes free later, and the reviews are good enough tomorrow morning, of course.'

'Well, you all deserve it. Hello, Fran,' he added.

'Hi,' Fran said coolly. 'You found time in your busy schedule to support Grace for once, then?'

Grace was mortified, but David merely smiled. 'I certainly did, and I hope I'm supporting her with the boutique hotel as well. Isn't that right, Gracie?'

Putting her arm through his she smiled up at him. 'It is, and I'm so pleased you were here. It's made my evening.'

'I think I'll go and sit with John,' said Fran. 'See you around midday tomorrow for notes, Grace?'

Grace nodded and watched her friend pushing through the crowd to find John. 'She's not in a very good mood,' she said to David. 'I think she really wanted Andrew to be here, but he's busy at the hotel.'

'And I think she simply doesn't like me,' he replied calmly. 'It's not obligatory you know, Grace. She's your friend and work colleague. We don't have to like each other, any more than you have to like my business colleagues.'

'I don't meet many of them.'

'You know Lucien very well.'

Grace felt herself blushing at the memory of exactly how intimately she knew Lucien. 'Don't!' she exclaimed.

'Don't what?'

'Talk about Lucien in front of all these people.'

'Why not?'

'Because it makes me think about our time in the Victorian Suite.'

He laughed. 'No one else here knows about that. Is that honestly the reason why you're blushing?'

'Of course it is. What other reason could there be?

He shrugged. 'I've no idea. I think there's someone here who wants to congratulate you. I'll mingle and try to hear what people are saying. Will you be free to leave in about half an hour?'

Grace nodded, watching him disappear into the throng. She couldn't wait to get back to the hotel so that they could celebrate his return, an early return that was totally unexpected and all the sweeter for that.

'I thought we'd go back to my place,' said David when Grace finally managed to get away.

'The hotel's nearer.'

'I don't want to mix business with pleasure tonight,' he replied.

'I'm thrilled you were able to get here for opening night,' said Grace. 'It means such a lot to me.'

'I enjoyed myself. What have you been doing while I was away, apart from getting the play on its feet?'

'Nothing much, it's been a bit of a nightmare getting everyone ready, but you heard all about that each time you phoned me, as you pointed out!'

'No chance of socialising then?'

Grace realised at once that he knew about her meal with Lucien, and knew too that this was why he'd made the effort to get back for the opening night of her play.

'I did go out for a meal with Lucien, soon after you'd left for Germany. He's asked me out a couple of times since, too, but I've been too tired. I thought perhaps you'd asked him to make sure I didn't get lonely,' she added.

'Don't lie to me, Grace,' said David sharply. 'You thought no such thing.'

She laughed. 'That's true, but I knew you wouldn't mind me having dinner with him. After all, he is your best friend.'

'I left the playground behind a long time ago. I no longer have "best friends",' he retorted.

'You do mind!' said Grace in astonishment. 'Why? I'm quite sure you went out to dinner with some attractive women while you were in Germany.'

'Not women I'd already been intimate with. There is a difference.'

'But it was only a meal, and I had a nice time,' she said defiantly.

'I'm pleased he didn't waste his money.'

Grace couldn't believe her ears. 'What's the matter with you? Why do you have to spoil things? I felt so happy when I saw you at the theatre, and now, when we're about to spend the night at your place, you're suddenly in a bad mood. I haven't done anything wrong. If you don't mind watching me have sex with Lucien, how can you object to me having a meal with him?'

'Because,' he said quietly, 'I wasn't at the meal, was I?'

'I'm not going to talk about this any more,' said Grace. 'I won't let you spoil tonight for me, and if all you want is an argument, then please take me back to the hotel and go home on your own.'

'I don't want an argument,' he said, his voice tight with tension, 'and I'm equally excited to see you again. We'll drop the subject, all right?'

'That's fine by me,' she said, feeling close to tears but determined not to let him know it. They finished the drive in silence.

The moment they were inside his front door, he made his move. Grabbing her by the shoulders he pinned her against the hall wall before beginning to unfasten the buttons down the front of her tightly fitted top, then he pushed her bra up over her breasts, lowered his head and started to lick and nibble at the soft flesh round her nipples. Stunned, she didn't attempt to fight him as his hands then pushed up her skirt, and he thrust a leg between hers, pressing his hard, muscular thigh against her vulva.

She could hear the sound of their breathing in the silent house, and despite herself she knew she was becoming aroused. Her breath caught in her throat as he bit hard on her left nipple. She gave an involuntary cry of pain, but he covered her mouth with one hand, muffling the sound. As the burning pain eased a little, he began to suck on the sore, hardened nipple, swirling his tongue over it in a contrastingly tender touch.

To her shame she felt the familiar ache begin deep down in her belly, and tried to move away from the wall towards the bedroom, but his grip was too strong. Keeping her pinned against the wall he repeated the process again with her other breast, and this time the pain was sharper and he failed to muffle her cry.

'Go with it,' he whispered. 'You know you want to. You're almost ready to come.'

She swallowed hard, not wanting to climax because there was anger behind what he was doing, but aware that he was right and she wasn't going to be able to stop herself. He had taught her to enjoy pleasure-pain too well for her to resist as the sharp darts of red-tinged pain lanced through her breast and down to her stomach.

Suddenly frantic for a climax she moved her lower body against his thigh, and as her back arched and her movements became more desperate she heard him give a low laugh as he moved his leg, leaving her poised on the edge of an orgasm, desperate for release and totally at his mercy.

For a moment their eyes locked, and she knew that there was naked pleading in hers, while his were bright with excitement. 'Tell me what you want,' he whispered.

'I want you to put your leg between my thighs again,' she whimpered. 'Please, David, let me come now. I'm so close.'

He kept one hand on her breast, his fingers pulling on the swollen nipple, but with his free hand he pushed her panties down below her knees and then cupped her vulva, pressing upwards and rotating his fingers while the heel of his hand pressed hard just above her pubic bone. She squirmed with pleasure, trying to hurry her climax as the pressure built inside her.

'Keep still or I'll stop,' he warned her, and immediately she froze, knowing that he always kept his word.

'Good girl,' he said softly, and then without warning he lowered his head to her red, aching nipple, nipping it again between his teeth while at the same time sliding his fingers inside her outer sex lips until he located her swollen clitoris.

'Do you know what I'm going to do now?' he asked.

'No,' she cried, sobbing with frustration.

'I'm going to rub your own juices round this little bud until you're about to come, and then I'm going to stop for a few seconds, and when I do you won't move, will you?'

Whimpering she shook her head.

'That's a good girl, and then I'll repeat that, and on the second time you can come. Do you understand me?'

The sound of her rasping breath seemed to fill the hallway, and she was nearly out of her mind with need, but she nodded, and felt his fingers touching her softly, exactly where the delicious ache was at its most intense. Her belly tightened and her hips moved forward as slithering sensations began low down in her belly.

'Careful,' he warned her, and with a groan she forced herself to be still.

'Very good,' he said approvingly, and she flinched as his teeth closed around her throbbing nipple for the final time, but the searing pleasure-pain was, she knew, only a prelude to the pleasure he was about to allow her.

'I think this is what you want,' he murmured, and very lightly he teased the tissue surrounding her clitoris with his fingers before finally drawing her juices to the side of the clitoris itself and then swirling his fingertips with delicate precision over the whole area.

The pleasure was almost too intense, and even as her whole body convulsed in its long-awaited orgasm the wonderful, hot moment of release was mixed with the dark edge of pain that she both dreaded and adored.

As all her muscles went into a spasm of release, she screamed with relief and then David covered her mouth with his and the moment she was still he lifted her out of her skirt, off the ground with her back to the wall and pulled her onto his rigid erection. His movements were sure and knowing, and she wrapped her legs round him as her well-tutored body responded imme-diately, so that her muscles tightened round him in an intense second orgasm that trigged his climax too.

Slowly he helped her to the ground, and her legs almost gave way beneath her. Without a word he took her hand and led her through to his bedroom's en suite bathroom. Then, while she removed her twisted bra, he turned on the shower and watched in silence as she moved slowly past him so that she could let the water fall on her abused but deeply satisfied body.

When she came out, he'd laid one of her nightdresses on the bed ready for her, but he still didn't speak and by the time he'd finished showering she was lying beneath the duvet, propped up on three pillows and watching him carefully.

'Don't ever take me like that again,' she said at last.

He frowned. 'Like what? You seemed to be thoroughly enjoying yourself.'

'You know what I mean. Do not touch me in anger like that, or we're finished.'

He ran his fingers through his damp brown hair, his eyes not meeting hers. 'I wasn't angry.'

'You seemed angry. There was very little love in it.'

'But it was good for you. I made sure of that. Don't try to tell me I'm wrong; I know you too well to make a mistake about that.'

'You've taught me to enjoy things like that, so of course I did, but you were angry with me because I went out for dinner with Lucien. Don't deny it; I'm not a fool.'

He sat on the side of the bed. 'It wasn't anger.'

'It wasn't love,' she retorted.

'I suppose I wanted to reassure myself that you were still mine,' he said slowly.

'I don't belong to you, and despite what you say I don't believe that this wasn't driven by your annoyance at me. But I *am* sure that I don't ever want it to happen again.'

He nodded. 'If that's what you thought, then I'm sorry, and it won't happen again. Clearly I made a mistake, but for me it was out of love.'

Grace hesitated. She could have said more, but she held back because she'd realised two things. Firstly, he was – despite his protestations – slightly ashamed. Secondly, although he might not realise it, he'd done it out of jealousy, and jealousy was an emotion that he had no time for. If she said too much, pushed him too far, he would end their relationship rather than face the fact that he was capable of an emotion that he had always despised.

'Of course I'm yours,' she said softly, and saw his tense body relax a little. 'Come to bed now. We're both tired, and tomorrow morning I have to give the cast notes, then in the afternoon we need to make sure everything is in place for next week's guests.'

Still naked from his shower, David slipped between the sheets, put his hands each side of her face and kissed her softly on the mouth. 'So lovely and yet so wise!' he murmured with a smile.

Within minutes Grace could tell by his regular breathing that he was fast asleep, and she knew that she'd said and done the right thing tonight. She'd waited so long for him to commit totally to her, to show he was capable of loving her as intensely as she loved him. Now that he had, albeit unintentionally, she had to face the fact that she would need to tread carefully in future, because as yet he didn't know how to cope with the new emotions he was experiencing. Nor did he want to vocalise them to her.

'I love you so much,' she whispered to him as he slept. 'I don't know how I'd live without you.'

Towards morning he woke her and made love to her so gently that she wanted to cry with gratitude and relief, but in the morning when she left for work she knew that a part of her, the part that he had taught her to embrace when they'd first met, couldn't wait for the next exciting experience at the hotel.

Chapter Five

When Grace woke the next morning, David had already showered, dressed and gone. Her breasts still ached from the night before, and when she ran her hands over them while under the shower they were tender to the touch. Despite her shock at what had happened, she was ashamed to realise that thinking about it all was arousing her. She knew that what he'd done was wrong, yet a part of her remembered only the pleasure.

She was still annoyed with herself when she arrived at the theatre to give the cast their notes. She knew that she didn't sound as thrilled as she should have done. Instead, she ran through her list quickly, complimenting the actors but also pointing out what could be improved while Fran sat next to her.

'I've left you until last, John,' she said, 'because—'

'Because no doubt you've read his rave review in this morning's *Telegraph* and want to congratulate him,' said Fran swiftly.

Grace hadn't read it. She hadn't read any of the reviews because she'd woken too late, and she was immensely grateful to Fran. 'That's right,' she said with a smile. 'I must admit that for me your Crofts is still a tad too charming in your final scene, but I'm only the director!'

There was general laughter, and then they all dispersed until the evening, leaving her alone with Fran.

'Thanks for that,' she said. 'I was so late getting up I didn't read the reviews.'

'I could tell by your notes. I had to stop you when it came to John, though, because he was singled out for praise in every review. I think "a snake hiding beneath a veneer of silver-tongued charm" was one of the more original comments. You still had to criticise him, though, didn't you? Why do you have such a problem with me having a fling with him? What does it matter to you if I'm tired of waiting around for Andrew to be free? You've got what you wanted. Isn't that enough for you? Or maybe it's not quite what you expected,' she added.

'Why do you say that? David flew back early from Germany last night to be here for opening night. Not that you were very nice to him, but it meant a lot to me.'

'I think he's a control freak, but I don't keep criticising him the way you criticise John, and let's face it he and I aren't going to spend our lives together. We're just having some fun while the play's on.'

'I'm sorry,' apologised Grace. 'I don't know what's wrong with me. Probably it was stupid to open the hotel at the same time as the play was about to open.'

Fran nodded. 'Probably it was. You certainly look tired. Why don't we have lunch together, and a good chat like we used to? Last night was such a triumph, we ought to celebrate it.'

'I really wish we could,' Grace said, putting a hand on her friend's arm, 'but I've got to go back to the hotel now. David's waiting and ...'

Fran shrugged. 'It's okay. I know that David always has to come first. No doubt he throws his toys out of his pram if everything isn't done exactly how and when he wants it. Spoilt, rich men like him aren't used to being kept waiting.'

'It isn't like that!' exclaimed Grace. 'We're joint partners in the hotel. Meetings about it are as important as any business meeting, and he does not throw his toys out of his pram when he doesn't get his own way. That's really unfair of you. You don't know him at all.'

'Right, and you do? I doubt it. Let's drop it. I don't want to fall out with you over him. After all, we were friends before you met him and we'll be friends after he's gone so—'

'Don't you understand that he isn't going to go away?' asked Grace.

'No, and perhaps it's something you should give some thought to before very long,' said Fran. 'If he cuts you off from all your old friends and then leaves you, you won't find them waiting. And it would make him even more dangerous than I already think he is. I'll be watching the play again tonight, so I'll email you any notes I think are important. Okay?'

Watching her friend leave, Grace felt a frisson of fear at Fran's words, words that she didn't dare think about too deeply because after last night they made her feel very nervous.

By the time she got to the hotel, David was already there talking to Tilly. He smiled at Grace. 'Everything go all right? The reviews are great; you must be thrilled.'

'Yes, I am,' she said hastily. 'What did you want to look over?'

'Before we start work, there's something I want you to see,' said David, taking her by the hand. 'It's in your study.'

Tilly smiled at Grace, who couldn't imagine what he was talking about. 'All right,' she agreed.

Once inside the room, he shut the door behind them. 'Close your eyes a minute,' he said softly, and still bemused she obeyed. 'All right, you can open them now,' he said, and when she did he was standing in front of her holding the most amazing bouquet of flowers she'd ever seen. It was huge, with a base of Vendela roses and viburnum, jasmine and lilies and then a long dramatic cascade of ivy and orchids. 'Congratulations on your brilliant reviews,' he said with a warm smile. 'I'm so pleased for you, my darling. You're a brilliant director, and I'm a lucky man.'

Tears filled Grace's eyes as she took the flowers from him, lowering her head to drink in the wonderful perfume. 'It's like something out of a Shakespearean play!' she said in astonishment.

'That's what I asked for, so they've done their job well,' he replied, still smiling.

Grace was totally overwhelmed. She'd never imagined David capable of such a gesture, which made the bouquet and the thought that had gone into it even more precious.

'You're not meant to cry,' he said softly, wiping the tears off her cheeks.

'I'm sorry; I was just taken by surprise. I never expected ...'

'What?'

'Something so wonderful!' she exclaimed, knowing that she mustn't say she'd never expected him to be the kind of man who'd give a woman flowers.

'I'm so pleased you like them,' he said, putting the bouquet carefully to one side and taking her in his arms. 'I am proud of you, my darling. I may not always say it, or show it, but I am.'

Leaning against his chest, Grace felt happier than she could ever remember, because she knew very well that

David had never been a man for this kind of gesture, and that made the moment incredibly special for her. 'I love you so much,' she murmured, and his arms tightened round her. 'It's the most beautiful bouquet I've ever had, and the most thoughtful one too.'

He gave a soft sigh. 'Unfortunately, I think we'd better put it in water and then get back to work, my love.'

'Of course,' agreed Grace, reluctant to let the moment pass but knowing he was right.

'I think I'd like to study the Pleasure Suite in more detail. That's where Lucien and Emily will be this time, isn't it?' Grace nodded. 'And the first couple there seemed very impressed, so I'd like to see it and assess its potential for us.'

The Pleasure Suite was on the first floor. It had a large bedroom and living room combined. A deep, pale pink carpet covered the floor, with a soft white fur rug in front of a long, white, curved-back sofa. Cushions were strewn around the room, and the white bed was soft and inviting. Three of the walls were also white but the one at the head of the bed was covered in thick stripes of alternating white, soft cerise and pale turquoise. The large window overlooking the back garden was covered by Austrian blinds, to protect the guests from people using the garden.

In the middle of the room a large, white wicker chair hung suspended from the ceiling. It was shaped like a cradle that had been hung from its head, the back curved to embrace the sitter, making it very difficult for anyone to get out of it without help.

David ran a hand down the sleek curve of the back, his fingers moving through the gaps between the strong wicker canes. 'It's a good height,' he remarked. 'Emily would need to be lifted in, or out, of course.' And he smiled to himself.

'There isn't a bathroom as such,' explained Grace, 'instead there's a sauna and shower room through here.' She opened a door on the left-hand side of the room to show him.

'What's through there?' he asked, pointing to a small door at the side of the entrance to the sauna.

'An ice plunge.'

'An exciting contrast then, the heat of the sauna and the cold of the ice plunge. That will certainly get the blood moving, making any lucky recipient incredibly sensitive to any kind of touch. What a clever young woman you are, Grace.'

'Well, it is for pleasure,' she said with a smile.

'Whose pleasure?' he asked.

'That's entirely up to the person who books the suite, so in this case undoubtedly Lucien's.'

'I think we're going to have some interesting times here,' said David softly. 'I can hardly wait. Who does he want to join the two of them, apart from us?'

Grace checked her notes. 'Tilly again – he must like her – and he's requested a strong young man. I'll find out who'll be most suitable.'

'I'm going to be busy for the next few days,' said David. 'Is there anything that you need me to sort out before the guests arrive?'

Grace shook her head. 'Everything's in hand.'

'Then I'll see you next Tuesday morning. Andrew tells me that Louise has some staffing problems at The Dining Club, so I'll probably have to take her out one evening to sort those out as I don't have any gaps in my timetable in the day. I'll phone you each evening.'

Grace nodded, making sure she didn't show any sign of anxiety or annoyance. If he was testing her, to see if she was jealous, then he was wasting his time. Louise was no threat, she knew that now. It was more likely relative innocents like Emily she had to be wary of, because David enjoyed a challenge, but right now, after the amazing bouquet, no one seemed a threat.

Gently he pushed her dark curtain of hair behind her ears so that he could nuzzle her earlobes, his tongue flicking in and out of each of her ears in turn until she started to squirm. He knew how much she liked that, but as soon as her breath began to quicken he released her. 'Until Tuesday, Gracie, and the joys of the Pleasure Suite. I hope Emily is well prepared.'

Grace was humiliated to realise that she was trembling with desire after he'd gone, and knew that she too could hardly wait for the hotel's guests to start arriving again.

'You look deliciously tantalising,' Lucien said as Emily got into the passenger seat of his convertible. 'I'm a very lucky man. There must be plenty of other men queuing up to take you out.'

'Quite a few,' admitted Emily, 'but they all seem very young now I'm going out with you.' Lucien laughed. 'I don't mean you're old, but ...'

'I know what you mean. Did your agent mind you pulling out of Grace's play?'

Recalling the scene in her agent's office still had the

power to make Emily feel uncomfortable. 'Yes, espe-cially after it got such rave reviews. She pointed out that Grace's plays always get great reviews and I'll probably never get a chance like that again. It doesn't matter, though; I'm a shoo-in for a lead role in a TV adaptation of *Little Women*, which will give me loads of exposure.'

'Who will you play?'

'Beth, she's incredibly drippy but I've got the look.'

'I think she's meant to be a thoroughly good and kind person, not a drip,' retorted Lucien.

Emily sighed. 'Can we talk about something else? Do you like my hair? I had it done yesterday, and it took hours.'

He looked across at her as she pushed her fingers through her shoulder-length, blonde and caramel-streaked hair, cut into feathered layers around her face. She knew that the cut emphasised her large blue eyes and sultry mouth, and the colours were perfect for her English rose complexion. 'Do you?' she repeated.

'You look absolutely beautiful, like a very expensive doll.'

Emily wasn't sure that was a compliment. 'I do have a brain; sometimes you talk to me as though I'm some kind of bimbo.'

He shook his head. 'I don't mean it like that, but your face is now an intriguing mixture of "come hither" and "touch me not". It's very exciting.'

Something about his tone made her nervous. 'This break is going to be fun, isn't it? I mean, I am going to enjoy it?'

'You enjoyed it last time, didn't you?'

'Yes, although there were times when I was a bit overwhelmed.'

'But that made it all the better in the end, as I recall.'

Emily chewed on her bottom lip. 'In a way it did. I'm not sure now. Is David going to join us again?'

'Why? Don't you like him?'

Emily felt herself blushing. 'Yes, I like him, but I feel that I shouldn't.'

'I think we're all going to have a wonderful time,' he assured her.

Twirling a strand of hair around her fingers, Emily hoped that he was right. She'd always been pretty open-minded about sex, and Lucien had introduced her to new ways of getting pleasure that she'd found exciting and satisfying. She only hoped that the boutique hotel wasn't going to prove a step too far, partly because she didn't want to stop seeing him but also – if she was honest with herself – because she was both excited and intrigued by David. David, who was not only fascinating but also Grace's boyfriend. If she could seduce him away from Grace then that would more than make up for the way the director had treated her at rehearsals, when she'd made her doubts about Emily's acting abilities only too clear. Emily didn't take kindly to criticism.

Chapter Six

'You're the first couple to arrive!' said David, coming into the entrance hall as Lucien was signing the guest book. 'Love the hair, Emily. It really suits you.'

Grace, who'd been talking to Andrew in the small lounge, heard his words and hurried out to join him. 'Lucien, lovely to see you again,' she said as he kissed her on both cheeks. 'And you, Emily. The hair is great. Is it for a part?'

'No, my agent wanted a slightly different look for me. Congratulations on the success of the play,' she added.

'All down to the cast really, but thanks. Now, Toby will bring your cases up and show you to your suite, then you can either have a coffee down here or have it up in your rooms.'

'I imagine we'll want to stay in our rooms,' replied Lucien. 'When will you and David be joining us?'

'In about an hour, once the other guests have arrived. If you want someone to join you before then, just ring on the house phone. We hope you enjoy your stay in the Pleasure Suite as much as you enjoyed yourselves last time.'

'I'm sure we will,' said Lucien with a warm smile.

At that moment Toby came to collect their luggage, and Grace noticed that Emily studied him very carefully before giving him a small, secretive smile. Toby was another friend from Andrew's gym, and with his blond crew-cut hair, hazel eyes and tanned, toned body, Grace felt sure he would make a useful addition to the staff.

David watched Toby lead Lucien and Emily upstairs and then turned to Grace. 'I don't think Lucien will need Tilly after all. I have a feeling Toby is going to be able to fill her shoes. He suits the Pleasure Suite.'

'And he's a trained masseur,' added Grace. 'I'll meet you outside their rooms in an hour, if that's all right?'

David nodded. 'Perfect, and then the fun begins.'

*

Exactly an hour later David tapped lightly on the door to the Pleasure Suite, and standing beside him Grace felt a thrill of eager anticipation. Lucien opened the door, and immediately she could hear soft moaning sounds coming from inside.

'Emily is enjoying a massage,' Lucien explained. 'Toby has very good hands.'

Grace saw that Emily was lying face down and naked on a towel on the bed while Toby knelt over her body, his hands moving up and down her buttocks and the backs of her thighs. Every time her soft moans became too intense, Toby would stop and Grace saw how this made Emily wriggle desperately into the towel as she tried to satisfy herself.

'I'm sure Grace would enjoy that,' said Lucien. 'Why don't you take off your clothes, Grace, and let Toby relax you? David can take over from Toby. I know he'll make sure Emily doesn't come. It's too early in the day for that yet.'

Emily turned her flushed face to look at the new-comers. 'It's never too early!' she protested.

'I'd hate to have to use the twigs from the sauna room on you,' said Lucien, 'but I'm afraid that if you should lose control I'd have to.'

Emily groaned, her large eyes looking appealingly at David, who was already taking off his clothes. 'Why can't I come when I keep being aroused?' she asked.

'Because delaying the pleasure makes it all the better when it finally happens,' said David. 'Isn't that true, Grace?' Grace, who was unfastening her underwired bra, nodded, her mouth already dry. 'Say it,' he reminded her softly.

'Yes, it's true,' she murmured, and then Toby was taking her by the hand and lying her down on a fresh towel next to Emily. Side by side on the large bed the two women waited as David and Toby poured almond oil into their hands and then began their work.

Toby began by using his thumbs on tense, knotted areas in Grace's upper back, rotating them slowly until she felt the tight flesh soften. Once she was totally relaxed he used his hands in long, sweeping movements over her back, the back of her waist and the cheeks of her bottom, keeping his fingers together and making sure the palms of his hands were in contact with her flesh the whole time.

Grace sighed with pleasure, but as he moved expertly to her thighs and calves she felt her body becoming aroused, and Emily's soft whimpers of pleasure from beside her only added to her excitement.

'Before you touch her buttocks, I want to explain something to the girls,' said Lucien, and immediately Toby's hands stopped moving. 'You're clearly both becoming aroused by this, but should either of you climax from it, then you will have to pay a forfeit. We have days of sensual pleasure ahead of us, and I don't want you to lose control too early. Enjoy it, by all means, but remember that orgasms are strictly forbidden at this stage.'

Grace had expected this, but Emily's cry of dismay reminded her of how she'd felt long ago when she'd first started experiencing all the things that David wanted her to learn to enjoy.

'I'd like both of them turned on their backs now,' Lucien added, and Grace knew that before long either she or Emily was going to have to pay the forfeit.

Toby's face was expressionless as she watched him slowly tilt a small bottle above her chest, letting five small drops of oil splash onto her breasts and chest, making her flesh jump. His hands then moved carefully over the undersides of each of her rounded breasts, and he took his time, teasing her swelling globes with the lightest of massages until she longed for a firmer touch and arched her chest upwards.

She heard Lucien laugh quietly, and knew that she should have kept still, because as soon as she moved, Toby's movements became firmer and he massaged closer to her nipples. When he brought her breasts together and squeezed gently she felt her belly tighten, and then as his fingers danced over her hardening nipples she felt the first flicker of an orgasm in her belly.

Next to her, Emily was making small mewing sounds of excitement mingled with fear, but this only heightened Grace's arousal. Fortunately she was sure that David would be able to bring the relatively inexperienced Emily to a climax now, but then she heard him murmur, 'Breathe through your mouth, Emily. You can do this,' and realised that he was helping the younger woman as he'd once helped her.

Toby pushed her breasts upwards and together, then slid his oiled hands down over her stomach and across her hips before digging his fingers firmly into the flesh just above her pubic bone. 'No, not there!' she protested, as the hot pressure began to build up between her thighs. Toby ignored her, merely caressing her stomach lightly with his fingertips for a tantalising few seconds before returning to the same sensitive area, a move that never failed to trigger an orgasm in her.

Her whole body felt swollen and her skin too tight. Desperately she breathed through her mouth, and tried to relax the tightening internal muscles, but this time when Toby's fingers pressed firmly on the base of her belly there was nothing she could do but cry out in protest as her body twisted and writhed and the blissful warmth of her long-delayed orgasm swept through her.

Only when her breathing began to slow did she open her eyes, and she saw David and Lucien looking down at her. 'I'm afraid you will be the one to pay the forfeit, Grace,' said Lucien, and she saw the look of excitement in David's eyes as he nodded in agreement.

'Emily did very well for a novice,' he said. 'I'm disappointed in you, Grace.'

But as he helped her up from the bed, while Lucien went to Emily and Toby quietly put on a robe and left the room, she could tell that he was actually pleased. She also knew that if he'd wanted to he could have teased an orgasm out of Emily long before she herself had come.

Huddled in a white towelling robe, Emily sat on the bed, still trembling with a mixture of excitement and relief, as David and Lucien moved to the window talking quietly to each other. 'What will your forfeit be?' she asked, but Grace couldn't answer her because she didn't know. All she knew was that she would have to pay it immediately, before they could move on to Lucien's next idea in the Pleasure Suite. And it was quite clear to her now that it was Lucien's pleasure that was going to count and not Emily's.

After a brief rest, Lucien helped Emily off the bed and lifted her into the hanging chair. 'You can watch the forfeit from there,' he said with a smile.

Emily wriggled. 'It's not very comfortable.'

'I assure you it could be made a great deal more uncomfortable,' remarked her lover, and seeing the expression on Emily's face Grace realised that the young actress was beginning to understand what was expected of her

Next Lucien gestured for Grace to get off the bed, and standing naked beside David she watched as Lucien removed the towels, piled the pillows up at the head of the bed and then started to remove items from the small chest of drawers. His lean, athletic body was surprisingly well muscled, and he was already in a state of semi-arousal.

'Don't let me down,' murmured David before moving away to idly stroke the suspended Emily's naked spine through the gaps in the back of the wicker chair.

'This game was very popular in bordellos on the Continent centuries ago,' explained Lucien as he approached Grace. 'David will help get us both ready. We'll be blindfolded with our hands tied behind our backs. You'll have fifteen minutes to bring us both to orgasm. It's easier than it sounds, because, without sight, the sensitivity of the skin is greatly increased. The game is also more fun if it's played in silence.'

Grace never liked being blindfolded, and she knew David was aware of this, but as he secured her blindfold he didn't whisper a word of reassurance, merely bound her wrists tightly behind her back before lifting her onto the bed. For a moment she panicked. Deprived of sight and without the use of her hands and arms, she felt very vulnerable, and was keenly aware that because of the way her arms were positioned her breasts were thrusting forward. There was total silence in the room, all that she could hear was the sound of her own breathing and then the bed dipped slightly and she knew that Lucien was now somewhere on the bed too.

She remained motionless in the place where David

had put her, but felt the bed moving beneath her as Lucien edged towards her. When his thighs touched hers she tried to think what she should do, aware that the minutes were passing, and failure was unthinkable with Emily watching.

Instinctively she parted her thighs, so that Lucien could move closer, and he leant towards her until his chest brushed against her nipples. She could hear the sound of his breathing, and then his lips touched hers and he kissed her softly. The tenderness of his kiss gave her back her confidence, and she began to rub her breasts against his chest, until her nipples grew hard and the hairs on his chest teased the now tight, sensitive little peaks.

Her thighs were beginning to ache, so she sat back and taking the weight of her upper body on her fastened hands put the soles of her feet flat on the bed, hoping that Lucien would follow her lead. To her relief he did, and now she was able to get close to him, wrapping her legs high over his hips and drawing her feet together behind his back.

All the time she was moving, Lucien continued to kiss her, not only on the mouth but also on her cheeks before nibbling softly on her earlobes. She felt his erection growing and leaning back on her hands, bound at the wrist, managed to raise her body up enough for him to slide inside her. Once there he began to rotate his hips so that she could feel him touching all the walls of her vagina, seeking out her G-spot, and when he found it she gave a tiny guttural moan of pleasure.

Her breasts were swollen and aching, longing for contact again, but in this position it was impossible. Sensing her need for more stimulation, Lucien managed to push his lower body forward more until his pubic bone was pressing against the top of her vulva, and at last she felt an orgasm starting to build.

'You have five more minutes,' said David dispassionately, his voice cutting through the erotically charged silence.

His words distracted her, taking her focus away from what she was doing, and she guessed that he'd spoken on purpose, because she was so close to paying the forfeit successfully. Then she heard Lucien give a muffled groan, and started to panic because she knew that if she didn't climax before him, she wouldn't manage to at all.

He nuzzled her ear, still pressing himself hard against her pubic bone with every small movement in and out of her, and he flicked his tongue in and out of her right ear, in an imitation of the way he was moving his erection inside her. At last she shivered with pleasure, trembling on the very brink of an orgasm but then he gave a shout and suddenly his hips were jerking uncontrollably as he climaxed, leaving her balanced right on the edge of fulfilment.

'Two minutes,' said David, still sounding totally detached.

Grace didn't know what to do, but Lucien withdrew and she felt him starting to kneel up again so she followed his lead, aware that he was trying to help her. As soon as they were more upright she moved around until she'd her legs each side of his left thigh and then knelt down on it, so that she could move herself back and forth against his hard muscles. Immediately her pleasure was reignited but she still wasn't sure she could come in time. As though sensing this, Lucien's mouth moved to the side of her neck, and he licked the small hollow by her shoulder bone before nipping sharply on the thin layer of delicate skin.

The familiar darts of dark pleasure that David had taught her to enjoy shot through her and immediately the small sparks that had been building in her lower body grew and spread until with a cry of intense relief and pleasure she finally came, grateful to Lucien for all he'd done. For several seconds, no one spoke or moved.

'You had five seconds to spare,' David said eventually, his hands untying her and removing the black, velvet mask. 'I have a feeling that Lucien helped you, though.'

As Grace blinked, her eyes readjusting to the light while David released Lucien, she caught a strange, slightly frightening expression on Lucien's face, which he quickly masked. 'I merely reacted to Grace's actions,' he said calmly. 'She did well. I hope you were watching carefully, Emily. I think you and I will play this together tonight, when we're alone, but not in silence. You'll need instructions.' Emily didn't respond.

'What now?' asked David, his voice still calm.

'I think Emily and I need some time alone. Perhaps we could all meet late afternoon, for a sauna, and generally relax together.'

Grace saw David smile. 'That sounds an excellent idea. See you both later.'

Scrambling into her clothes, Grace glanced across at Emily who was still sitting in the hanging chair. Her cheeks were now very flushed and she looked excited but also unsure of herself, and as Lucien lifted her down and kissed her it was clear that she'd found the scene that had just been played out both arousing and worrying.

'I don't think Emily is too sure what's happening any more,' said Grace as she and David went up to their suite to shower and change.

'Are any of us?' David asked, looking intently at her, and remembering how she'd felt when Lucien had helped her, Grace didn't have any answer for him.

'I've been trying to contract you for hours!' exclaimed Amber, when Lucien finally took her call on his mobile.

'I could hardly speak to you in front of Emily,' he retorted. 'I've had to come out into the garden as it is, and I'm not supposed to be out here.'

Amber didn't want to hear anything about Grace's new hotel. 'Just answer the question,' she snapped. 'I'm working really hard to get your basement the way you want it, the least you can do it keep me updated on how things are going.'

'It's not easy. I don't want to arouse David's suspicions, and as far as I know he isn't aware that you and I are still in touch. I think it's going very well. Emily definitely likes David, which makes my work all the easier.'

'Especially as you're smitten with Grace.'

'She's a wonderful mixture of innocence and extreme sensuality. I'm not smitten, but she fascinates me, although David's feelings for her interest me even more.'

'I think you are smitten, but that's your problem. Don't let it interfere with the plan, though, and if Grace stays with David she won't keep any of her innocence for much longer,' retorted Amber.

'I think she will.'

'Is he tiring of her yet?'

There was a short pause at the other end of the phone. 'I don't think so, but I believe she may be moving away from him as she becomes more confident, and he won't know what to do about that.'

'Is she moving towards you? We need her to trust you, otherwise I'm wasting my time in this basement.'

'Yes, she trusts me,' Lucien said, a note of regret in his voice.

Amber laughed. 'You don't need to sound sad about it. That's the whole idea of the plan.'

'I know. Regrettably, David isn't really that keen on Emily. He's helping her sometimes, and shows his usual interest in the corruption of relative innocence, but she's not his type.'

'She doesn't need to be his type,' retorted Amber. 'If he's helping her, then Grace will begin to feel insecure and that will make your job easier. Emily's just a pawn in the game, but we can't afford to lose her before the Ultimate Fantasy scenario.'

'I think I know how to keep someone like Emily keen,' said Lucien, and Amber could tell that she'd annoyed him. She didn't care.

'Of course you do,' she replied, knowing they had to remain on good terms or she would never get her revenge. 'Right, I'd better get back to work. Enjoy the rest of your mini-break.'

'Oh, believe me, I will,' said Lucien, switching off his phone, and it was with mixed feelings that he returned to the hotel suite, where Emily was waiting for him.

Part Four

Chapter One

After some time to herself, oblivious to Lucien and Amber's secret plotting, Grace went to find Andrew to check on how things were going in the rest of the hotel. She found him in the staff room, sitting at the table writing.

'Will you be working in the Victorian Suite today?' she asked him.

'They've asked for Toby, but we do have a bit of a problem there. I think David will need to spend an hour or two with them. The girlfriend can't accept that in Victorian times a woman's body belonged to her husband. She's kicking up quite a fuss, which makes it difficult to maintain the right atmosphere. I think David could help out.'

Grace flicked through the register. 'They've both had plenty of experience at The Dining Club. She should be enjoying herself.'

'I suspect she's actually gone off her partner.'

'Well, David's free until this afternoon so I'm sure he'll be happy to try to smooth things over. Are they using Tilly?'

'No, she's at the desk working on the timetable.'

Grace, who was feeling sleepy after her time with Lucien, forced herself to concentrate. 'I didn't expect this sort of problem,' she confessed.

Andrew shrugged. 'It's always a risk with this kind of venture. David will sort it out. He's had a lot of practice.'

'A lot of practice at what?' asked David, coming into the room. Grace explained and he checked the names on the list. 'No problem,' he assured her. 'I recognise their names, and the trouble is she needs a firmer hand than her partner is able to provide. She complains and pushes him because actually she wants him to be more dominant.'

'She claims he's being too dominant,' said Andrew.

'I gathered that, but deep down it's not what she wants. I've seen that with her before. Send someone up to the suite to bring Toby back down. I'll take his place – if that's all right with you, of course, Grace?'

She was grateful he'd at least pretended that her opinion mattered, but wished she'd found out more about the couple before they arrived. She should have spoken to Louise at the Club, who could have told her all she needed to know, but she hadn't thought of it. 'Yes, that sounds perfect,' she assured him. 'I'll make sure I get better background notes in the future.'

'It might be a good idea,' he agreed as he left the room.

Grace bit on her bottom lip, suddenly feeling rather foolish.

'Don't worry about it,' said Andrew. 'The hotel's a massive success, we've got a waiting list of guests and there's nothing like it anywhere else that I know of. The whole concept was an absolute brainwave, and David must be very proud of you.'

'Maybe,' she said doubtfully. 'I hope he remembers that he and I are both due in the Pleasure Suite this afternoon.'

'He never forgets anything,' retorted Andrew.

Grace rather hoped that wasn't true. For a brief

time, while she and Lucien were pleasuring each other in intense intimacy, due to their lack of sight, she'd felt herself being drawn towards him emotionally as well as physically, and that was a betrayal of her relationship with David, a betrayal that she was sure he'd noticed.

It was four o'clock in the afternoon before Lucien phoned down to say that he and Emily wanted Grace and David to rejoin them. By then David had set things right in the Victorian Suite and Grace had found time to phone Fran for an update on the way the play was going.

'This should be very enjoyable,' said David as they approached the Pleasure Suite. 'A time to relax and enjoy ourselves.'

Grace didn't reply, well aware that in the world she and David had created at the hotel, nothing was ever quite what one expected, and whilst enjoyment was guaranteed, relaxation wasn't generally included in the scenarios played out behind the closed doors of the suites.

'Fun time, girls!' exclaimed Lucien as soon as he'd let Grace and David in. 'You can both take a sauna, and for once you won't have us with you. I'm told ladies enjoy having some "girl time", so this is your chance. Of course, there's a camera in there, so David and I can watch you enjoying yourselves, but apart from that you're on your own.'

'I love saunas,' said Emily enthusiastically, stripping off her clothes and taking the thick, cream-coloured towel that Lucien handed her. 'It's a small one, though. Is it big enough for the two of us?'

'Of course,' said David, 'although you will have to sit close together, or one of you could always stand some of the time. I'm sure you'll find ways of enjoying it.'

'Ways that we can enjoy too,' Lucien added with a smile.

Emily frowned. 'What do you mean?'

'He means that you and Grace must help each other to enjoy the experience to the full. I don't suppose you'll want more than ten minutes in there, so make the most of it.'

By this time Grace was naked too, and letting the towel hang by her side she walked erect across the living room and opened the door to the sauna, while a slightly more reluctant Emily followed her. 'I'm not sure I understand,' she murmured.

'Yes you do,' said Grace. 'We're to pleasure each

other while we're in there. We don't have to climax, it's too hot for that really, but we can come close.'

'I've never done things with only another woman before,' admitted Emily.

'Wonderful!' exclaimed Lucien. 'You'll discover a whole new world in the next ten minutes. In you go, girls.' And with that he pushed the reluctant Emily in behind Grace and closed the door on them.

Emily immediately laid her towel on the slatted shelf and sat on it, wrapping her arms round her knees, which she kept tightly closed.

'Lucien won't like that,' said Grace softly, sitting down on her own towel next to Emily, her legs hanging down and the edges of her towel pulled teasingly over her body from waist to upper thigh. 'He wants us to fully enjoy the sauna.'

'I am enjoying it,' retorted Emily, but Grace could see that the younger woman was nervous.

'This could be really nice for us both if you cooperate,' she said quietly. 'Let me take care of that bead of sweat running down you.' Leaning across Emily she licked delicately at it, her tongue gently caressing the top of Emily's right breast. Emily promptly tried to pull her towel over her chest, but Grace stopped her.

'Didn't that feel nice? Twist round a little and I'll do the same on your back,' she said. 'You really don't want to annoy Lucien and David.'

Reluctantly Emily twisted her body so that Grace could run the tip of her tongue down the length of Emily's spine, and this time the younger woman gave a soft sigh of pleasure. 'You see, it feels good. Now do the same for me.'

Emily complied, and very soon her inhibitions started to dissolve as the two of them softly licked and caressed each other's bodies, until Emily actually decided to take the initiative. Leaving her towel on the shelf she got to her feet and stood in front of Grace, her hands wandering over Grace's waist and hips as the sweat ran in rivulets down Grace's body.

Pausing only to pour water over the hot stones to create more steam, Emily then leant forward until the hot, damp flesh of their burgeoning breasts were touching, while Grace's hands cupped the cheeks of Emily's bottom, pulling her lower body closer until Emily could experience the hardness of Grace's leg and her eyes started to widen with pleasure.

'We mustn't come,' Grace whispered into Emily's ear under the pretext of licking the side of her neck.

With her blonde hair sticking to her head and the sides of her neck, Emily nodded, but the two women continued to caress each other's bodies with soft, gentle touches that were arousing and at the same time reassuring.

Just as the heat was starting to feel uncomfortable the door was opened by Lucien. 'Well done, girls. Time to come out and cool down a little now.'

Full of new-found confidence, Emily walked out ahead of Grace, and then screamed as Lucien grabbed hold of her and tied a blindfold round her eyes. 'Relax,' he said with a laugh. 'You want to cool down, don't you?'

Grace watched as David opened the door into the ice plunge. She wanted to warn Emily, but didn't dare. All she could do was stand in the doorway of the sauna and watch as Lucien lifted Emily off the ground and then with one swift movement pushed her down into the ice plunge.

Grace heard the crack of the thin covering of ice followed by Emily's scream of terror as her body was submerged in the freezing water. When her feet reached the bottom her head was only just above the water line, and she continued to scream as she tried to scrabble out.

'Relax, this is all the rage in Scandinavia,' said Lucien. 'I'll get you out in a couple of minutes.'

Standing next to David, Grace could feel the excited tension in his body as he watched the scenario unfolding. Then, when Lucien gripped Emily under her arms and pulled her out, David grabbed her ankles and the two of them carried the sobbing blonde through into the main suite.

'You'd better take a shower, Grace,' said David. 'Your pleasure comes later.'

She showered quickly, pulled on the cosy robe that was hanging on a hook and went to join the other three. By now Emily had been spread-eagled on the bed, her eyes still covered by the mask, and the two men were teasing her squirming body with the fringed tips of long pieces of rope of varying thicknesses.

'She's incredibly sensitive after the sauna and the ice plunge, aren't you, Emily?' said Lucien.

'Yes,' she sobbed, 'so please stop what you're doing.'

'Why?'

'I want to come. I want you inside me. This is called the Pleasure Suite, so—'

'But this *is* my pleasure,' Lucien explained. 'Your nipples look very tight, would they like some attention?'

MARINA ANDERSON

Taking Emily's moan for a yes, Lucien moved down the bed, pushed Emily's legs apart and started giving her oral sex while David stood above the young blonde, watching her intently.

Grace was shaking with desire now, frantic for some kind of stimulation herself but aware that she had to stand and watch, because this was Lucien's fantasy and all she could do was play whatever role he'd allocated to her.

As Emily whimpered and squirmed, Grace grew damp between her thighs, and the sound of her own breathing was almost as loud as Emily's. David, who was still watching Emily keenly, glanced up at Grace. 'Don't worry, your turn will come,' he assured her again, and then he began to gently caress Emily's tight nipples with small feathers at one end of the cane he was holding.

That, combined with Lucien's skilful tongue, quickly had Emily gasping and groaning as her orgasm approached. 'Not yet,' cautioned Lucien. 'I haven't quite finished here.'

Grace saw that Emily was really trying to obey, but the caress of the feathers combined with the tantalising movements of Lucien's tongue were too much for her and she gave a sob as her whole body tightened and when her toes curled she began to thrash around on the bed.

'Punish her,' said Lucien calmly, and Grace watched as David turned the cane in his hand and with total precision flicked a thin leather whip across Emily's swollen nipples, and despite her cries of protest he didn't stop until her orgasm was over and her body finally still.

'There,' said Lucien, removing the mask from Emily's eyes. 'I'm quite sure you've never experienced pleasure like that before, have you?'

Exhausted and replete, Emily opened her large blue eyes and stared at the two men in a sated daze. 'No,' she admitted breathlessly. 'Never.'

'She did well,' said David. 'She managed to last for fifteen minutes despite the ice plunge, which must have made her whole body incredibly sensitive following the sauna.'

'And how long do you think Grace would last now, after watching us?' asked Lucien.

David shrugged. 'That's difficult to tell. She's highly experienced so obviously it would be longer than that.'

Grace stood completely still, hoping that the conversation wasn't heading for the conclusion she feared.

'How much longer?'

'I don't know. She's been watching everything, so that's arousing, but I'd say an extra ten minutes at least.'

'Twenty-five minutes, then?' asked Lucien.

'Yes.'

'I'd like to see if you're right.'

'You're the guest,' said David. 'If that's what you want, then that's what we'll do. I'm sure Grace is in the mood to be pleasured.'

'Excellent,' said Lucien. 'Emily, I want you to watch this from the suspended chair. Grace is something of an expert at controlling her body's reactions to being pleasured. You might learn a thing or two by watching her. Time to change places, ladies.'

'Don't let me down, darling,' said David, removing Grace's robe while Lucien lifted Emily into the chair.

Grace lay down on her back, then the blindfold was placed over her eyes and as the first tendrils of rope were trailed softly over her already excited body, she doubted if even with all her training and skill she was going to succeed. The light caress of the rope was both pleasurable and soothing, and she started to relax slightly. Then, as it continued, her body began to react more strongly and she moved herself around a little, attempting to make them touch her where she wanted them to.

Lucien gave a low laugh. 'Time to move on, I think,' he said, and as the ropes were withdrawn she remembered what had happened next to Emily and to her shame felt her nipples hardening in anticipation of the touch of the feathers that would come from David's skilful hand.

At the precise moment that he swirled them around her left nipple, she felt Lucien pushing her legs wider apart so that he could squeeze her outer sex lips gently between his finger and thumb before slowly rubbing them up and down. A sigh of pleasure escaped her, and as David moved the feathers to her other nipple, Lucien pressed the palm of his hand on her pubic mound and then applied pressure in alternating up and down and circular motions.

Small sounds of pleasure escaped from her mouth, and she heard him laugh quietly as he then inserted a finger inside her, moving it slowly in and out while at the same time pressing the knuckles of his other fingers against the whole of the area surrounding her swelling clitoris.

'She's very well aroused,' he commented, and she wished her treacherous body wasn't so quick to betray her.

'I imagine she is, but she still has nearly twenty minutes to go,' said David, as he began to move the soft feathers across the width of her breasts, so that both of them were being teased and excited at the same time. Her nipples were so tight that they were hurting her, and remembering what would happen to them when she finally climaxed she didn't know if she would be able to bear the sharp, stinging streaks of pleasure so deep they became pain.

I'm going to move you down the bed a little, Grace,' said Lucien. 'I want your feet on the floor while I use my mouth on you.'

Slowly, gently, he pulled her towards him. Once she was in place he took her totally by surprise by kissing and licking her lower belly, and she gave a small gasp of surprise and delight as her whole body began to respond. Desperately she tried to disassociate herself from what was happening to her, concentrating on the image of Emily being plunged into the icy water, and imagining her sitting in the suspended chair, unable to move, but then Lucien gently parted her pubic hair, opened up her outer sex lips and with his head deep between her thighs, he moved his tongue upwards in long, firm strokes.

Grace could feel her orgasm beginning, the strange ache deep inside her that always preceded it was growing far too fast, and when his tongue circled her clitoris she gasped and her hips jerked upwards as she tried to stop him. Again he laughed softly. 'You're nearly there, Grace,' he murmured, 'and when I put my tongue inside you, how will you control yourself?'

'You still have ten more minutes to wait,' said David, and Grace could hear the displeasure in his voice.

'She can't wait that long, not if I do this properly, can you, Gracie?' Lucien asked affectionately, and she felt as though her body was melting.

Thrusting his tongue inside her, he drew out her juices so that they could moisten her even more, then paused for a moment. 'Now I'm going to swirl my tongue all around the base of your clitoris, Gracie,' he said. 'Not right on it, that would be too intense, but round the sides, just the way you like it, and you won't be able to stop yourself from coming, will you?'

Grace knew that he was right, and tears escaped from her eyes, tears of frustration and disappointment. She only hoped that none of them showed through the mask.

'Answer him,' said David. 'Tell him he's wrong.'

'I wish he was, truly I do, but—'

Before she'd even finished speaking, Lucien's tongue began to move around the throbbing centre of all her pleasure, and at the same time he sucked lightly on the frantic flesh. With a loud cry of delight mingled with despair at her own failure, Grace felt her orgasm gather into a tight knot and then rush through her. She twisted and turned on the bed, moaning softly, but then when it was nearly over David used the leather whip end of the cane on her, just as he had on Emily.

Grace's nipples were so sensitive after the torment of the feathers that they reacted swiftly and violently, and to her shame she realised that he'd triggered a second orgasm, one that followed so quickly behind the first it was almost impossible to separate them.

'How she loves the darker pleasures,' murmured Lucien, slipping a finger inside her rear entrance and pressing firmly on the walls of her rectum as all her muscles contracted with the force of this second wave of pleasure.

She felt so full that it was unbelievable, and again she cried out at the wonderful sensations that were sweeping through her. Eventually, though, it all ended, and her body was finally quiet.

Lucien moved her legs back up onto the bed. 'How long did she last?'

'Twenty minutes,' said David.

'That was still very good, all things considered.'

'But not what she knew was expected of her.'

'True. Blame that on me. She's so responsive to me I probably overwhelmed her with some of the things I did.'

Grace couldn't believe what Lucien had said, making it sound as though he was better at arousing her body than David had ever been, and she knew that David would pick up on that.

'Time for us to go, I think,' David said quietly as he removed the mask from Grace's eyes. 'You'd better get dressed, Grace. I think Lucien has plans for Emily while she's still in that chair.'

'I wish I could put you in the chair,' Lucien whispered to Grace as she walked past him.

Once they were outside the door of the Pleasure Suite, David caught hold of Grace's shoulders and turned her towards him. 'What did he just say to you?' he asked. Grace told him. David's eyes narrowed. 'And what did you think when he said that?'

'I was very glad he couldn't,' she replied truthfully.

'Only because he's already exhausted you.'

'Keep your voice down, we don't want other guests to hear,' she retorted.

Grabbing her by the arm he led her up to their rooms. 'I was right, wasn't I? You were relieved he couldn't because he'd already exhausted you. Why didn't you manage to last twenty-five minutes? It shouldn't have been that difficult.'

'Well, it was! You were both working on me, and you know how sensitive my nipples are. I'd been in the sauna, watched Emily being pleasured and then had to last longer than her despite having been aroused by all that beforehand. You're the person who taught me all these different ways of being pleasured. You've made me what I am. It's not my fault if you don't like it now. I can't go back. I can never be like Emily is or—'

'I don't want you to be like Emily, but nor do I expect

you to come quicker with Lucien than you would have done with me.'

'I didn't!'

'I think you did, and I think I know why as well. You like him, don't you? He took you out to dinner, he's made you feel special and so you're turned on even before he begins.'

'If that were true, and it's not,' she said quietly, 'perhaps you would need to ask yourself why you're not able to make me feel special these days.'

David's eyes widened and he looked at her in astonishment. 'I can't believe you said that,' he murmured, almost to himself.

'It's not true, I'm only saying—'

'I know what you're saying, and I think you'd better go down and see that all's well with the other guests. I've got some business calls to make. I'll join you later,' he said quietly.

'David, I don't care for Lucien in the way you're trying to make out. You were the one saying I did, and all I wanted you to consider was why you thought that might be a possibility.'

'I know what you were saying. I'll be down later, Grace,' he said. He suddenly sounded very tired.

Going down to check on her guests, Grace wanted to cry. David was still the only man she wanted, and she loved him more than she'd imagined it was possible to love anyone, but he'd forced her into a position where she'd had to defend herself. What she hadn't realised was how deeply her words were going to affect him, and if she could have gone back in time, she would never have said them.

Chapter Two

'Lucien doesn't want you and David until tomorrow morning,' said Andrew when he and Grace were going through the guests' various requirements after dinner that evening. 'He says he has to leave mid-afternoon tomorrow, as something urgent has come up. David might know about that. It's bound to be business.'

'Right,' said Grace, still distracted by David's reaction earlier.

'All in all, it's pretty quiet tonight. Everyone seems to be having a great time without too much assistance, so I was wondering if I could have the evening off?'

Grace glanced at the book. 'You're wanted in The Ultimate Fantasy Suite at nine. It's a Roman orgy, isn't it?'

'Yes, but Toby could take my place.'

'He's there as well. An orgy needs quite a few men and Grant is helping in the Country Retreat Suite.'

Andrew sighed. 'All right, but I'm leaving as soon as the orgy is over. I want to see Fran.'

'Is there a problem?'

'Grace, I never have any free time, what with my work at the gym, helping at the Club and being here once a month, I hardly see Fran, and she's not happy about it. She's never been involved in any of this and so she doesn't understand. She's spending a lot of time with some actor from your play, and—'

'Andrew? He's over sixty!'

'So what? I'm sure he's still perfectly capable of giving her a good time, and they're in the same business. Anyway, I've seen him a couple of times and he looks much younger than that. The point is, how can I hope to keep Fran if I hardly ever see her?'

'You won't,' admitted Grace. 'If she means that much to you, you're going to have to give up some of your work. Would you be able to do that?'

Andrew nodded. 'Yes, I would. I'm not like David and Lucien. Sure, I enjoy everything I do, but it's not a lifestyle I want for the rest of my life. I love Fran, and I want us to spend time doing ordinary things that other couples do, like going out to dinner at weekends, visiting art galleries or spending a few days in Paris on the spur of the moment. With the hours she works, especially now you're running this hotel and she has to cover for you one week a month, plus the hours I keep, it's just not possible. If I'm not careful, I'm going to lose her.'

'And you're sure she wouldn't be interested in this lifestyle?'

Andrew laughed. 'You're one of her best friends; you must know she wouldn't be. She'd hate it.'

'She certainly doesn't think much of my relationship with David. No, she'd never understand the things we enjoy,' admitted Grace. 'Well, get away as soon as you can tonight and when the first four months are over here, and we take stock of how things have gone and what people have liked and disliked about the four suites, maybe you'll choose to leave us.' She put a hand on his arm. 'I hope you don't, Andrew, but I'll understand if you do.'

'It won't be easy to give it all up,' he confessed. 'Sometimes, though, when I see you and David, it's not easy for me. You know how I used to feel about you in your early days at The Dining Club. There are still times when I wish it had worked out differently, and I think that unless I cut myself loose it's always going to be difficult.'

'Like I said, decide when the four months are up,' she repeated, closing the book sharply.

'What's up?' asked David, coming in to the office as Andrew left.

'He wants to get away as early as possible tonight. He's worried Fran's losing interest in him.'

'She was bound to. She's not into his kind of lifestyle.'

'I think he's tiring of it,' said Grace.

David shook his head. 'He might be saying that today, but he won't find it that easy to walk away. Maybe right now he imagines he'd be happy with what might be called a *normal* life, but that feeling won't last. He'd be bored within a few months.'

'You don't believe people change?' asked Grace.

'Of course they change. We all make mistakes, hopefully learn from them, and adjust our lives accordingly, but you're talking about a very specialised part of life, the sexual side. It's like food. Once you've tasted fine dining, you don't want to live on bread and cheese for the rest of your life!'

'But he wants a normal sexual relationship with Fran, and—'

'Does he indeed? I'll believe that when it happens.'

'You don't think it's possible?'

'No, not for people like us. He'd be bored to tears within a few months, as would we all. When does Lucien want us again?'

'Tomorrow morning; it seems he has to leave after lunch tomorrow because of work.'

David frowned. 'Really? I've no idea what that can be about. Well, if we're not needed tonight, I have to go out for a couple of hours and make some business arrangements for next week. I'll be back late. You don't have to wait up for me if you don't want to.'

'I do want to.'

He looked surprised, but then gave her a quick smile and her stomach lurched. She loved him so much, yet after all this time she still didn't fully understand him. She wanted to, because she was sure that if she did, or at least understood more fully how he felt about her, then they'd both be even happier.

'Fine. I'll see you later, then.'

After he'd gone, Grace let out a deep sigh as her body relaxed. She sensed that something pivotal to their relationship had happened in the Pleasure Suite earlier, but she had no idea how it was going to affect them, and it was the not knowing that was making her tense.

It was nearly midnight before David returned, and Grace was propped up in bed reading. 'Good, you are awake,' he said. 'Everything go all right tonight?'

'Very quietly, and Andrew managed to leave around ten, so he should have been in time to catch Fran after the play ended.'

'I've bought you a little something,' he continued, handing her a small dark blue box with a ribbon tied round it. 'I was unfair earlier today and it's my way of saying sorry.'

Grace's eyes widened in surprise. She couldn't recall ever hearing him apologise before, and although he was always generous, this gift was totally unexpected.

'Aren't you going to open it?' he asked.

'Of course.' She untied the ribbon and inside the box found the most exquisite necklace imaginable, with an aquamarine and opal pendant made up of five gemstones, pear cut, suspended from a rose gold double link rope chain. It was breathtakingly beautiful, and she stared at it in astonishment.

'Do you like it?' he asked quietly.

'It's stunning!' she whispered. 'So delicate, and the design is absolutely gorgeous.'

'Let me put it on you,' he said, and she bent her head forward so that he could fasten it round her neck. 'I want you to wear it every day, so that every day you remember that although I know I can say thoughtless things, I never mean to hurt you the way I hurt you today. And I do mean every day,' he added.

'But it's too lovely to wear all the time,' she protested.

'Nonsense; and it's very delicate so it won't ever look out of place. Promise me that you'll wear it every day,' he pleaded.

Grace was totally overwhelmed by the gift. She didn't really understand why she had to wear it every day, but she had no intention of spoiling such a lovely moment. 'I promise,' she assured him.

Leaning forward he kissed her softly on the lips, and then he was taking off his clothes and within minutes was lying naked beside her, slipping the straps of her silk nightdress from her shoulders and gently caressing her shoulders and breasts.

With a sigh of contentment she relaxed beneath his clever, knowing hands and much later, when they'd finished making love, he curled himself round her back, one arm draped across her waist, and she was soon fast asleep.

Unknown to her, her lover lay awake for a long time, staring into the darkness, his mind a jumble of mixed emotions that at times threatened to overwhelm him.

At ten o'clock the following morning, Lucien opened the door of the Pleasure Suite to Grace and David. 'Emily's nearly ready for the hot tub,' he said. 'We had a wonderful time yesterday afternoon and evening. I made full use of the suspended chair, which was a superb idea of yours, Grace. Many congratulations!'

When Emily joined them she was wearing a thin silk housecoat over her naked body. 'I'm still sore,' she complained, pouting prettily at David. 'Look what Lucien did to me.' Slipping off the housecoat she turned and showed a series of fading thin red lines over her back and the cheeks of her bottom.

David licked his middle finger and drew it gently down over the lines, and Emily shivered with dark delight. 'So, you enjoyed that experience, did you?' he said with a low laugh.

She wriggled, and Lucien laughed. 'Once she'd

stopped pretending she wanted me to let her go, yes she certainly did enjoy it. She wanted more this morning, but I thought you might like to take over this time, before we all use the hot tub. Maybe Grace would like a turn as well?'

'If that's what you'd like then of course she would,' David assured him. 'You first, Emily?'

He lifted the curvaceous blonde up into the seat, leaving her legs dangling in the air then took the very thin whip from Lucien and drew it softly down over Emily's spine between the gaps in the wicker chair. Looking on, Grace felt her body respond: she began to tremble with excitement, mingled with a touch of fear. She knew the pleasure that would come for Emily, but she also knew the sensation of pain that must come first.

David spent a long time caressing Emily's creamy skin with the tip of the whip, keeping her waiting until Grace could tell that she was becoming nervous, perhaps anticipating the pain that would precede the pleasure. He was an expert at timing, and waited until she let a tiny whimper of fear escape her lips before flicking his wrist sharply. Emily's body jerked, and Grace saw a thin red line appear across the younger woman's lower back, a line broken up where the wicker had protected her flesh.

Emily let out a small moan of pleasure, but then had to wait for several minutes, and turned her head to see why David was delaying. 'Keep looking to the front or I'll blindfold you,' he said dispassionately, and at his words, Grace felt her own desire rising.

The second time he flicked his wrist, David struck upwards, so that the softly rounded cheeks of Emily's bottom were struck. She gave a cry of surprise and pain, but without pausing he then worked his way up her back, with only a few seconds gap between the blows.

Emily shook with excitement, uttering small guttural sounds of pleasure as the sensations grew, and Grace wished that the blonde would hurry up and climax so that she could have her turn. Unfortunately for both young women, David was an expert at delaying the final rush of satisfaction, and soon Emily was crying out with frustration until he told her to stay silent or he'd stop.

Standing behind Grace, Lucien rested his hands on her shoulders. 'You're trembling,' he whispered. 'You want to feel what she's feeling, don't you? It won't be long, and I'll be watching you while you're in the chair. Later you can join me in the hot tub and that should be very enjoyable for us both. I hope David appreciates how lucky he is,' he added.

Grace didn't reply, and within seconds Emily's whole body arched as, with a shriek of pleasure, she finally reached the point of no return.

Lucien lifted Emily down from the chair and then turned to Grace. He undressed her and settled her into the suspended seat that she'd spent so many hours selecting.

'I timed Emily,' said David, 'and for a change I want you to come more quickly than she did. I'm sure that won't prove a problem for you,' he added.

Naked except for the pendant around her neck, Grace found the chair comfortable but she didn't like the way it swayed when David touched it. Her hands gripped hold of two of the side struts to try to make herself feel more stable.

'Naughty,' said Lucien, opening her hands and resting them on her thighs. 'Emily didn't hold onto the sides.'

Grace could hear the sound of her own breathing in the silent room. Emily, now wearing her robe again, was standing in front of Lucien who had his arms round her. They were both watching her closely. She couldn't see David, but could feel his breath on her back as he carefully ran one hand down her spine, his fingers caressing her just as he'd caressed Emily.

With a soft sigh she tensed, waiting for the whip to fall, but for what seemed like an eternity nothing happened, and she remembered how he'd made Emily wait. Her nipples grew tight and her breasts began to feel full as her body anticipated what was to come. When Lucien coughed she jumped, and David laughed softly. 'How tense you are, and how eager, my darling. But where will the first blow fall?'

She had no idea, but suspected it would be near her shoulder blades. In the event, he let the thin whip strike round the back of her waist, and the sudden burning sensation made her cry out after such a long delay. Then the burning eased and a warm glow of pleasure followed it, but within seconds the whip had fallen again, this time on the back of her thighs, and the lash fell harder so that the pain was more intense and it took longer for it to turn to pleasure.

He was toying with her, making her wait, and soon her body was so full of the conflicting sensations of red-hot pain and dark, forbidden pleasure that it didn't know what to do. Her climax kept building and then fading, and she was sure that David was playing her body differently from the way he'd played Emily's, in order to make her take longer to climax than the younger woman.

Determined not to lose, she made herself embrace the feel of the whip, so that every time her skin flinched her excitement grew. The pain was now exquisite, truly the pleasure-pain that she'd been learning about for a long time, and as she embraced all the sensations so she grew damp between her thighs, beads of sweat formed between her swollen breasts and when he flicked his wrist even harder the hot pleasure rushed through her and she convulsed in a blissfully sharp orgasm.

'Very good,' said David, and she could hear surprised approval in his voice. 'You were quicker by twenty seconds.'

'Wonderful!' exclaimed Lucien. 'Now, a short break for the ladies and then we can all enjoy ourselves in the hot tub. I'll take Grace in with me. David, you and Emily can use it after us, although naturally I hope you'll be watching us.'

'I don't think you need have any fears on that account,' said David drily, lifting Grace down from the chair, and twenty minutes later she and Lucien climbed into the hot tub.

'Pure pleasure now,' he said with a smile, pushing his thick brown hair off his forehead. 'We can relax and enjoy ourselves. I enjoyed lubricating you just now, of course. I hope you enjoyed that too?'

Remembering the way his fingers had stroked the inside of her vagina as he'd applied the lubricant that was so necessary to make sex in water pleasurable, she blushed. 'Yes, I did.'

'Did you hear that, David?' he asked, sitting down on the shelf with his knees bent and his legs spread-eagled while his arms rested on the edge of the tub.

'Hear what?'

'How much Grace enjoyed me lubricating her with the gel. No doubt you'll give Emily as much pleasure when it's your turn.'

'No doubt,' David replied, looking intently at Grace who was facing forward as she straddled Lucien, lowering herself slowly, teasingly onto his penis while keeping hold of his shoulders for support.

The warm water lapped round her waist, and she put her feet flat on the shelf, bent her knees and then moved slowly up and down on his erection. Lucien let his head fall back a little, clearly relishing the sensation, and then Grace became aware of a strange tingling warmth spreading up through her abdomen. The more she moved up and down the more intense the feeling grew, and after a few moments Lucien lifted his head and gazed into her eyes.

'It was a special lubricant,' he whispered. 'I brought it with me, in case you hadn't supplied any. I hope you don't mind?'

Grace gave a tiny cry of surprise as the tingling intensified. She could feel her whole body responding to the heat that was now spreading upwards to her breasts, making every centimetre of her skin feel more alive than she could ever remember.

'Move backwards and forwards on me,' he said softly. 'It will be even better for both of us then.'

She did as he suggested, and immediately even more nerve endings were covered in the special lubricant and she felt as though her whole body was swelling with pleasure, and it also seemed that Lucien was filling every part of her.

'Has it never felt this good before, not even with David?' he asked.

Her eyes, which had been closed to allow her to wallow in the pleasure, flew open and she saw David, his arm round Emily's naked waist, watching her closely.

'Of course it has,' she gasped, wondering what was

happening to her body, because usually it took her a long time to climax in this way. It had always been a slow, tender way of making love, but this was totally different.

She knew that her face was flushed, and could see that her nipples had never been so large. David's eyes were cold. Before she could say anything about the lubricant, or get Lucien to explain, Lucien lifted and rotated his hips and without warning an intense climax rushed through her. 'Yes, oh yes!' she shouted, and her body continued to ripple with tendrils of ecstasy as Lucien climaxed too, so that they were shuddering together. Even when he was spent, she continued to jerk, uttering tiny cries of pleasure for what seemed like an eternity.

Finally the sensations died away and she felt her body calming down. Cupping her face in his hands Lucien kissed her hard on the mouth, his tongue moving teasingly between her lips so that he could flick it in and out, in an imitation of what had just taken place below the water. It was too intimate, too personal, and Grace pulled away, stumbling in her haste to leave the tub. David put out an arm to save her. 'I should think you're exhausted,' he remarked. 'Lucien is clearly something of an expert in the hot tub.'

'It wasn't that,' she whispered, 'he—'

'You were meant to enjoy it, Grace. I don't begrudge you your pleasure, you know,' he replied, but the look in his eyes didn't match the reassuring tone of his voice.

After she'd showered, Grace returned to watch David and Emily having sex in the tub, and when David put his hands beneath the blonde's armpits so that he could lift her up and down on his erection, she felt a stab of jealousy. That was something he often did when they were alone together in a hot tub, something she'd always thought of as being theirs alone. Seeing him doing it to Emily, and watching Emily's excited reaction, really hurt her but she knew she had no right to feel jealous, especially after what David had been forced to witness.

When everyone was totally fulfilled, they all got dressed and Lucien poured a round of drinks. 'I must say, this hotel has provided me with more pleasure than even I have experienced before,' he said to Grace. 'The entire concept is incredible. David must be very proud of you.'

'Indeed I am,' David assured him.

'After Emily and I have tried the final two suites I'll tell you which of them I've enjoyed the most, but so far they've both exceeded my expectations – as have you, Grace,' he added, his voice softening and deepening.

Remembering the hot tub, Grace flushed.

'Unfortunately, I have to leave earlier than planned, so we look forward to seeing you next month, when I believe it's our turn for the Country Retreat?'

'That's right,' said Grace. 'I hope the weather's fine; it makes such a difference to that particular break.'

'Now, Emily and I would like to round things off with a masseur. Perhaps Toby?'

'Yes, of course,' agreed Grace, and then before Lucien could keep them talking any longer she hurried from the room with David close behind her.

'It seems Lucien has a magic touch in hot tubs,' said David the moment they were out of the room.

'No, he hasn't. He just used a different lubricant from the one I'd provided.'

'Really? And what was in this different lubricant?'

'I don't know but it made me feel—'

'I saw exactly how it made you feel, thank you, but I also saw a used tube of lubricant identical to the one I used on Emily, so you might just as well admit that either he has a better technique than I do or you find him more exciting.'

'I am not a liar, David. In any case, I thought you despised all forms of sexual jealousy,' Grace retorted, refusing to let him see that she was close to tears at his words.

'My word, Gracie, you are growing up,' he said softly, and with that he turned on his heel and went down the stairs, leaving her to go to their rooms and get changed on her own.

In bed that night, before turning off the bedside lamp, she cuddled up to his rigid body. 'Don't be angry,' she begged him. 'My reactions in the hot tub had nothing to do with Lucien himself, truly they didn't. He told me that he'd used his own lubricant. He thought he'd been very clever – and he was because look what's happened to us. As for me growing up, would you really have wanted me to stay the same?

'You enjoy this hotel,' Grace went on, 'and I would never have thought of the idea when we first met because I knew nothing of this secret world of yours. You can still get pleasure from making me face challenges here, and when I struggle it excites and arouses you, but then when I succeed you're pleased for me. We're closer than ever before, because we're working and playing together for the few brief days the hotel is open each month, yet we both have independent lives outside the hotel. I don't understand what's wrong, or what more you need, but if you're not happy any more then please tell me what it is you want from me?'

She felt him relax a little. 'Go to sleep, Gracie. It's late and we're both tired,' he said gently.

She knew that she had to be content with that, but deep inside her a terrible fear was growing. A fear that despite the success of the hotel so far, and the progress she was making as she became even more involved in his darkly erotic world, David was losing interest in her, and if he cast her off she didn't know how she would survive. Only now did she totally understand how Amber must have felt when David discarded her.

'I won't let it happen to me,' she whispered to herself in the darkness. 'I'll do whatever it takes to keep him.'

The following evening, after all the guests had left, Grace held a brief staff meeting. She checked that everything was in place for the following month, asked for feedback – which was all positive – and then when everyone had left she switched on her laptop to check for any reviews of *Mrs Warren's Profession* that she might have missed.

David had gone back to his own place, preparing for a forthcoming business trip to China, so after she'd finished the reviews and jotted down a few notes she was alone in the hotel. It felt strange to wander from room to room – all of them spotless once more thanks to the efficiency of the cleaners who came in within an hour of the guests' departure – and think about the various activities that had taken place there over the past few days. When she checked the Pleasure Suite and saw the hot tub she remembered the exquisite sensations that Lucien's lubricant had sent flooding through her body, and remembered too the expression in David's eyes as he'd watched her.

It was almost impossible now for her to recall what she'd been like when she'd first met him. Sexually she'd come so far in a relatively short space of time that the girl she'd once been seemed like a stranger to her. She'd been happy then, she knew that, but not happy in the way that she was now. Life with David brought her moments of pure sexual bliss, and as a lover and companion he was everything she could ever have dreamt of. Yet she was well aware that although he'd allowed her to get closer to him than had seemed possible at the start of their relationship, she still didn't really understand him.

He understood her, and knew all there was to know about her, but despite her best efforts there was still a part of him that remained hidden from her. She knew nothing of his deepest hopes or fears, but instead had learnt to live in the moment and be grateful that fate had brought them together. She was well aware that this wasn't enough, not for a permanent commitment, but she still believed that if she persevered, and made him feel safe, one day he would open up to her. Then their partnership would be equal and both of them could feel safe.

And there, she thought to herself, was the crux of the problem. Despite everything, she didn't feel safe or secure. No matter how exciting the sex, or how many gifts he gave her, she suspected that he might still tire of her, and there would be nothing she could do about it, because he was afraid to love in the way that she loved him and wanted to be loved herself.

The next morning she met up with Fran at a café on Tottenham Court Road where they both ordered the smoked salmon and cream cheese baguette and bottled water. 'How's it going, then?' asked Grace.

'Very well. Full houses every night and for the Saturday matinée. The whole cast are enjoying it, and

I hardly have to give any notes. I bumped into Michael Bromley, the agent, when he was leaving the other night and he said he was delighted to hear we might be getting financial backing for a West End transfer. I had to confess that I hadn't heard anything about that. Have you?'

Grace shook her head. 'Definitely not. It would be nice, but he's misinformed.'

'One bit of gossip that seems to be accurate is that Emily – you remember her, she was our original Vivie – decided not to take up the *Little Women* series she was a cert for and has got a starring role in an American movie that starts filming in the States early next year.'

'What? How did she manage that?'

'Probably slept with someone rich and influential,' said Fran. 'I know that sounds catty, but she'd hardly get it on talent. She's a type – and not the best actress of her type either.'

Grace immediately guessed that Lucien must be behind it. 'Well, good luck to her. She's very photogenic and does have a following here after *Kesby Close*.'

'Grace, does Andrew ever talk to you about me?' asked Fran.

'Yes, of course. He's always saying he wishes he could

see you more often. I think he's feeling a little jealous of our John. I told him that was ridiculous but—'

'Why did you tell him that?'

'Because John's old enough to be your father!'

'I like mature men. At least John's around, he's good in bed and he's interesting. Whenever I do get to see Andrew he's exhausted and it's just not the same. I miss him, Grace. I miss the fun we used to have, and the way it used to be between us.'

'He is trying to hold down three jobs,' Grace pointed out gently.

'I know that, but even when we are together, I don't feel the same,' confessed Fran. 'Believe me, I wish I did, but something's changed. Maybe it's me, but I don't think so, truly I don't.'

'He really is keen on you,' Grace assured her.

'I wish he had more opportunities to show it, then. Unlike you, I don't enjoy having to play guessing games where my love life is concerned. It upsets me.'

'Meaning what?'

'Nothing, sorry. Ignore me; I'm in a rotten mood today. I really do like Andrew, and I thought it was going to develop into something serious, but I'm not sure we're ever going to be able to make it work. I need to think about it a bit more and then make a decision, for my own sake. I love your necklace, by the way, very pretty.'

'David gave it to me.'

'He's got good taste. And you're still happy with him, are you?'

Grace hesitated. 'I am, but I get confused. Sometimes he can be so nice – absolutely the perfect lover – and then it's as though a switch has been thrown and he becomes so distant. It unsettles me. I know he loves me in his own way, but ...'

Fran sighed. 'Oh Grace, step back and take a long, hard look at what's happening. He's controlling you, playing both good cop and bad cop, so that you're always on edge, always eager to placate and please him, never daring to stand up to him, because then the bad cop might linger and spoil things.'

'I do stand up to him,' said Grace, remembering how she'd told him never to touch her in anger again.

'And how does he take it when you do that?'

'It doesn't happen often, but he accepts it.'

'Then I guess you have to decide whether you want him as he is, because I doubt if he's going to change, or if the stress of always feeling on edge means that you have to walk away.'

Grace lowered her voice. 'I can't walk away.'

'Why on earth not?' asked Fran in astonishment.

'I just can't. He's shown me a different kind of life and I couldn't live without it.'

Fran raised her eyebrows. 'I didn't expect you to be that influenced by money.'

'It's not his money; it's the sex!' Grace retorted in a rare, unguarded moment.

The two friends stared at each other in silence, Grace wishing she could turn the clock back two minutes and Fran clearly shaken to the core. 'What the hell do you mean by that?' she asked after a long pause. 'Sex is sex. Sure there are lots of different ways of enjoying yourself, but unless you start getting into heavy S&M, role play-ing, serious bondage games, and all that kind of thing, it's pretty much the same when it comes down to it. I think the only thing that makes it different, apart from some good technique, is how you feel about the person you're having the sex with.'

Grace swallowed hard. 'Let's talk about something else, shall we? I shouldn't have said that. I know you don't like David and normally I wouldn't have said any-thing but I suppose I needed to confide in someone and you're my closest friend.'

'Then why do we need to talk about something else?'

'Because I don't want to take this any further,' said Grace firmly.

Fran looked thoughtful. 'I see. Okay then, let's talk about what you'll do if we do get financial backing for a West End transfer, shall we? I mean, will you have time to direct it now you've got your little boutique hotel to manage as well?'

'We won't get financial backing,' Grace said, glancing at her watch. 'Right, it's time I left. Andrew won't be working at the hotel for a month now, so with any luck you'll get to see more of him and then you can decide whether you'd rather stay with John . . . until he moves on to the next play and his next conquest, of course. He's famous for it.'

Fran shook her head. 'There's no need to be nasty, Grace. If I've said something that's too close to home, I apologise, but how was I to know? You've changed so much since you met David that I often feel quite awkward when we're together. It's as though you're trying to live two lives: your old one, which used to be really interesting and fun, and the new one with him, which might well be interesting but doesn't seem to be making you very happy.'

'It does make me happy!' exclaimed Grace. 'I wish that it didn't, but it does.' And with that she grabbed her bag and walked out into the street, leaving a thoughtful Fran alone at their table.

For the next three weeks, Grace spent quite a lot of time working with her actors, making small adjustments that she felt would improve the play without upsetting the cast or Fran. Fran had been right when she'd said it was a happy cast, and it was a joy to work with them.

Fran was happy to use the time to start writing a new play; she worked from home and the two friends rarely met for more than a few moments once or twice a week. Grace wondered if Fran had said anything to John about her comments, but he behaved exactly the same as he always had, and because his performance didn't need any attention, she didn't have that much to do with him anyway.

As the next open week of the hotel drew nearer, Grace became more preoccupied with the weather fore-cast than anything else. The Country Retreat Suite was always problematic, because if the weather was bad it meant that everything had to be done indoors, which although possible did make it less realistic than the guests would have hoped. This month she wanted it to be perfect for Lucien and Emily.

Fortunately, it seemed that fate was going to be kind to her, and the day before the guests were due she was able to tell the hotel staff that outdoor pursuits were definitely on the cards.

'Lucien wants a large picnic table set up at the bottom of the garden,' she told Andrew. 'Put it in between the trees and the bushes, because I don't want complaints from the neighbours. He also wants a haystack, but I don't think we can manage a full-size one. Any ideas?'

'I've got a friend who farms. I'll tell him I'm going to a themed party and get enough hay to make an interesting one,' he promised.

'Great. Tilly, can you make sure there's a wood fire burning in the grate when they arrive, even if it's a warm day. You know you've been chosen to be Emily's personal maid, I assume?'

Tilly nodded. 'Yes, I know. It should be very interesting, more like the Victorian Suite, in a way. There are so many unwritten rules about staying with people in the country.'

'Not exactly the same rules as Lucien's, I imagine,'

Grace replied with a smile. 'Now, we also need to discuss the Ultimate Fantasy Suite: they've requested an Arabian Nights theme, which is going to be complicated.'

By the end of the day, everything seemed to be in order, and after the others had gone, Grace went up to check that the large, glossy, dark oak rocking horse – perfect in every detail, with stirrups, bridle, reins and its special saddle – was in place by the window of the Country Retreat Suite. She touched it between its ears and it rocked gently to and fro, but before she could touch the special switch set behind its blinkers, the door to the suite opened and David walked in.

'I hope you weren't thinking of trying it in advance of Lucien and Emily's arrival,' he said teasingly.

Grace felt slightly guilty. 'Of course not, but I did want to see it rocking faster.'

Striding across the room he wrapped his arms round her from behind and pulled her close to him. 'You will, but all in good time. After all, you found it.'

'How was China?' she asked, twisting round to face him.

'Interesting; hectic. I was afraid I was going to miss my flight back, and like you, I'm eager to sample the pleasures of the Country Retreat.'

As he pulled her against him she could feel that he was already aroused, and thrust her lower body closer to his hardness. 'I've missed you,' she said.

'And I've missed you, but I think it will be more fun if you're this eager tomorrow morning, don't you?'

'No,' said Grace. 'I want to welcome you home.'

'You can certainly do that, my darling, but let's keep your pleasure for tomorrow. Anticipation will heighten your senses, as you well know.'

She didn't believe that he was serious, but later in their room, although he kissed and caressed her until she was squirming and moaning with pleasure, he never let her come, although his cry of satisfaction when she eventually took him into her mouth and used her hands and tongue on him until he climaxed was so loud that she could hardly bear it.

She too wanted release like that, but she realised that he'd meant what he'd said and so she spent a restless night, her confused body unable to settle while David slept quietly beside her. It would be worth it, she knew that, but all the same, after so long apart it seemed cruel to deprive her of even one moment of full satisfaction.

In the morning, when he woke, he kissed her and

stroked her bare shoulders. 'Did you pleasure yourself while I slept?' he asked.

'No, but I wanted to.'

'Then why didn't you?'

'Because I'd wanted to make love to you, I'd pleasured myself lots of times when we were having phone sex while you were away.'

'And?'

She stared up at him. 'And what?'

'Tell me the truth, Grace.'

She lowered her eyes, not wanting to see the look in his eyes when she spoke. 'And I knew you were right.'

'Look at me,' he said softly, and she lifted her eyes to his. 'There's nothing to be ashamed of. You should be proud of yourself. You know what a difference it makes to be aroused but unsatisfied. You understand how much keener your pleasure will be today because we didn't make love last night. You've embraced my world better than you could ever have expected, and later today you'll reap your reward. Think how good that's going to feel.'

As he spoke, he trailed the fingers of one hand over her hip bones and belly, making tiny circles on the sensitive skin until he heard her breath catch in her throat, and then he stopped. 'Let the Country Retreat begin,' he said with a smile, and Grace, her whole body clamouring for satisfaction, forced herself out of bed and into the shower.

As the jets of water caressed her body, she closed her eyes and thought about what lay ahead during Lucien and Emily's visit. Eventually she would reap her reward for her self-control, just as David had taught her from their early days together, and she shivered with dark excitement. Yet the nagging fear remained: what would happen to her if she should ever lose him, and with him this sexually sophisticated world they shared?

Part Five

Chapter One

Lucien and Emily arrived for their third visit to the hotel just before four in the afternoon, by which time all the other guests were settled in their suites. 'Emily was making a new showreel for America,' Lucien explained, signing the guest book. 'I'd planned on us getting here around two o'clock.'

'At least the weather's lovely, so it really doesn't matter,' said Grace, who'd been on edge all day because every time he'd passed her, David had managed to touch her, or whisper in her ear promises of what was to come, so that she was constantly aroused but unsatisfied. Dealing with the other guests in that state had been almost impossible, and she'd struggled to focus on their needs.

Emily, wearing light-coloured jodhpurs and a tight-fitting white blouse with a cut-away neckline that revealed the tops of her pert breasts, glanced out of the window. 'I don't want to get cold,' she told Lucien.

'Then let's unpack and take a nice warm shower before we go outside,' he said indulgently. 'If you really were visiting an old country house then you'd probably be frozen. They're always cold.'

'Are you sure you only need David and me outside with you?' asked Grace.

'Plus Tilly, she'll be taking care of Emily's changes of clothes and so forth upstairs but I think I'd like her to join us outside too. An extra pair of hands is always useful,' he added with a smile.

'I wore these jodhpurs in case I got the chance to ride a horse,' explained Emily, smoothing her hands down over her hips.

'You will, later on,' promised David, walking into the hall to join the three of them. 'Even if you don't, you look delicious in them!' he added with a smile, and Emily smiled back at him.

By the time the five of them met up at the bottom of the hotel garden, the sun was shining directly down on the rough wooden table, beside which lay an old-fashioned picnic basket.

'Are we overlooked?' asked Lucien.

'It's possible,' admitted Grace. 'If people in the Ultimate Fantasy Suite have any spare time, they could see us, and if our neighbours to the right come out into their garden they will definitely hear us.'

'All the more exciting,' Lucien responded, and Emily giggled.

'I think I'm hungry,' Lucien continued.

'So am I,' agreed David.

Emily stopped giggling. 'I'm not. I want some fun,' she retorted.

'Oh, you'll have fun,' Lucien reassured her. 'You're my first course.' And he and David laughed.

Emily looked puzzled, but before she could say any more Lucien had lifted her up and laid her down at one end of the rough wooden table, flipping up the floaty skirt that Tilly had wisely got her to change into, revealing that she was naked beneath it. Then, with Tilly parting the blonde girl's thighs, he lowered his head.

'I'll use the other end of the table,' said David, and almost before Grace realised what was happening she too was lifted up and placed at the opposite end of the

MARINA ANDERSON

table to Emily, so that their heads were nearly touching.

'Whoever comes first pays a forfeit,' said Lucien.

David lifted Grace's legs over his shoulders as he bent his head down, parted her outer sex lips and then lazily circled her already eager and swollen clitoris with the flat part of his tongue. Swift darts of rising pleasure pierced through her lower belly, and despite not wanting to pay the forfeit she instinctively raised her hips, so that the blissful pressure was increased.

Giving a low laugh he put his hands beneath her buttocks, pulled her as close to his mouth as possible and then increased the pressure and length of his tongue strokes.

Grace could hardly bear the intense pleasure, and her body began to twist restlessly with rising excitement. She could hear Emily moaning with delight too, which only added to her arousal. The table was rough beneath her delicate skin, but she didn't care. She needed to come, but despite this she knew that she had to try to wait until Emily had climaxed.

Emily began to utter tiny whimpering sounds, which Grace knew meant her orgasm was near, and she thought that she was going to manage to outlast the

6font
Tagg

younger girl, but then David let his tongue stray along the thin, unbearably sensitive skin that led to her rectum, and she cried out with the overwhelming pleasure this gave her.

After a few seconds of that, as she gasped and twisted in his grip, he stopped and for a fatal second she dropped her guard. With lightning speed he flicked his tightly furled tongue deep inside her and as her muscles tightened she fought desperately to quell her pleasure for a few more seconds. Then he withdrew his tongue and using her own juices from deep within her, covered the sides of her throbbing clitoris as he once more swirled his tongue over the whole nerve centre of her excitement.

Forgetting everything but the wonderful sensations sweeping through her, Grace gave a loud cry of ecstasy as she finally climaxed, and her whole body continued to twitch and jerk for several minutes as David's clever tongue extended her orgasm for longer than her over-excited body could almost bear.

As she finally slumped onto the table she heard Emily give a cry of pleasure, and only then did she remember that now she would have to pay a forfeit, because her desperately aroused body, kept waiting for over twenty-four hours for its pleasure, had betrayed her.

Still half-dazed she was helped off the table by David, and within seconds Lucien was in front of her, holding out his hands. 'I choose the forfeit,' he said with a smile. 'I see there's a convenient birch tree right by us, so we'll use that, I think. Tilly, bind Grace's hands behind the tree trunk with the rope you'll find there, and fasten her legs too, but apart, not together. Oh, and I'd like her naked except for that temptingly tight top she's wearing. There's no point in al fresco sex if she's fully clothed.'

'I think that as Emily won, she deserves a roll in the hay!' laughed David, and Grace had to stand and watch as he led the clearly very willing Emily towards the small haystack that Andrew had acquired from his friend. With her tousled blonde hair, flushed cheeks and shining eyes, Grace had no doubt that Emily was going to have a good time. She wasn't quite so sure about what was going to happen to her.

Once she'd fastened Grace to the tree, Tilly withdrew and now Lucien approached her. Naked from the waist down, and unable to move her arms or legs, Grace watched him nervously. 'Don't worry,' he said reassuringly. 'After all, it's only a forfeit in a game.'

Slowly he unfastened her fitted, bodice-style blouse and studied her breasts with interest. 'I remember thinking you had beautiful breasts the first time I saw you,' he said quietly. 'Of course, you couldn't see me then, because I was in darkness, but I'm sure you know when I mean.'

'The Dining Club was a long time ago,' she replied.

'Not that long, and you've only grown more lovely and more experienced since, yet you've retained your innate innocence. I find that incredibly exciting,' he whispered, his hands cupping her breasts before he began to gently massage them until the nipples grew hard. Then he teased the rigid tips with his fingers, pulling on them, rolling the palm of his hand over them and all the time he was talking quietly to her.

'No matter what I do, you have to cry out with pleasure, so that David can hear,' he said softly. 'That's your forfeit, you see. You're going to tease him, make him a little jealous, because I'm jealous that he's got you.'

'That's not fair!' she replied.

He put a hand over her mouth. 'You lost, that's the forfeit. You can tell him later, but I doubt if he'll believe you.' Before she could say anything more he twisted her left nipple hard between his fingers and the pain filled her whole breast. Without thinking she gave a sharp cry.

'Goodness, you did like that, didn't you?' he said

loudly, his fingers still poised over her throbbing nipple as he stared into her eyes. His brown eyes had lost their soft expression now, instead they were bright with satisfaction, and she wondered how she could ever have liked him.

'Yes,' she said, a sob catching in her throat at the lie but not daring to say no.

For the next ten minutes he teased and tormented her, forcing her to move her naked body back and forth against the rough bark of the tree when he entered her forcefully, pushing his moistened fingers deep inside her and moving them roughly around, so that although her body did respond the actual moment of pleasure was so heavily mixed with pain that her cry as she climaxed was almost piteous.

'Say how good that was,' he ordered her quietly, 'and say it loudly or I'll do it again.'

Trembling, unable to believe what was happening to her in her own hotel, she nodded. 'That was so good,' she sobbed, tears rolling down her face, tears that he wiped away tenderly.

'Good girl,' he said at last, and then finally he began to softly touch and arouse her without any pain, coaxing one totally blissful orgasm out of her by pressing the heel of his hand down hard above her pubic bone while his fingers were spread down between her thighs, teasing her clitoris as it tried to shelter behind its hood.

She didn't want to come, but she did and again he ordered her to cry out with gratitude, only this time it wasn't a total lie.

'Forfeit over,' he said with a smile that didn't reach his eyes, and then he walked away, leaving Tilly to release her.

Stunned by what had happened, Grace pulled her top tightly round her, collected her skirt and began to walk indoors. She was nearly at the back door when David caught her up. 'You had a very good time, by the sound of it,' he remarked.

She opened her mouth to tell him the truth, and then closed it again. Lucien was right, he would never believe her, and all she wanted to do now was forget any of it had happened, especially as at the end Lucien had given her abused but treacherous body pleasure, for which she could never forgive herself.

'Yes, for a forfeit,' she said carelessly.

Catching hold of her chin he turned her face towards him. 'Are you all right? You're very pale.'

'I think I got cold.'

He studied her very closely. 'And I think we'll have a quiet evening tonight,' he remarked. 'I'm sure Lucien and Emily can manage without us until the morning. I'll say I've got jet lag.'

'We can't do that. In the brochure it says—'

'We are doing it, and that's final,' he said firmly.

'There's a wonderful log fire with a fur rug in front of it. We can all share that tonight,' said Lucien as he and Emily joined them on their way back into the hotel.

David shook his head regretfully. 'I'm afraid I've got jet lag. I'd be no use to anyone tonight, especially after all this. We'll see you tomorrow, after lunch perhaps. We can go riding, just like Emily hoped,' he added with a smile.

'You don't have jet lag, Grace, do you?' asked Lucien. 'I'm sure that after our exquisite forfeit you're eager to sample more of the Country Retreat's delights.'

'I want her with me,' said David, and Grace saw Lucien give a small smile at what he assumed to be proof that his forfeit game had worked.

'Fine, then tomorrow afternoon it is,' he agreed, taking Emily's hand and together they vanished into the hotel.

'Is there anything you want to say to me, Grace?' asked David once they were in her office.

'No, nothing.'

'Then go and have a long bath and get into bed. I can take care of everything here for the next few hours and I'll join you later. You look absolutely exhausted.'

She wanted to tell him, but something held her back. She felt guilty that she hadn't shouted for David the moment she'd realised what Lucien was doing, and even more guilty that her treacherous body had allowed him to give her pleasure after tormenting her so cruelly. Now anything she said would sound feeble, to say the least, and more likely untrue. She also realised that she'd failed to put any precautions in place, such as a safe-word that meant everything had to stop. She'd been so sure the hotel would be a place for people who understood the unwritten rules that it had never crossed her mind, and now she'd paid the penalty for her mistake.

She was half-asleep when David finally came to bed, but when he cuddled up to her back she winced.

'What's the matter?' he asked.

'I scratched myself on the birch tree while I was paying my forfeit.'

'Let me look. Why the hell didn't Lucien put a rug behind you?' he added as he surveyed the damage. 'I'll put something on that for you. He knows better than this. He's had sex out of doors often enough before.' With the stinging pain easing, she settled down more comfortably ready to sleep. 'Are you quite sure there's nothing you want to tell me?' he asked quietly.

'Quite sure,' she replied, and heard him sigh as he put one arm carefully over her shoulders and cradled her until she fell asleep.

The next morning Grace was thankful that she was kept busy by the other guests, which meant she didn't have time to dwell on the coming afternoon, when she'd see Lucien again in the Country Retreat Suite. The Arabian Nights scenario in the Ultimate Fantasy Suite had, as expected, gone on for most of the night, and while the guests were sleeping it off, their request for two extra dancing girls later that day had to be met.

'I'll phone The Dining Club,' said Andrew. 'The twins might be free. They still work there on and off; they'd enjoy themselves and don't need any training.'

'I'd rather we found our own people. I want this hotel to be as separate as possible from the Club.'

'Perhaps your ex-casting director can come up with something then. I'm not sure why you're bothered, though. After all, I'm working here – and Lucien.'

'Lucien's a guest, that's different. Yes, I'll ask her,' said Grace, lifting up the house phone.

All too soon it was lunchtime and the afternoon with Lucien and Emily beckoned.

David, who'd vanished on a work-related problem, returned just after two o'clock. 'Sorry I'm late. It was more complicated than I expected. Are you ready to go up?' he asked her.

'Not quite.'

'Grace, we're running late and you haven't changed into your riding clothes either. Hurry up; Lucien won't like being kept waiting.'

She knew that she had to put the previous afternoon behind her, or David would become suspicious and Lucien would have the pleasure of knowing how much he'd upset her. 'Sorry, I'll get changed and then we can join them,' she said with a quick smile.

David frowned. 'There's something different about you today. Are you quite sure you're feeling all right?'

'I'm fine; there have been a few problems this morning, but they're all solved now.'

'Good. A ride will probably do you good,' he said with a quick smile. She hoped he was right.

Once in their bedroom, she got out her clothes for the

afternoon. David watched as she wriggled into the specially designed tight-fitting jodhpurs, then waited for him to help her into her side-lacing, gold under-bust corset, made of leather with fabric side panels. Her gently rounded breasts were thrust upwards and as he fastened the leather straps that ran from the sides up round her neck he tugged so tightly that it was difficult for her to breathe.

'You'll get used to it,' he assured her, running a hand over her exposed right breast and teasing the nipple with the tips of his fingers. 'You'll look amazing once you're on the rocking horse. Then he bent down and checked between her thighs. 'And the gap in the crotch of the jodhpurs is exactly the right size,' he commented, sliding one finger inside and lightly caressing her outer sex lips until her thighs began to tremble. 'Let's go and join the others. I think perhaps this is your best idea so far.'

Remembering the rocking horse, Grace wasn't so sure, although the tightness of the clothing and David's touch had already combined to arouse her.

Entering the Country Retreat Suite, Grace saw that Emily was dressed in exactly the same way, but her jodhpurs were pale blue and her under-bust corset was white, giving her a look of misplaced innocence. Her full breasts were firm and her nipples already erect, so Grace knew that – like David – Lucien had been eager to start arousing his partner.

The rocking horse was motionless in the window, the glossy dark oak animal set on large, shiny brown rockers, an instrument of pleasure waiting to be used.

'Emily first, I think,' said Lucien. 'You've been riding before, haven't you?'

'Not on a rocking horse!'

'But you enjoy riding? You like the feel of the horse beneath you?' Emily nodded. 'Excellent, then you're certainly going to enjoy this. First, I want to slip something inside you, but you'll need to pull your jodhpurs down.'

'There's an opening,' Emily reminded him.

'No, these go further back,' he said with a smile, pushing Emily face down on their bed and tugging at the waist of her jodhpurs. She struggled a little when she realised what he was going to do, but David stroked her hair and told her it would only give her extra pleasure, so eventually she lay still.

Grace watched, her desire rising as Lucien eased a string of anal beads inside Emily's rectum. The blonde girl's first reaction was to try to keep them out, and Lucien tapped her sharply on the backs of her thighs. 'Stop that! You said you were an experienced horsewoman.'

'I didn't know what you were going to do. I don't like that, it's uncomfortable.'

'Nonsense, it will make you feel so full that your pleasure will be even greater. Isn't that true, Grace?'

Her mouth felt dry and she could only nod, aware that she too would soon be lying on the bed having the same thing done to her. Eventually, when the beads were inside Emily, David signalled for her to take the younger girl's place but he sat on the bed and laid her across his thighs, so that she couldn't struggle as he opened her up and slid the well lubricated beads deep into her rectum, which immediately made her muscles cramp.

'Breathe through your mouth, relax,' he reminded her. 'You know how good this is going to be.' She obeyed, and soon the cramping died down. Now her breasts were even more swollen with excitement, but she knew that she had to stand back and watch Emily before her own pleasure could truly begin.

Putting one foot in a stirrup, Emily swung herself into the large, well-padded saddle and then gave a squeal of surprise. 'What's that?' she asked, pushing herself back towards the tail end of the rocking horse.

'It's an unusual saddle pommel,' explained Lucien. 'You have to slide it inside you, like a vibrator. When you start to rock, it will stimulate you exactly as a vibrator does, and the faster you rock the greater the vibrations.' While he was talking he lifted her up, lined the opening in her jodhpurs up with the inbuilt vibrator and lowered her down onto it.

'It's too big!' she complained. 'I'm not comfortable. I can feel the beads inside me at the back and now this. I don't want to ride after all, Lucien. Help me off.'

'I will if you like,' he assured her, 'but there's a lot at stake here, remember.'

Emily stared at him, and Grace wondered if this was the price the young actress had to pay for her American film role, because she hastily stopped complaining and slowly started to move back and forth, until the large rocking horse began to move.

At first Emily only uttered small sounds of mixed pleasure and anxiety, but as she found her rhythm colour flooded up over hear breasts and neck and then into her cheeks as she began to utter cries of excitement. 'You must tell us when you come,' said Lucien, and David laughed.

'I suspect we'll know,' he remarked drily.

271

Watching Emily, the waiting Grace felt her own body growing tight and knew that she was damp between her thighs. Hearing Emily's breathing quicken as her orgasm approached made Grace long for an orgasm herself, and she swallowed hard as Emily's upper body stiffened and her head started to go back.

'Yes!' Emily cried suddenly, so caught up in the wonderful rush of pleasure that she didn't even notice Lucien moving closer until she felt the flick of a riding crop across her totally exposed breasts. She gave a small cry of protest, and immediately he flicked at her again, but harder this time, catching one of her swollen, dark red nipples. Emily cried out once more, and Grace knew that the other girl hadn't yet learnt that if she relaxed and gave herself up to the shock of the well-aimed crop, the strength of her orgasm would increase.

Slowly Emily's movements died away until the rocking horse was totally still. 'You shouldn't have done that,' she said to Lucien.

'Did I spoil your ride?' he asked with apparent concern.

'Yes.'

'Then you must have another one, but a faster one this time, I think.'

'I can't make it go faster,' she replied.

'We can,' said David, stepping forward and pausing only to lick gently at the thin red line across Emily's rounded breasts he pushed the button hidden behind the rocking horse's blinkers.

Emily gave a shocked scream and gripped the slippery wooden mane with both hands as the horse started to rock at twice the speed of her first ride. Now Grace could imagine how Emily must feel, with the vibrator deep inside her, the anal beads filling her back passage and a total lack of control over what was happening to her. She and the two men watched Emily's face contort as her next climax swept over her, and soon she was half-laughing and half-crying as the clung to the polished mane, helpless to do anything except give her body over to what was happening as one climax followed hard on the heels of another.

'Please stop the horse,' she begged at last, exhausted. 'I don't want to come any more.'

'So sweet,' murmured Lucien as David stepped forward and pressed the button, bringing Emily's ride to a halt. As she stumbled across the room, Lucien grabbed her by the waist, threw her down on the bed and took her immediately. His groan of pleasure came quickly but

Emily remained silent, clearly unable to reach the pinnacle of pleasure again.

'I want you to come with me inside you,' said Lucien, withdrawing from her, but she merely shook her head and closed her eyes, her hair plastered to her head from all the orgasms she'd already had.

'Game on, then!' David exclaimed. 'I think Emily has made her position clear. She was on the horse for twenty minutes. If Grace does the same and then I can bring her to another climax, I win the bet we made earlier.' Lucien nodded.

'I'm not usually lucky at the races, but perhaps this time it will be different,' David continued, leading Grace slowly towards the rocking horse. Just before she climbed on, he slid a finger inside her. 'You're very wet,' he murmured. 'I hope you can pace yourself. Twenty minutes is a long time, but I don't want Lucien to win this bet.'

Already incredibly aroused, Grace slowly mounted the rocking horse, let the vibrating saddle pommel slide inside her and very slowly started to move back and forth until the horse began to rock.

She'd been so excited by watching Emily that within a very short time she felt her body building to a climax and with a sharp shudder she came, a small sound of pleasure escaping from between her lips.

'Unless she slows down she won't even last the twenty minutes,' said Lucien.

'I think her body is far too well trained to let me down,' responded David, and Grace hoped that he was right. The prospect of Lucien winning the racing bet after hurting and humiliating her in the garden the previous day was unthinkable.

The vibrating pommel was long and curved, and after two more orgasms Grace felt as though her body was starting to calm down a little, until Lucien pressed the speed button and she no longer had control of how fast the rocking horse moved. Now the length of the pommel, so carefully chosen by Grace herself, made itself felt as it started to massage her cervix, deep within her. The sensations from this were entirely different from any other sensation, as she'd known at the time she chose it, but now she wished she hadn't tried so hard to find something different and exciting, because whenever David's long, clever fingers massaged her in this way she always came sharply and quickly.

She tried to lift herself slightly off the pommel, but Lucien saw the movement and crossing the room he flicked the riding crop across her bare back and pushed her down again. 'That's naughty!' he chided her with a laugh, but the sting of the crop as it fell a second time told her that in truth he wasn't amused. This was a bet he was desperate to win.

Time and again the hot pleasure kept engulfing her tightly encased and well-tutored body, so ready for pleasure that it was almost impossible for her to ignore the ways in which she was being aroused. Each time a climax peaked and her flesh started to quieten, David would draw the tip of his crop over her breasts, letting it linger on her nipples until despite her best efforts they grew rigid, sending tendrils of pleasure deep into her belly.

Then, as she struggled to stop them from spreading lower, he would let the tip move in circles over her back, waiting until she responded by arching upwards before letting the crop fall in a sharp, stinging blow over her tight nipples. Each time he did this, she was unable to stop herself from coming. As the hot, liquid sensation coursed through her body she also squirmed in discomfort because she was so full and the anal beads caressed the highly sensitive nerve endings of her rectum while the pommel filled her from the front.

She lost track of time, aware only of the sound of her

own breathing, the short gasps that she uttered as she neared a climax, and the deeper groans of dark, pain-tinged pleasure when David teased the all-enveloping orgasms from her frantic, over-pleasured body.

Eventually she couldn't bear it any more. 'Please, stop the horse,' she cried out, as an intense, dark wave of pleasure left her so tired she knew she had to stop. 'I can't take any more.'

Without a word, David stopped the rocking horse and lifted her off. 'Thirty minutes, I'm very impressed,' he said with a smile.

'Thirty? Why didn't you tell me once I'd passed Emily's time?'

'Because we were waiting for you to want it to stop. You had to be exhausted,' said Lucien. 'That's how it was with Emily. Now David has to see if he can succeed with you where I failed with her.'

'But surely I've already won your bet for you?' she asked David.

He shook his head. 'Not quite, just one more moment of pleasure and then you have.'

'I can't,' she said softly. 'I know I can't.'

'And I know you can, and exactly how to do it,' he replied.

'She looks incredibly sexy,' commented Lucien. 'Totally ravishable.'

'Lucky me, then,' said David, peeling off Grace's clothes until she was totally naked. Then he laid her face down on the bed, pushed two pillows beneath her stomach and very slowly began to pull out the cord containing the anal beads. She felt each one of them leaving her, but her body wasn't affected by the teasing caress of the nerve endings. She remained motionless, all arousal gone, and feeling totally sated.

Working in silence, David pushed her legs forward until she was kneeling face down on the bed, and then she felt him parting the walls of her rectum before sliding a small syringe inside. Then he pressed the plunger and emptied it, so that a cool gel flooded into her rear entrance, beginning to heat up as soon as it touched her hot inner flesh. Her hips twitched restlessly as the walls of her rectum sent flickers of desire through to her stomach, and at last her tired flesh finally began to respond. Gripping her firmly round the waist with one arm, David thrust himself deep inside the already aroused tight channel, and she whimpered because it was too tight, too full.

'Hush,' he said softly. And as he began to move in

and out of the almost cruelly aroused rear entrance, he slid his fingers beneath her and up into her vagina, quickly finding her clitoris, which he massaged in the soft circular motions that he knew she loved.

Within a few seconds she felt herself growing very wet, and heard his light laugh of pleasure as he continued to move in and out of her back opening while his fingers played with her clitoris. She felt as though she was going to be torn apart because she was so full, and the sensations that were building threatened to overwhelm her tired body.

'Come as soon as you like,' he whispered in her ear. 'I could never have believed that I'd taught you to embrace your sexuality like this in such a short time. Come now, Gracie, I know you can.' With that he squeezed the sides of the tight, throbbing nub of her clitoris while at the same time rotating his hips so that all the walls of her rectum felt as though they were on fire. With a cry that was half ecstasy and half despair she finally managed to come for one last time, and the sensations swept through her over-excited body in wave after wave of blissful ecstasy as David spilled himself into her and then she slumped face down on the bed.

The room was silent for a long time, and when

Lucien finally spoke Grace could hear the anger behind his words. 'Congratulations; it seems you've finally got lucky at the races today, David.'

'I find a bet always makes it more exciting,' David replied. 'Now we'll leave you and Emily to enjoy yourselves together. I'm sorry you have to leave early tomorrow. Is it business?'

'Nothing we need to discuss now,' replied Lucien. 'After all, Emily and I are here on a break.'

Grace managed to stumble off the bed and took her clothes from David's outstretched hands. All she wanted to do was go to bed and sleep, but she managed to smile at Lucien and Emily. 'Enjoy the last part of your stay,' she said quietly. 'It's such a shame it's been cut short.'

'We'll make up for it next time,' Lucien assured her. 'The Ultimate Fantasy Suite was always going to be my favourite.'

'What is your fantasy?' asked Emily, clearly beginning to recover from all she'd seen and done that afternoon.

'You'll find out next month,' he responded, stroking her hair back off her face.

'Whatever it is, make sure you let us know everything you'll need,' said Grace.

'Oh, believe me I will, and thank you for once again providing such a superb and discreet service,' he replied.

She looked away from him, knowing that when he talked about discretion he was talking about the fact that she hadn't told David how he'd abused her in the garden. 'It's my pleasure,' she said quietly.

'That's good to hear,' he said with a laugh, and when David opened the door and waited for her to leave, Grace had to struggle to stop herself from hurrying out of the room. There was something about Lucien that genuinely frightened her now, but he was David's friend and business partner, and he only had one more visit to make to the hotel with Emily, so she was determined not to say a word about her feelings to her lover. Unfortunately, this was a big mistake.

Chapter Two

Late the following evening, after all the guests had gone and Andrew had hurried off to take Fran out to dinner, David sat in the visitors' lounge sipping a glass of brandy. His mind, usually occupied with work when he wasn't relaxing at the hotel or on a rare visit to The Dining Club, was racing.

Something was wrong with Grace, he was certain of it. One of the things he'd always loved about her was her openness, the way she was incapable of deception or deceit. Yet now, just as he was beginning to wonder if he could trust her enough to allow himself to open up more to her, she was holding something back from him. He wasn't worried that she was deceiving him, that wasn't her style and he trusted her as much as he was capable of trusting anyone, but there was something important on her mind that she wasn't sharing with him.

Aware that his own inability to discuss emotions might be making it difficult for her to confide in him, he decided that they needed more time together doing ordinary things. Usually he seemed to rush from the hotel to business meetings around the world, and then when he was free she was frequently working on a play. For once, he was going to change that pattern, and hopefully then he'd find out what was troubling her.

'You're tired,' he said when she finally joined him, sinking down next to him on the sofa with a sigh. 'Wine?' She nodded, and he poured her a glass, handed it to her and sat down beside her again. 'We both need a change,' he said, slipping an arm round her back and feeling her gradually relax against him. 'I can take some time off in the evenings for a couple of weeks. We'll eat out, go to a film premiere, the opera, things like that. We could visit the new Jacobean Theatre at The Globe, too, if you like. They say the seats are hard, but I'm willing to suffer if you are!'

Grace looked at him in surprise. 'You sound like a party animal all of a sudden.'

'No, but I think I've become too reclusive. There are a few problems at work right now, and I've been very caught up in them, then used this hotel for relaxation, but we need more time alone together.'

'Is this a trick?' she asked nervously.

David was surprised how much her words hurt him. 'Of course not. Grace, when we first met we used to go out a lot together. We're in danger of becoming a pair of workaholics, and I don't want that to happen. I think you've got too much to deal with. The hotel and the play keep you on your toes all the time, and it's clearly tiring you, so this is my solution. If you don't like it then ...'

'Of course I like it!' she exclaimed quickly. 'You just took me by surprise.'

He handed her an embossed card. 'Go here and choose yourself a couple of new dresses, something suitable for the opera or a premiere. Put them on my account, they know me there.'

'I'm sure they do,' she said drily. 'How many women have already used their services in order to look good on your arm?'

He felt a swift flare of annoyance, which he quickly subdued. She was right, and he was too intelligent not to realise that this was why he was annoyed. 'Thousands!' he said with a light laugh. 'You can go elsewhere if you like, but I wanted you to have a nice time choosing. I thought young women enjoyed that kind of thing.'

'I will enjoy it, but it's rather like being a kept woman.'

'It wasn't meant that way,' he said shortly, feeling himself shutting down emotionally.

Grace kissed him on the cheek. 'I'm sorry, I know it wasn't. You're right, I am tired and for some reason I can't relax very easily at the moment. It's a lovely idea, and I'll go there tomorrow after I've talked to the cast. As for the Sam Wanamaker Playhouse, I'd love to go. It's not easy to get tickets, though.'

'I'll get some,' he assured her. 'It's Hvorostovsky in *Traviata* at Covent Garden, so that should be a night to remember. I don't know what film premiere we'll be going to though.'

'It doesn't matter,' she said, snuggling up against him. 'Just being out together will be enough for me. You're right, we've both got too caught up in our professional lives. This will be our own mini-break.'

'We do share the guests' pleasures,' he pointed out,

and for a moment he saw a shadow cross her face before she smiled back at him in agreement.

'You make me very happy,' she said softly.

'Good,' he replied, aware that he should tell her that she made him happy, but unable to form the words.

'Have I changed a lot since we first met?' she continued.

David sighed. He found personal discussions difficult. 'Everyone changes,' he said quietly, remembering his mother's furious outbursts at and about his father. 'And not always for the better.'

Grace was obviously shocked. 'I've changed for the worse?'

'Of course not,' he said swiftly, wishing he could forget his upbringing completely, just erase it from his mind. 'I was being philosophical, not literal. Sorry, Gracie. Yes, you've changed, but that was always my intention, and how I feel about you hasn't changed.'

She gave a sigh of relief. 'Sometimes I worry that when you've changed me as much as you can, you won't want me any more.'

'Silly girl,' he replied, kissing the top of her head. 'Let's go to bed, because I definitely want you at this moment.'

Much later, after they'd made love and when Grace was fast asleep, David went over and over their earlier conversation, and knew that yet again he hadn't said everything that he should have said or, more importantly, would have liked to say. The only justification he could give himself was that he knew Grace was hiding something from him. Until he found out what, how could he even consider changing the way he wanted to live the rest of his life, knowing she didn't trust him enough to be open with him? The fact that this was probably his own fault was something he preferred not to consider.

'Look at her, smiling smugly on his arm at the Opera House!' exclaimed Amber, flinging the paper furiously to the floor. 'That's three very public outings in two weeks, and he's not even trying to avoid the cameras.'

'Temper, temper,' said Lucien. 'Why should he want to avoid them? She looks incredibly beautiful with her hair up in a French pleat, and that turquoise dress clings to her like a second skin.'

'That's right, you drool away too,' snapped Amber. 'He never wanted to be seen out with me, and he certainly never offered to buy me a dress like a second skin,

287

as you put it. She's even got a diamond-studded clip in her hair, to match the ones in her ears.'

'He can afford it; let him enjoy his money while he can,' said Lucien.

'I don't mind him enjoying it, but I do mind her sharing it so publicly. One of the tabloids even suggested that the UK's most eligible financier might finally be thinking of getting engaged.'

'I'm quite sure that's not true,' responded Lucien. 'He told me they both needed a break. It suits me. The less he's in the offices at the moment the better.'

'She's getting more newspaper coverage than the Duchess of Cambridge!' snapped Amber.

'Only because of David. You know how much people like a romance, but until now, although he's rich, handsome and successful, he's failed to give them any. Now they're ecstatic, but for a man like that it's not romance, it's all about sex and possession. He's parading a beautiful young woman in public, dressed to perfection thanks to his money, and demonstrating she's his creation. A sort of *Pygmalion* with sex,' he added with a laugh.

'Grace doesn't look as though she thinks of it that way,' retorted Amber.

'Well, she'll find out the truth. I doubt if she'll enjoy it when he throws her to the wolves, or rather this particular wolf, in order to save his financial empire.'

At that moment a high-pitched cry rang through the room. 'I'm training a new girl, teaching her how to please me,' explained Amber. 'She's willing but has a low pain threshold. Would you like to see her?'

Lucien nodded, and Amber led him down to the cellar beneath her kitchen where, in the dim light from a single red bulb, he could just make out the figure of a young, slim girl hanging by her wrists from a beam. The tips of her toes were touching the floor, her whole body taut as she struggled to take some of the weight off her arms.

Amber ran a hand over the trembling girl in a soft caress, circling her belly button and hip bones as the girl whimpered quietly. 'You made a bad mistake this morning, Ginny, didn't you?' she said in a deceptively soft voice. The girl nodded, her waist-length hair falling forward over her large breasts. 'I expect you're sorry now, though,' she added.

'I am, truly I am,' the girl cried. 'It won't ever happen again, I promise you.'

'She told me that she wanted to go back to the

289

woman who used to own her,' Amber explained. 'Such ingratitude when I'd rescued her from some cheap S&M club and opened her eyes to what true bondage and servitude meant. Haven't I pleasured you well?' she added, moving to the back of the girl and running a finger down the length of her spine.

'Yes, yes,' the girl sobbed. 'You have, and I'm grateful, truly I am.'

'She's a good little masochist at the moment, but she could become a great one,' Amber said to Lucien. 'Do you want to try her out before I release her?'

'I'm tempted, but I'd rather save myself for our planned reunion with old friends,' he said regretfully, absent-mindedly pinching the unfortunate girl's swollen nipples hard between finger and thumb until she cried out with pain before hastily thanking him. Amber repeated the process, and tears rolled down the girl's face.

'I'll be back in an hour to let you down,' said Amber as she and Lucien left, and slammed the door on the girl's loud sobs of pain-filled despair. 'It's not the same as when I worked for David,' she continued. 'Introducing unsuspecting people to S&M and bondage was far more exciting than expanding the knowledge of people like Ginny, and introducing them to important clients from time to time.'

'I'm sure you'll enjoy the surprise party,' Lucien said with a laugh, and Amber nodded. 'You do realise you won't win David back this way? Quite the contrary, I imagine.'

'I know that. He'll never come back to me now, but at least I'll make sure she loses him, and I'll be able to watch her face as she hears him reject her just as he rejected me. That's all I want.'

'And I'll get what I want too; not all of it, of course, but part of it. I don't imagine Grace will stay with me out of choice when it's over.'

'You'll have all of it for a brief time,' said Amber.

Lucien smiled. 'Yes,' he said with satisfaction. 'I suppose that for a brief time I will.'

'I can't believe how quickly the time's gone,' said Grace as she and David sat in a small trattoria near Covent Garden eating their pasta, sipping wine and generally watching the world go by.

David glanced at his watch. 'It's only two thirty.'

'I meant our mini-holiday,' she explained with a smile. 'It's been lovely and I feel so much better for it.'

'Really?'

'Yes, really,' she said truthfully, because now the memory of Lucien's casual, secret cruelty was just that: a distant memory.

'And what have you enjoyed doing the most?' he enquired.

'I think it has to be the opera. I've followed Hvorostovsky's progress for years, and I think he's probably at his peak now. That was a wonderful evening.'

'And a wonderful night,' he added.

Grace felt herself blushing, remembering how she'd cried out, begging him to touch her where she wanted to be touched as he teased her clamouring body for several hours, allocating pleasure only when her demands became too frantic to be ignored. 'Yes,' she admitted, 'and a wonderful night.'

'How do you feel about going back to full-time work after our break?'

'It feels good. Getting financial backing from that group of businessmen to transfer the play to the West End next year is like a miracle, and I'm hoping to direct some Shakespeare as soon as *Mrs Warren* finishes. I was going to direct Fran's next play, but it's not finished yet.'

'I suspect Andrew has been distracting her, just as I've been distracting you,' replied David, leaning across the table to pull a strand of hair down over the side of her face. 'You looked too perfect,' he explained with a tender smile, and she felt her heart pounding.

Their time together away from all distractions, exciting or otherwise, had only increased the depth of her love for him, and he'd been more openly affectionate than ever before. He'd even spoke once or twice about the future, talking about moving house in London and also buying a larger house in the country so that they had a quiet place they could retreat to together at times. He never actually mentioned love or marriage, but she was happy to accept him for what he was now that he was so clearly wanting to make her happy in all ways, and not merely sexually.

'And the hotel?' he asked.

'I'm looking forward to the final mini-break in this first session,' she said. 'We've got bookings for as many sessions as I want to hold, but I'm not certain I'll have the time to be in charge of them all.'

'I certainly won't have enough time to be with you for them if you are,' he said, his eyes following a tall, leggy brunette in a short, tight skirt walking past them. 'Too sophisticated already,' he commented when she was out of earshot.

'What do you mean?' asked Grace.

'I like a challenge, my darling. I'm quite sure she's already good at either controlling or being controlled. The pleasure comes from teaching someone from the very beginning, watching them take each step, and helping them when they stumble a little, as you did. And still do at times,' he added. 'I think you always will. That's part of your fascination. Now, how can we make the most of our final afternoon of freedom?'

Grace swallowed hard. 'I'd like ... '

'Yes?'

'That is, I want—' She stopped, unable to vocalise her needs in such a public place, even though no one was listening to her.

He looked intently at her. 'I'm not a mind reader, Grace, and this holiday was originally planned for you, so you need to tell me.'

His gaze seemed to see into her soul, and she knew nothing she said could ever shock him as he'd taught her all she knew, but still she struggled to say it aloud.

'I'm waiting,' he said gently.

'I want to be yours for the afternoon,' she admitted.

'Mine?'

'Yes, you can do anything you like to me that gives you pleasure. I want it to be like it was when we first met. I need it to be like that.'

Pushing his meal away and quickly draining his wine glass, David took her by the hand and hurried her along the pavement back to where his chauffeur-driven car was waiting. 'My wonderful Gracie,' he whispered, his fingertips straying beneath the hem of her skirt as he fondled her lightly, teasingly, in preparation for what was to come.

In the early hours of the morning, as an exhausted Grace slept, David paced around his study. His mind kept going over and over what they'd done together, what she'd allowed him to do and how much pleasure she'd taken from it all in the end. Even he was amazed by how far she'd come since they'd first met. She was everything he'd ever dreamt of, the perfect partner in every way imaginable, and now he had to make a decision.

Either he had to commit himself fully to her, changing the lifestyle that he'd built up so carefully over the years, leaving behind people and places that had formed the fabric of that lifestyle, or he had to let her go. Except letting her go would mean hurting them both, because just as he knew that she would be heartbroken if he ended their relationship, so he knew that his life too would never be the same again.

Of course there would be other young women like Grace, just as there had been before he'd met her. There was unimaginable excitement in teaching receptive, sexual women how to explore and enjoy the more extreme forms of sexual pleasure that brought him satisfaction, but to what end? Now that he'd found someone who not only embraced his lifestyle but also loved him deeply – and he knew that Grace did – shouldn't he progress? Just as timing was vital when building up a large business empire, surely it was equally important in your private life, he reasoned.

Except, he'd never planned on having a new phase in his private life. He'd been very happy with it, and hadn't expected to have the time or the inclination to alter it. He didn't want children, and he knew that he was so easily bored that one permanent companion day after day, year after year, would drive him out of his mind. And yet, he had to accept now that life without Grace was equally unimaginable. He needed her as much as she needed him.

She gave him more than sexual satisfaction. She was highly imaginative and creative, she understood him and accepted him for what he was and, most importantly of all, she loved him. She loved him in a way he'd never been loved before, and all he needed to do in order to keep that love was to tell her how he felt about her. He had to admit that he loved her too, and plan a future that included them both.

Pouring himself a brandy, he gazed out into the silent street and watched a young couple walking with their arms around each other, kissing as they went. They were little more than teenagers, but their love for each other was clear from their body language, and the happiness in the girl's face as she looked up at her boyfriend just as they passed under the street lamp.

David had never experienced young love. In order to survive emotionally, as his hysterical and resentful mother flew into countless rages about her husband, or took to her bed in order to force him to take care of her, causing him to give up all his hobbies over time, David had cut himself off from what he now accepted was normal emotional development.

Highly sexed, exceptionally intelligent and good at reading people, he'd become incredibly successful at work, and then invested money in a club that catered not only for his need for sexual excitement without commitment, but also for other like-minded people. There had been, and always would be, plenty of them. The difference was that whereas most of them only remained interested for a time, or also had what many people considered normal private lives outside of the club, he didn't. Only Amber had never moved on. In many ways she was more like him than any other woman he'd met, but she was incapable of love, and now he knew that he needed love. But love came at a price.

As dawn broke he went back to bed, so that he was there when Grace woke, and he still hadn't reached a decision. If he was honest with himself, he knew that he was afraid. Afraid that by returning Grace's love and committing himself to her, the day might come when she fell out of love with him, and he knew that he wouldn't survive such a rejection.

Chapter Three

It was the night before the fourth session of themed mini-breaks at Grace's hotel, and she was busy checking her notes when David arrived.

'I've got an early-morning meeting tomorrow, and it's important,' he said by way of greeting. 'Sorry, but I don't have any choice. I hope that doesn't make things difficult for you. What's Lucien chosen as his ultimate fantasy?'

'Kidnapping, so I hope Emily is up for that.'

'Has he got all the restraints he wants? If Emily isn't keen he'll need quite a few,' said David with a wry smile.

Grace checked her notes. 'Yes, everything is in place. I hope she doesn't panic.'

'Who else is involved?'

'He wants Tilly to be a second kidnap victim, so I assume he's eager for some girl-on-girl action, and Toby will be there with them.'

'Does he want us at all?'

Grace shook her head. 'Not until the afternoon, which is lucky. You'll be back before then, won't you?'

'I hope so. Look, do you mind if I stay at my place tonight? I'll be nearer the office, and then I'll come straight here when the meeting is over. Any other potential problems that you can see?'

Grace shook her head. 'Everyone is pretty comfortable with things after three visits. Quite a few of the guests seem to be forming friendships and meet up between the breaks. I think that's nice.'

'And I think you've been very clever,' he said, kissing the nape of her neck. 'Now, if there's nothing else I'll get off home. Where's the kidnapping taking place?'

'Right here in the lobby. Lucien said they'd arrive a little late, so that other guests aren't disturbed if Emily screams. I've warned the staff to ignore any noises!'

'Which rather suggests Emily doesn't know what theme he's chosen. That's going to be fascinating,' mused David. 'See you tomorrow, then. I'll text when I'm on my way.'

Grace missed having him in their bed that night. She wasn't looking forward to seeing Lucien again, and was relieved that David would be with her before she was needed in the Ultimate Fantasy Suite. She woke early the next morning, and by eight o'clock she was in the hotel's small lobby arranging the fresh flowers that had just arrived.

She heard the front door close behind the delivery man, and then heard it open again. Before she could even turn round to see what he needed a blanket was thrown over her head, strong hands pinned her arms to her sides and another pair of hands gripped her by the ankles. Cord or rope was then tied tightly round her upper body and lower legs, to immobilise her.

She screamed, but knew that the thick blanket would muffle the sound. Unable to struggle she decided to save wasting energy by trying. Although she was shaken, she was certain that this was all part of Lucien's fantasy. He'd changed the time of the kidnapping, and had obviously intended all along to make her the second victim and not Tilly, and as the initial shock wore off, she realised she was actually becoming excited by it all, and guessed this was why David hadn't warned her in advance. He would have known that just a touch of fear would make all that was to follow even more arousing.

She waited to be carried up the stairs, but when she realised that she was being bundled out through the main door, panic began to set in, especially when she was thrown into the back of what seemed like a van, the doors were slammed and with a jolt the vehicle began to move.

She was thrown around from side to side for what seemed like an eternity, but was probably less than half an hour, and then the van came to a halt and the back doors were opened. Again hands gripped her helpless body and she was pulled out and upright until her feet found the ground, then the rope round her legs was cut.

'You go down steps here,' said an unknown voice. 'Be careful. We have to deliver you unharmed. They're steep ones,' he added.

Unable to see a thing, Grace was growing nervous. Carefully, she put one foot forward and down. The man was right, the steps were steep, but although she had to negotiate them herself, he still had hold of her upper body in case she began to fall. She wondered where she'd been taken, and if David was already waiting there with Emily and Lucien.

'Right, last one,' the voice said at last. 'I just have to knock on this door and then you'll be taken inside. That's my job done.'

Although she could just hear him through the blanket, Grace didn't think he'd be able to hear her muffled voice and in any case she was certain he wouldn't answer any questions, so she remained silent. She was shaking now, trying to work out what was happening.

The man knocked on a door, and after a short pause she heard it open. Then she was pushed hard between her shoulder blades and nearly fell as she stumbled through the door and into the unknown. As the door slammed behind her, the blanket was taken off and her eyes struggled to adjust to the dim red light that illuminated a large, dark basement. She could see a few metallic beds, chairs and cages dotted around the room, while thick beams with metal hoops hanging from them covered one end of the ceiling.

'Hello, Grace,' said a familiar voice. Grace's head whipped round and she found herself staring into Amber's eyes, eyes that were so cold she instinctively tried to take a step away from the other woman. 'Fasten her somewhere,' said Amber sharply. 'Lucien will be here in a minute, we have to wait for him.'

'My ultimate fantasy,' said another familiar voice as a small door opened at the far end of the basement and Lucien walked in. 'A kidnapping, as I told you.'

'Where's Emily?' asked Grace, looking in vain for the blonde girl.

'She's not included in this special fantasy of mine. I never intended her to be. She and I have parted company now, and she's been well rewarded with her American contract, which is perfectly genuine. No, you're the person Amber and I really wanted to kidnap. We both wanted you here for revenge, you see. Amber's revenge is personal, as I'm sure you're beginning to understand. You took away her lover and her way of life, and she's waited a long time to punish you for that.

'Much as I will enjoy helping her with that, and much as I've always desired you, you're now more a pawn in my game. I'm tired of losing out to your lover. I want either his business or his girlfriend. The choice will be his.'

'You're completely mad,' said Grace, stunned by

what Lucien was telling her. 'You can't think that this pantomime is going to make David hand you his business.'

'More a tragedy than a pantomime, I think. Well, perhaps not, in which case he'll have to agree that I can have you.'

'I'm not a possession or a business,' retorted Grace. 'He can't give me away; I'm not his to give.'

'Of course you are. When you're mine I can take you abroad. We'd have a lot of fun together, once you realised I'm far more exciting than David.'

'David and I are in a relationship!' she said incredulously. 'I'm not some sex slave he can hand over to another person. Besides, I'd be missed. I'm due at work on Saturday. Fran would start asking questions.'

'Would she really? How close are you both now? If David told her that you'd decided to open up a hotel abroad, she'd believe him, wouldn't she? She doesn't feel she knows you any more, or so my sources tell me. She knows how much he's changed you, and I suspect she resents it. Why, she might even take over your directing work once you're gone.'

'You just want to hurt David!' she retorted, trying to disguise the fact that she knew his words held a grain of truth in them. 'That's all this is about. You're jealous of him, because he's a better businessman than you, and more popular with the women.'

'Be very careful, Grace,' said Lucien softly. 'Amber can be difficult to control, and she hates you with every fibre of her being. I can help you, but only if I choose to, and right now I'm not sure I do. Tie her up, Toby.'

'Toby!' exclaimed Grace.

Lucien smiled thinly. 'Yes, so much more corruptible than Andrew. That's why I used him more. I knew he'd come in useful at the end.'

'Oh, get on with it!' snapped Amber, who was across the room setting up a video recorder. Grace's eyes darted to her and the camera nervously.

Toby quickly began to undress Grace. When she resisted, Lucien gripped her chin tightly in his hands and stared into her eyes. 'I won't warn you again,' he said, ice in his voice. When he let her go she stood limply, letting Toby unzip the back of her maxi dress and push it down her arms until it fell in a pool round her feet. Then he removed her bra, and while Lucien played idly with her nipples, occasionally pinching one until she wanted to cry out with the pain of it, Toby pulled down her bikini briefs and reluctantly she stepped out of them. As much as she knew she shouldn't, Grace had to admit that she was excited by everything that was happening to her. She knew Lucien would never let her be truly hurt, and the kidnap set-up was wonderfully elaborate. Part of her was also desperate to impress Amber, to show her how far she'd come and how confident she now was with her sexual abilities and preferences. She wished David was here, but she must stay strong without him, just this once, she told herself.

Once she was naked her wrists were bound behind her, a rope collar fastened round her neck and then a thick rope was pulled tight beneath her rounded breasts and over the tops of her arms before being drawn up over her spine and joined to her collar. She could feel the collar rubbing against the delicate necklace that David had given her so unexpectedly, and suddenly wanted to cry out for him, needing him so badly, but she knew he was busy at a meeting and probably had no idea she was even missing.

'Stand her on top of the metal platform,' Amber instructed, 'and fasten her ankles to the sides, legs wide apart.'

When Toby had finished, Grace was naked, exposed

and more vulnerable than she'd ever felt in her life. Always before in sexual situations like this, David had been near, and she'd known that she was with friends. Now she wasn't so sure.

'Put the tall, narrow leather stand in front of her,' said Amber, coming over to Grace. 'Not very nice now, is it? You've always done what you were told because you wanted to please David. You didn't do it because you liked it, you did it for him.'

'That a lie!' retorted Grace.

'Really, then let's see how much you enjoy it when he's not here,' said Amber, clasping the younger woman around the neck and forcing her to bend sharply from the waist until her breasts were rubbing against the leather sides of the stand.

Lucien moved to the head of the stand, and now he was naked too. His erection was huge, and within easy reach of Grace's mouth. 'Use your skill on me,' he said quietly. 'Let me experience what David undoubtedly enjoys regularly, and Amber will pleasure you at the same time.'

Grace wanted to refuse, but she didn't dare, she was determined not to break down. As she let her tongue caress the underside of the head of Lucien's erection, flicking lightly beneath the ridge and moving her head back and forth, Amber slowly started to tease between Grace's outspread thighs, licking softly at her trembling, delicate flesh and drawing the slowly swelling clitoris into her mouth.

Worried about the pain that Amber could inflict on her if she chose, Grace redoubled her efforts to satisfy Lucien, and soon he began to groan. As his testicles drew up against his body she knew that he was going to climax quickly. Sure enough, as she licked and swirled her tongue around him his hips jerked frantically and then he was spilling himself into her mouth, his hands forcing her to keep her head down until she'd swallowed every drop.

In the meantime, Amber let her tongue go deep inside Grace, thrusting it like a penis while all the time her fingers circled the throbbing clitoris. As Grace's body tightened in an automatic response to the pleasuring, Amber spoke.

'I don't really want you to come after all,' she said. 'If you do then I'll definitely have to punish you severely.'

A tiny gasp of fear escaped from Grace's lips, because she knew – just as Amber knew– that she was now past the point of no return. With one final swirl of a fingertip and her tongue still deep inside the fastened woman, Amber got the result she'd wanted. To her everlasting shame Grace felt her body gather itself together and then she was jerking as the contractions rushed through her while all the time she remained in the position they'd chosen for her. As soon as it was over she began to cry, ashamed and humiliated that she couldn't hold back, and that her body was experiencing such deep pleasure when she knew she should be insisting they let her go. But she couldn't resist what they were making her feel ...

'She's afraid of what you're going to do next,' said Lucien with a laugh. 'Shall we make her wait a little, while we decide?'

'Yes, let her wait and wonder,' agreed Amber, and Grace was quickly gagged and tied to a chair.

For what seemed an eternity she was ignored, apart from Amber occasionally strolling over to flick her breasts with her riding crop until her red and swollen nipples throbbed, and she had to force herself not to wriggle on her chair as, to her horror, she felt the pressure of an impending orgasm growing in her lower belly.

Eventually, Lucien came over to her. 'How long do you think it will take David to notice you're missing?' he asked.

'Not long, although he had a meeting.'

'Ah yes, the meeting. He'll have waited quite a long time before he realised there wasn't one, so I don't think he'll know something's happened to you until he finally goes to the hotel. Perhaps after lunch? That was the itinerary I'd given you, I believe.'

'He's not stupid. He'll—'

'Indeed he's not, and I've left him a number to call once he grasps the situation. That's why I want to get as much pleasure from you as possible before he and I start negotiating, just in case he should choose to keep you and give me control of his business empire. Pleasure that Amber will, of course, make as difficult as possible for you to fully enjoy. Get her ready for the suspension bar, Toby.'

His words increased Grace's apprehension and, when Toby approached her, she saw him glance upwards. Lucien was now lowering a triangular suspension bar with chains from a beam in the middle of the ceiling, and as she stood motionless, Toby removed the ropes and restraints that had just been used on her before

311

picking up a leather harness that he and Amber then fastened round Grace's unresisting body.

The tall, curvaceous blonde woman looked thoughtfully at Grace. 'You're afraid, aren't you? That's good, because fear is an excellent aphrodisiac for you, as I recall. David taught you well, and I've no doubt you're kept in regular practice, so your body will enjoy itself against your will. Not at first, of course, but eventually. I shall delay the pleasure for as long as possible. I want you to suffer, although no amount of suffering can equal the suffering you've caused me.'

'I didn't cause it,' replied Grace. 'David made the final decision.'

'He had no choice. You defeated me, and he had to keep his word. No one was more surprised than him, and I imagine he's been quite bored at times since then. Not that he'd have let you know. He's a man of his word, unfortunately.'

'He'll never forgive you for this,' said Grace, wincing as the straps that ran down between her legs were pulled up tightly.

'Can you ever forgive him for what his obstinacy has forced us to do to you?' mused Amber. 'Now, grip those chains on the triangle tightly, we're going to lift you up until your toes are balancing on a stool, then we're going to blindfold you.'

'No!' exclaimed Grace, unable to contain herself.

Amber smiled thinly. 'I remember how much you hate that, but it enhances all the sensations and of course you won't be able to see what we're doing either. Try not to move around too much. If you accidentally kick the stool over, you'll be taking all your weight on your arms. Don't worry. Before long we'll suspend you vertically and put a spreader board between your knees. You'll feel almost weightless then.'

The leather straps criss-crossed Grace's body from neck to crotch, but her hands were free so that she could grab the chains when Toby lifted her up, and then the black velvet mask was put over her eyes, the triangle was raised and she was frantically scrabbling to get a toehold on the stool they put beneath her.

The room was silent except for her rapid breathing. 'Where shall we begin?' mused Lucien, and she felt him running a hand over her breasts, slipping his fingers beneath the straps that cut across her nipples. 'Some of our special ointment on these should make life interesting, especially as you'll have the pressure of the straps to contend with too.'

She felt his deceptively gentle fingers spreading a gel over the nipples, then the straps were put back in place, and within seconds she felt them start to grow and harden. They were so rigid that the pressure of the straps became painful, and she let out a whimper of pain. The moment the sound had escaped her lips a long whip fell across the cheeks of her bottom, the tip curling round over the thin skin that covered her hip bone and this time she screamed loudly with shock.

'We don't want to hear you cry out, not even when you have a climax,' said Lucien. 'Amber will punish you for any sound she hears, and she has excellent hearing.'

'Please don't do this to me,' begged Grace, as she felt him spreading the gel over her quaking belly. 'I don't think I like this position. I thought we were becoming friends. Why are you being so harsh now?'

'Oh, he did like you,' said Amber, 'that's why he wants you now. He liked you but David got you. Lucien is good at bearing grudges, and he's lost a lot of women to David over the years.'

'But you were special, Grace,' whispered Lucien, and now his fingers were pushing apart the straps between her legs and spreading the gel over her outer sex lips. She tried desperately to twist away from him, but someone –

Toby, she assumed – gripped her hips and now the hot, swollen feeling was travelling along her most tender tissue and she uttered tiny gasps as she felt her belly swelling and the first flickers of a climax began deep inside her.

She hardly noticed the flick of the whip, she was so frantic to stop the dark and forbidden pleasure from spreading, but her body was too well trained, too accustomed to reaching a pinnacle of pleasure through ways such as this, and she heard Lucien laugh.

'You know you're going to come, don't you?' he whispered in her ear, making her jump as she'd thought he was in front of her. 'How close is it now? Very close? Let me touch you again. Your clitoris must be so large. The gel is something no one can fight, no matter how exhausted their body. We can play this game for hours.'

Grace could barely think straight as his finger moved lightly inside the straps, travelled up her inner sex channel and then finally located the throbbing nub. With exquisite tenderness he circled it, spreading the heat from the gel and at the same time making her gasp aloud at the intense pleasure his touch was causing.

'Let it come, Grace. Give your body at least one moment of ecstasy before the pain begins again.'

She was helpless to resist, her tormented flesh couldn't hold out any longer and her whole body twisted and turned as she hung on tightly to the chains while her orgasm flooded through her.

'Spread her legs,' snapped Amber. 'This time I'm going to use a latex paddle on her as punishment.'

'No – please!' cried Grace. 'I couldn't help it, you know that. I'm sorry, truly I am.'

'She still doesn't understand the enormity of what she did to me,' said Amber. 'Do as I say, Toby, and then we'll truss her up and suspend her vertically.'

Unable to see, still trembling from the pleasure they'd forced from her, Grace bit hard on her lip to stop herself from screaming. With the blindfold on she wouldn't be able to see what was happening when they moved her position, and panic started to overwhelm her. 'I've had enough now!' she shouted.

'Why? Haven't you just had an orgasm? How can you say we're ill-treating you? In any case, if you want to blame anyone, blame David. He's the one who—'

There was a loud crash, and Grace felt a strong current of air sweep through the musty basement, making her body twist with its force. 'The one who what?' asked a familiar voice.

'David? Help me down!' she cried, hot tears of shame flooding her eyes and trickling down her cheeks from beneath the mask.

She could hear the sound of running feet and a door slammed at the far end of the basement, Amber gave a scream of fury and then Grace was being lifted upwards off the stool. 'You can let go of the chains now, Gracie,' said David gently. 'You're safe. Let go, darling.'

Shaking and sobbing, she fell against him, and he quickly removed the mask as someone else put a towelling robe round her. 'I have to finish dealing with all of this,' he said softly. 'Andrew will take you back to the hotel and stay with you until I've finished. The guests have all gone. We explained there was a family emergency. Do you need a doctor?'

Grace shook her head. 'No, but they made me do things . . .'

'You can tell me everything later, I promise you, but I have to sort this out. I'm so sorry, my darling.'

'How did you find me?' she asked, as Andrew waited patiently beside her.

David put out a hand, and she flinched. A shadow crossed his face and his mouth tightened. 'I could kill them both,' he muttered.

'How?' she repeated.

'Using this,' he said, his outstretched hand touching the tiny necklace she was still wearing. 'It sends out a signal. That's why I told you to wear it every day.'

'You knew this was going to happen to me?' she asked incredulously.

'Of course not. I'll explain later,' he promised her, and then Andrew put an arm round her shoulders and helped her up the steps and into the back of one of David's limousines.

'Would you like me to sit in the back with you?' Andrew asked.

Grace nodded. 'I'm cold,' she said as the car drew smoothly away.

'It's shock. I think you do need a doctor.'

'I'm not hurt, not in that sort of way.'

'You're definitely in shock. I'll have David's physician meet us at the hotel,' he said, picking up his mobile phone. 'Don't worry, he won't ask any awkward questions, but you need to be seen by him.'

'Perhaps you're right,' she admitted, closing her eyes, and then she knew he was because during the entire journey back to her hotel all she could see were images of Lucien and Amber's faces, and sudden flashbacks to the basement room and how she'd taken Lucien into her mouth while Amber teased an orgasm from her.

'It wasn't my fault,' she said despairingly. 'I couldn't help it.'

'Of course it wasn't your fault!' exclaimed Andrew, but Grace knew that he didn't understand what she really meant, or the full extent of her shame.

Chapter Four

Twenty-four hours later, David sat behind the mahogany desk in his main London office, flanked by two of his security men, and studied the couple sitting opposite him. Amber's eyes were still defiant, and her luxurious mane of blonde hair tumbled over her bare shoulders as she crossed one leg over the other, displaying her tanned and toned thighs. He wondered how he could have been so bewitched by her for so many years. Other women had come and gone, but she was always there to provide him with the kind of urgent, darkly exciting sex that they both embraced. She was beautiful and sexy, but as cold as ice, and he was surprised that he'd never realised before quite how lacking in normal feelings she was. All the same, he'd enjoyed her body, and used her keen brain to run The Dining Club for him. She hadn't changed, he thought, so perhaps he had.

His gaze moved on to Lucien. Lucien, who had been his friend, business partner and companion in the joys of extreme sexual pleasure for ten years. Unlike Amber, Lucien looked defeated. His hair was uncombed, his eyes dull and he kept his gaze on the ground in front of him, unable to meet David's eyes.

'I never knew you hated me, Lucien,' said David, his voice finally breaking the long silence. 'That was a bad mistake on my part.'

'I didn't always hate you,' muttered Lucien.

'No? Well, whenever the hatred began, I failed to spot it.'

'I taught him to hate you,' said Amber. 'When Grace defeated me, taking away everything I'd ever worked for and loved, I needed help, but you simply cast me adrift. I knew Lucien liked Grace, so I contacted him. It all snowballed from there.'

'I think Lucien is intelligent enough to have known what you were doing,' said David, his eyes flicking over Amber.

She lifted her chin. 'Most men are easily led. He was

no different from the rest of them. Only you were different. You never cared about convention, or what other
people might think or feel. You went ahead and did
what you wanted, and I admired that.'

'Until I wanted Grace rather than you,' he pointed
out.

'Yes, until then,' she admitted. 'Didn't you think
about me at all after you'd abandoned me?'

'No. Why would I? As you've just said, I've never
cared about how other people feel.'

'Why didn't you call the police?' asked Lucien.

David raised his eyebrows. 'Do you really think I'm
willing to put Grace through the ordeal of having to
answer their questions and tell them what happened?'

'Why not, since you don't care about anyone's feelings?' Amber retorted. 'Mind you, as our film shows us
giving her intense orgasms, they might not take any
action. Private pleasure in a private place isn't illegal.'

David went white. 'Don't you dare mention that film
again. As for not caring about anyone's feelings, perhaps I've changed.'

'Or perhaps you just don't want to have to listen to
it all for a second time yourself,' snapped Amber.

'When Grace has recovered enough to tell me everything, I'll listen to her version. I've already watched the film, and she's told me more than enough for me to know that you two will always be dangerous.'

Lucien finally lifted his head. 'What are you going to do, then?'

'Firstly,' said David crisply, 'I expect your resignation from all the positions you hold in my companies. You can write the letter when we've finished talking. Secondly, you and Amber will leave this country and never return. I don't care where you go, or if you choose to stay together or not once you've left, but believe me if either of you ever tries to come back here, or attempts to interfere in my life or Grace's life again, you won't be given a second chance.'

'A second chance of what?' demanded Amber.

'Leaving.'

There was a long silence while she digested his words. 'You mean you'd kill us?' she asked incredulously.

'Don't be ridiculous. Unfortunately, accidents do happen and I think that you two have pushed your luck as far as you can, so anything could happen – anything at all.'

'Where can we go? What can we do?' asked Lucien, who knew perfectly well what David meant. 'I don't imagine you're going to give me a reference.'

David shrugged. 'Go as far away from here as you can. Open a brothel in some far-flung place out East for all I care. Amber will be able to make a living for as long as her looks last.'

'But I'm a businessman!' exclaimed Lucien.

'Then start up a business of your own, or become a shareholder in whatever Amber decides to do. You've got enough money; it should be easy for both of you given your particular talents.'

'The sex is a hobby for me. I enjoy big business too,' protested Lucien.

'Well, let's hope you're as clever as you clearly thought you were, and manage to build a large business empire somewhere. But to be truthful, Lucien, you'd be wiser to go into partnership with Amber. On your own you're nothing,' he added contemptuously.

Lucien jumped to his feet, and one of the security men's hands moved towards his inside pocket. 'Is it any wonder I grew to hate you?' he said. 'You've never appreciated my talents.'

'Indeed I have, and I valued your friendship, too. I was a very poor judge of character. I shall be more careful in future.'

'You've never had friends,' snarled Amber. 'You

always told me you didn't want them, and that's why you kept us all at arm's length. What are you going to do about Grace? She's not likely to want to return to her old ways with you now, is she? Her nerve will have gone.'

'Do not mention her name again,' said David softly, but although his words were spoken quietly the fury behind them was clear to both Amber and Lucien.

'We got carried away,' admitted Lucien, shifting uncomfortably in his seat.

'Yes, and not for the first time in your case, I suspect,' mused David. 'Now, I'm going to take a walk round the building. By the time I get back I expect you to have written your letter of resignation. Amber, your passport, financial papers and some luggage will be collected from your house and brought here this evening. You'll both be on a flight to Berlin by midnight. After that you can decide whether to remain together or split up, but keep moving on, because Berlin is too close to London for my liking. And don't make the mistake of thinking that I won't know where you are. From now on, I will always know, day and night, where both of you are living.' With that he got up out of his chair and walked towards the door.

'You'll miss me,' said Amber, 'miss having me, or someone like me, for the days when Grace's talents aren't quite enough to satisfy those urges you get from time to time, urges that only I have ever been able to satisfy for you. What do you plan to do when we've gone – get married and raise a family?' And she laughed.

'What I do in the future is none of your concern,' he pointed out, and then he was in the corridor outside and found that he was shaking with fury. He had never been this angry in his entire life, and the effort of keeping himself under control had exhausted him.

As soon as Lucien had written his letter of resignation, David put it in his briefcase, snapped the lock closed and hurried from the building.

'We need to stay together,' said Amber, watching him leave through the window of his office. 'We complement each other, and together we can build a sex empire abroad somewhere. We'll be happy too, Lucien, because we'll still be doing what we love most. David won't be happy. Within a year, two at the most, he'll be bored out of his mind, and then we can invite him to come and stay with us.'

'Perhaps,' said Lucien slowly. 'Right now, I'm not sure I think you're right.'

'I have to be right!' she said angrily. 'If I believed he and Grace were going to live a "happy ever after" life, I couldn't bear it. No, he might be going to try to change, but he'll never manage it. He's damaged goods, and far too old for even someone like Grace to help him.'

'Then you think we should go on hoping he'll forgive us?'

'Yes!' exclaimed Amber. 'I know a few girls in Berlin, I'll contact them and we can take them with us when we move on. We have to believe we can do it, and that one day we'll both get the old David back.'

Lucien nodded, but Amber wasn't sure that he really believed it. She didn't care, because she had more than enough drive and talent for both of them, and already she was starting to become excited by the prospect of what might lie ahead once they left David and Grace behind.

Chapter Five

A month later, Grace was about to leave David's house for work when he called her name. She found him sitting on the side of the bed, and noticed how tired he looked.

'What is it?'

'I wondered where you were going.'

'To work. It's time I got back, and Fran's finished her play. We'll be going through it together.'

He patted the bed. 'Come and sit beside me.' She hesitated. 'Please, Grace, we need to talk before you start getting involved in work again.'

She shook her head. 'There's nothing to talk about. You've seen the film. You know I let them give me pleasure despite being scared of them, what more is there to say? I think we just have to move on.' Her heart was pounding as she spoke, because no matter how hard she tried, she hadn't been able to let him near her since the day of the kidnapping, and she was so scared of losing him that pretending everything was all right was the only way she could cope.

'Just sit,' he said, his voice firmer than it had been since Lucien and Amber left the country. As a result, she automatically obeyed him, pressing her knees tightly together to try to stop her legs from shaking.

'Lucien and Amber won't ever be able to hurt you again,' he said quietly. 'The reason I sent them away was so that you wouldn't be looking over your shoulder in fear all the time. I thought it would make you feel safe.'

'It has!'

'But not safe enough to let me make love to you?'

She clasped her hands tightly together. 'I don't want to.'

'I'd take it slowly, Grace. There's no pressure for anything to happen, I just want to be able to touch you, to feel close to you again,' he explained.

Grace shook her head. 'I don't want to be touched by you.'

'Why?'

'Because I don't. All I'll do is remember what they did to me again, and how I reacted. I don't want that.'

'So you'll let them ruin our lives after all, will you?'

Grace shook her head. 'No, but it's still too soon. I'm sure I'll feel differently eventually, and if you don't want to wait I'll understand, but—'

'Grace, I'm willing to wait as long as it takes, but you're not making any progress. You've seen a counsellor, you've talked to a therapist, and they all tell you that the best thing for you now is to live a normal life.'

'That's why I'm going back to work.'

His mouth tightened. 'Don't pretend to misunderstand me. I've been very patient with you, but we can't go on like this for ever and I don't believe you've told anyone, including me, the truth about this problem. I only want to hold you close, Grace.'

She knew that he was right. They couldn't go on like this for ever, and she hadn't told him the whole truth about why she wouldn't let him make love to her, so with a sigh of resignation she dropped her handbag to the floor. 'All right then, go ahead,' she said, her voice expressionless.

He studied her intently for a moment, and then pulled

her slowly towards him. He was still naked, and despite not getting any help from her, managed to undress Grace within a few minutes before laying her carefully across the width of the wide bed, while he lay on his left side and tenderly placed her legs over his thighs.

His right hand caressed her thighs while he moved his upper body close to her, so that he could look down at her, studying her reactions to his slow, gentle caresses. For a long time he kissed and stroked her, until her body began to relax a little, and reaching up with her left hand she started to stroke his shoulders and upper back.

Eventually she began to feel that she wanted more, and her hips shifted restlessly on the bed. David immediately moved a lubricated finger in steady circles around her clitoris, gazing down at her so that he could watch her reactions carefully. When she began to breathe more rapidly, feeling a climax building deep within her, he left her clitoris and easing two fingers inside her he began to softly stroke the walls of her vagina in a sweeping circular movement, and was still stroking them as her body tightened and the hot, welcome release of an orgasm finally swept over her.

His fingers stopped moving until the last pulsations of

her climax had died away, and then he began stimulating the walls of her vagina again, stroking her gently at first and then with more pressure before moving back to her clitoris and caressing that until her body arched in another blissful moment of release.

Time and again he played her in this way, moving from caressing her vaginal walls to circling her now soaking clitoris until eventually he changed tactics, using one finger to tease her clitoris while the other remained deep inside her, massaging her cervix until, with a cry of ecstasy, she was consumed by a wave of multiple orgasms that left her crying with joy.

'I want you inside me,' she whispered, as he held her body close to his. Only then did he move on top of her and as he slid slowly inside her, she tightened her pelvic muscles around him and heard him give a deep groan of satisfaction. When he finally came, his head went back and he gave a muffled cry as he spilled himself inside her.

Almost as soon as his pleasure was complete, he was back lying beside her, cradling her close to him and tenderly brushing her dark hair off her face. 'Welcome back, darling Gracie,' he said softly.

Part Six

Chapter One

'You're late,' said Fran as Grace hurried in to the café where they'd arranged to meet.

'Sorry, I got held up. I'll get myself a latte.'

'Is it true you're thinking of selling the hotel?' asked Fran when Grace returned with her coffee. 'You've only just opened, and Andrew said it's a huge success.'

'I don't know what I'm going to do.'

Fran raised an eyebrow. 'I assume it will all depend on what David wants you to do?'

'Not really, it depends on how much I want to stay at the cutting edge of directing. The hotel takes up more time than I'd expected. I was naïve. I didn't realise I'd be needed so much once the reconstruction was finished, but the guests can be very demanding and I have to be there for them twenty-four/seven.'

'You certainly don't look well. You've got huge dark circles under your eyes. Andrew said you'd had a bad virus.'

'I'm feeling much better now.'

'Did you know that Emily has definitely signed her Hollywood contract? I read it in the *Metro*. She must have done something really special to get that sorted so quickly.'

'I hate to think about it,' said Grace truthfully.

Fran started rummaging through her bag. 'Here's my new play. You'll need to take it home with you. It's too long for you to read here.'

'How is Andrew? I haven't seen him for ages,' said Grace. 'I've hardly seen anyone. The virus really knocked me out.'

'I don't know how Andrew is.'

Grace looked at her in surprise. 'What do you mean?'

'What I say. I don't know how he is. I'm not seeing him any more. It's over between us.'

'Oh no!' exclaimed Grace. 'Why? He's such a great guy and I thought you two—'

'We tried, but it didn't work out. Let's face it, he

wasn't so great that you fell for him last year, was he? Why should he be good enough for me but not you? Of course, David is rather stiff opposition for anyone without his money and influence.'

'Please leave David out of this,' said Grace. 'So, you're on the lookout again, are you?'

'No, I'm with John.'

Grace looked at her in amazement. 'You don't mean the two of you are an item?'

'Yes. He's appearing at Chichester this summer, and I'll be staying there with him. I've fallen in love with him, Grace. It might last a few months, or it might last a few years, but I don't care. I'm happy and we're never short of things to talk about because we're in the same business. That's what I don't understand about you and David. You two are from such different worlds.'

'You know nothing about him, nothing at all,' said Grace, remembering how tenderly he'd made love to her earlier. 'Just drop it, Fran.'

'Okay, but I will just say that one of the reasons I dropped Andrew was because over the past few weeks all he's talked about is you and your virus. He wouldn't even let me call you. He said you were too ill to take phone calls! Anyone would think no one else in the world has ever been ill. When a man behaves like that, you can be pretty certain his thoughts are with the patient. He still fancies you, Grace, and I don't want your leftovers.'

'He's a kind person,' said Grace weakly.

'Right, how silly of me not to realise that's all it was. Anyway, you've got the play, so let me know what you think. I hear you've been offered a chance to direct at The Globe. Is that true?'

'Yes, next summer.'

'Congratulations,' said Fran, reaching for her play.

'What are you doing?' asked Grace.

'I've changed my mind. Things don't stay the same, Grace. Time passes, we meet new people, and you and I aren't the same as we were in the old days, before you met David. You know that's true.'

Grace nodded. 'That doesn't mean we can't stay friends, though.'

Fran smiled. 'We're not going to fall out, but I think we're going our separate ways now. You have the hotel, the West End transfer of *Mrs Warren's Profession* and The Globe coming up, plus the ever-present, all-powerful David White is your lover. I've learnt a lot from you, and I'll direct my own play if I can get some money together. I've got John now, and I'm happy with my life. Are you happy with yours?'

Grace hesitated for a second. 'Of course I am,' she said vehemently.

Fran looked thoughtfully at her. 'I really hope that's true. You of all people deserve to be happy. You're so loyal, clever and loving. Take care, and we'll keep in touch. You must come to Chichester and we can watch the play and have dinner after.'

With that, Fran gathered up her things and walked out of the café. Despite Fran's words, both she and Grace knew only too well that she was most probably walking out of Grace's life for ever.

Alone at the table, Grace thought long and hard about everything. She knew that she had to be as truthful with David now as Fran had been with her. It wasn't going to be easy, and she had no idea how she was going to do it, but she had to. He needed to know, although she wasn't sure she could find the courage or the words to tell him.

Chapter Two

That evening David took Grace out to dinner, and as she sat down at a discreet corner table, she remembered her evening out with Lucien only a few months earlier.

'I'm not very hungry,' she said after reading the menu. 'A salad will be fine.'

'Wine?'

Knowing what she had to say over the meal, she nodded, hoping it would give her the courage she needed.

'Did you have a good time with Fran?' he asked after they'd given their order.

'Not really. She feels that we've both changed so much there's no point in us trying to continue with our working relationship. She's going to direct her own play.'

'She might have a point,' said David. 'You've got a lot of directing commitments, and we haven't decided what to do about the hotel, so—'

'You haven't said anything about Andrew,' interrupted Grace.

He frowned. 'You didn't mention him.'

'No, but you know he's been keen on Fran for ages, that's why he wanted more time off, and he's been taking her out for meals a lot lately.'

David shrugged. 'If he doesn't do it for her, then she's right to let him go. Has she got someone else?'

'Yes, an ageing actor.'

'Clearly not too ageing to make her happy!'

'I just feel sorry for Andrew,' said Grace.

'He'll be fine. He's never been short of girlfriends. Why on earth should it upset you what Fran does?'

'I'm upset because everything's changing, I suppose.'

'Grace, you've changed more than anyone I know over the past year. You can hardly complain if other people's lives change too.' He glanced up at the waiter who'd just arrived with the wine. 'I'll pour, you can leave us.'

'How's your work?' asked Grace.

'Busy, but that's how I like it. Would you like to discuss the weather next?'

She stared at him. 'Don't be ridiculous!'

'It just feels rather strange, especially after this morning, sitting here making small talk.'

'Well, we can hardly sit here and talk about sex,' she retorted.

He gave a half-smile. 'I will if you will!'

Grace sipped her wine, put down her glass and took a deep breath. 'Actually, I do want to talk about sex,' she admitted.

He raised his eyebrows. 'Do you now? This should be interesting. Go ahead, then.'

Grace shifted uneasily on her chair. 'I don't want to do it here, but I know I'll never have the courage to say it to you when we're alone together.'

Suddenly David went very still. 'Go on.'

'I don't understand myself any more,' she confessed. 'It was wonderful this morning, and you were so good. You made me feel loved and desired, and took things so slowly. It was exactly what I needed, and I can never thank you enough for that, but I didn't deserve it.'

'What do you mean?'

'You've seen the film. You've watched how I reacted to what Lucien and Amber did to me. How could I have behaved like that? I was terrified, and I hated them, but I still let them pleasure me. What kind of a person does that make me?' Her eyes were full of tears, but just at that moment the waiter arrived with their meals and she looked down at her lap so that he couldn't see she was upset.

'I'll signal when we need you again. We'd like some privacy now,' said David. The waiter nodded and walked quickly away. 'Go on,' he said to Grace.

'Weren't you appalled when you saw the film?'

'Only by their cruelty. They knew what they were doing, Grace. They both knew how to play you, and in any case fear has become an aphrodisiac for you. I taught you all about that way back in the beginning.'

'And I should have told you that Lucien hurt me in the hotel garden when he and Emily were staying in the Country Retreat Suite. If I had done, maybe he wouldn't have gone as far as he did. You could have stopped him sooner.'

'I knew he'd done something, which is why I bought the necklace. I don't understand why you didn't tell me, though. Did you think I wouldn't believe you?'

'I was ashamed!' she exclaimed. 'I hated him, and the pain, but my body took pleasure from it.'

'That's the way we live now, and there's nothing for you to be ashamed of, although I imagine it's a way of life you're rather keen to put behind you after all that's happened to you.'

Grace swallowed hard, and lowered her voice. 'That's the shameful thing, I don't want to put it behind me. This morning was wonderful, but I still want what we used to have as well. I want the excitement that comes from the fear, and the pain that precedes the pleasure, but I shouldn't want it. Not after everything they did to me.'

David leant back in his chair. 'So, you still want to enjoy S&M and bondage?' he queried quietly.

'I need it,' she confessed, looking down at the table because she didn't want to see the expression on his face. 'I need it, but I don't know how that's going to be possible any more. I'm afraid to keep the hotel, because everything got out of hand there. What am I going to do? And when you and I are finished, how will I ever find the same kind of pleasure with someone else without putting myself in danger? Fran was right: I've changed, but it isn't making my life easy, and I'm scared and confused.'

'I think you may find that although you think you need it, that's not true. You grew used to what I taught you, but I'm sure you could unlearn it given time, retrain your body to more conventional pleasures,' said David.

'You don't understand; I need it now!' she said, and with that she burst into tears.

He let her cry quietly to herself, and when she'd regained her composure he signalled for the bill. 'There's only one way to find out,' he said. 'We'll visit a small club that I own; it's not far from here.' With that he took her by the arm and led her out to where his car was parked. 'If you don't like it, and want to stop anything at all, say "it's over" and it will stop. That's your safety net; remember it.'

Grace nodded. 'I didn't know you owned two clubs?' she commented, feeling his left hand caressing her knee as he drove through the dark streets of West London.

'Yes, but this one's tiny. I don't often go there now, but it's perfect for us tonight.'

The Club turned out to be very small, and David's arrival sent the doorman scurrying downstairs in a hurry. An auburn-haired young woman quickly came up to greet them. 'Any special requirements?' she asked David, giving Grace a quick smile.

'One male companion and the smallest dungeon that's free,' he replied.

Five minutes later Grace was being led into a tiny dark room, with a horribly familiar red light glowing at the far end. She saw ceiling beams and wall bars, cages similar to the one Emily had been put on, and a long, waist-high leather table tucked in a corner.

'Before we go any further, are you sure this is what you want to do?' David asked. Grace nodded. She was scared, but not in the way she'd been scared with Lucien and Amber. This was an entirely different sensation, and for the first time since her kidnapping she felt herself becoming totally alive again. 'Fine, but remember the phrase. What was it?'

'It's over,' she said quietly.

'Exactly, now we'll see if you do enjoy this as much as you seem to think you will.'

'Do you think it's wrong of me?' she asked softly.

David looked surprised. 'Nothing is wrong, as long as it makes you happy and doesn't harm anyone else. Surely you know that by now.'

Even as he spoke he was stripping off her rose-pink

sheath dress and running his hands over her body, which was naked beneath it. She heard a door open somewhere else in the room, but before she could turn her head to see who was coming in, David had slipped a velvet blindfold over her eyes. 'You have to learn to like this if you're going to continue down this path,' he said softly, and she tried not to panic.

Then a new pair of masculine hands were fondling her, cupping her buttocks and stroking her breasts. 'Tie her to the wall bars,' said David, and within seconds she was being lifted up, and felt the rub of hard wooden bars against the back of her body. Her arms were spread wide then fastened to one of the bars, and when her legs were parted and cuffed to a bar she felt the stranger's hands pressing down on her belly, just above her pubic bone.

Instinctively she moved her hips backwards, only to find there was nowhere for them to go except against the bars. She could hear the two men moving around the room, but they didn't speak so she had no way of knowing what they were doing until her breasts were fondled and squeezed. Once her nipples had grown tight and hard, she felt the touch of sharp metal teeth against them as nipple clamps were attached, and she gave a moan of pain, which resulted in a sharp tug on the chain of the clamps.

'You like that, don't you?' asked David, touching her between her thighs, and she knew that he could feel how damp she'd grown. 'Answer me,' he continued. 'You must always answer when questioned.'

'Yes, yes I do,' she said hastily, and then his fingers were probing her inner sex lips until they became swollen and parted, allowing his tongue easy access to her inner lips.

'Clitoral ring,' he said curtly, and a frisson of fear ran through her. Again, within a few seconds she felt the most delicate part of her, the tiny centre of all her pleasure, being imprisoned within the confines of a small metal ring, and now there was no way it could escape. Not matter how much she was touched, teased and tormented there, the clitoris could no longer withdraw beneath its hood.

David used his tongue on her there relentlessly, until the sensations were too much, too overpowering, and she knew that normally it would have retracted out of reach to protect itself. Now there was no escape, and she'd never felt such intense sensations between her wide-spread thighs. She moaned with a mixture of pain and pleasure as her clitoris started to pulsate, sending sharp shards like flashes of lightning up through her whole body.

'It's too much!' she protested, but she was ignored, as she'd known she would be, and now she was growing frantic with excitement.

'Don't come yet or you'll be punished,' said David.

'I can't help it!' she whimpered, and sure enough, as he sucked softly on the imprisoned clitoris, a climax tore through her.

'Nipple clamps,' said David harshly, and now the other man released the clamps and as the blood flowed into the abused tips of her full breasts a stinging blow spread across the middle of them. In their highly sensitive state her nipples reacted violently, and now her upper body jerked against the hard wooden bars as yet another climax was drawn from her.

'Not very obedient,' said David crisply. 'Get her down; I want to try out the new piece of equipment.'

Trembling with the fearful excitement that she'd come to need so desperately, Grace felt the men part her legs and then a spreader bar with ankle cuffs was fastened between them while another bar was pulled up between her legs until it rested against her rectum.

'The position looks about right,' said David. 'It's going to be interesting, to say the least.'

Unable to see or move, Grace waited as she felt hands moving around at the back of her. Then one of the men, she didn't think it was David, was easing two fingers inside her rectum, spreading lubricating gel around. Once that was done she was moved slightly backwards, and for a moment it felt as though she was going to fall and she gave a muted cry. 'Get up onto your toes,' said David, 'unless you want to stop now?' She shook her head, and obeyed immediately. 'Excellent,' he murmured, stroking the backs of her thighs before easing a throbbing dildo into her back passage.

'It's on the end of the impaling spike,' he explained. 'If you try to lower yourself so that your feet are flat on the floor it will move deeper inside you. If you prefer to keep it where it is, then I suggest you remain balanced on your toes.'

'I don't want it deeper,' she cried, because the rotating dildo was already well inside her and sending strange sensations shooting through to the front of her body.

'Then do as you're told.'

Naked and unable to see, all she could do was let the

dildo do its work, but just as her body began its rise to a peak of pleasure she was hit across her lower belly by a thick latex paddle. She gave a scream of shock and without thinking let her feet go flat on the floor.

With the dildo now even deeper inside her she could hardly bear the intensity of the sensations, but every time she attempted to get back on her toes the paddle would strike her, sometimes across the front of her thighs or her still painful breasts, sometimes over the backs of her legs.

'Doesn't she look amazing,' said David. 'Tell me, Grace, is this what you need? Is this what you secretly crave sometimes? Admit the truth, whatever it is, and then we'll let you have an orgasm.'

'You know it is!' she sobbed. 'You did this to me. You made me what I am, and now I can't go back. Please, please let me come now. I'll do anything you say, any-thing, but I need to come.'

'Then of course you can,' he said gently, and drawing her abused right nipple into his mouth he closed his teeth over it and with pleasure-pain assaulting her from both the back and the front, Grace's body went into a massive convulsion as she was finally allowed to climax.

Only when she was still was she released from the

equipment, and after that she heard a door close as the other man left. Then David removed her mask and cupped her face in his hands. 'Now do you understand?' he asked. 'You should never feel ashamed of what happens to your body at times like this. You were born for pleasure, and it comes in many forms. You embrace them all, and that's a rare gift.'

Totally exhausted by the events of the past few weeks, Grace didn't speak, but she nodded and let him hold her shattered body close to him before she dressed herself and they left the club as quickly and quietly as they'd arrived.

It was only later, with her lover asleep beside her, that Grace allowed herself to consider the future, and wonder what was going to become of her and David now.

When she woke the next morning, she found that David had managed to get up, dress and leave without waking her, leaving her a note on his pillow, which she quickly read. 'Had forgotten an appointment I'd made for this morning. Back around six tonight. We're out to dinner with Andrew and his new girlfriend at eight thirty. Will be back in good time for that.'

No scrawled kiss, she noticed, not even a 'love' and his name, just a businesslike note. She smiled to herself, wondering why, even now, she expected him to suddenly change. He was what he was, and in truth he had changed a lot from their early days together. Sometimes she felt that they were really close emotionally, and it was impossible to doubt his love and concern for her, and his fury with Lucien and Amber, after the kidnapping. But he remained a complex man, who compartmentalised his life and in general kept within a rigid framework he'd clearly constructed for himself over the years.

As she showered, her nipples stinging when the hot water touched them after the previous evening at David's club, she reminded herself that only someone who was afraid of their emotions, fearful of loving, would go to such lengths to protect themselves from hurt. And that, as she was now beginning to understand, was what he was doing. He wasn't deliberately trying to hurt her, or people who wanted to get close to him, but protecting himself from them. She wished he'd take her to meet his parents, or that they'd meet up with friends of his from the past at some time, but nothing like that ever happened. It was as though he hadn't

existed before he arrived in London and started building his business empire.

She had workmen coming in to do some minor work on
the hotel that morning, and in the afternoon she met up
with a friend who'd already directed a play at The
Globe, so by the time she'd got back to David's house,
showered and changed for dinner, it was already eight
o'clock.

By eight fifteen she was about to phone Andrew to
say they'd be late when she heard David's key in the
lock. 'You're cutting it fine!' she exclaimed.

He glanced at her, his eyes taking in her ivory, stretch-
lace, one-shoulder dress, cut in an A-line design. 'Don't
nag, it's very unattractive,' he said as he headed for the
shower. 'And your hair would look better up with that
dress.'

To her astonishment she felt tears pricking her eyes,
and hastily blinked them away. She had no intention
of putting up her hair after that, and merely waited
for him to emerge, showered and changed, ten minutes later. Even if she'd wanted to, which she didn't,
Grace couldn't fault his beautifully cut pale grey suit,
light blue shirt and dark blue tie with thin gold lines

on it. He hadn't been voted one of the ten best-dressed men in London for nothing, she thought to herself.

'We'd better get going then,' he said, picking up his car keys and checking his watch. 'I see you prefer your hair loose?'

'Yes.'

They drove in silence for the first ten minutes. 'I'm sorry I snapped at you,' he said at last. 'I knew I was running late, and the bloody traffic was terrible all the way back, but that's no excuse.'

'It doesn't matter.'

As soon as he could, David pulled the car over to the side of the road. 'Clearly it does matter. I've upset you, haven't I?'

Grace was horrified to realise she was close to tears again. 'I'm being stupid. It was rude of you, but not that rude. I don't know why I'm so upset.'

'It's because you're suffering from shock. That's why you wanted to do what we did last night. You needed to prove to yourself that you could still enjoy something that had once given you pleasure but which Lucien and Amber tried to use to harm you. All the same, it was probably too early. I should have said no.'

'I pushed you to let me,' said Grace, wiping her eyes and knowing he was right.

'Anyway, I apologise for what I said earlier. Your hair looks gorgeous down.'

She smiled through her tears. 'But nagging is still very unattractive?'

'It's something I find difficult to deal with, but you don't nag. You never have nagged. You stated a fact, and I chose to see it as nagging. So, a double apology is really required. Accepted?'

'Of course. I think you should have been a barrister. You talk like one sometimes.'

'I think I might have enjoyed that,' he mused, starting up the car again.

Fifteen minutes later they were walking into the hotel lobby to meet Andrew and his new girlfriend. 'I was looking at country houses in Oxfordshire today,' said David just before the four of them met up. 'I'm thinking of buying a place there. We can talk about that later.'

She couldn't believe that he'd told her something so important at such a moment, but then Andrew was greeting her with a hug and a kiss before introducing his new girlfriend, Suki, and all she could do was concentrate on them, forcing what David had told her to the back of her mind.

Suki was a friendly, cheerful young woman. Small-boned, with huge dark eyes and a short hairstyle that framed her perfect features, she was beautiful, and nice with it. As the meal went on, Grace noticed that David was spending a lot of time talking to her and, when she was speaking to Andrew or Grace, he rarely took his eyes off her.

'What do you do for a living, Suki?' he asked over coffee.

'I'm training to be a solicitor.'

'Hard work but interesting, I imagine.'

She smiled at him. 'Yes, although it's not always interesting when you're on the bottom rung of the ladder.'

'That's the same in every walk of life,' he replied. 'Although beginners often have the most fun: learning new things all the time, finding pleasure in things that will become boring with the passing of time.'

Suki nodded. 'That's so true. It's not cool to say it, but nearly everything I learn is actually pretty exciting at the moment.'

'I'm sure it is,' said David thoughtfully, and when

Andrew went to pay the bill Grace found herself standing alone while David chatted animatedly to Suki.

That night he made love to Grace in a totally different way from the previous time, taking her hard and fast after toying with her until she was almost out of her mind with frustration and she knew, beyond any shadow of a doubt, that this was because of Suki.

In the morning he was gone before she woke once more, and without any further reference to his remark about a house in Oxfordshire. Alone, she played the previous evening over and over in her mind. In the end, in desperation, she phoned Andrew and after a few conventional pleasantries she decided to be honest with him. 'Did you think David found Suki exciting last night?' she asked.

There was a short silence. 'She's my girlfriend,' Andrew replied at last.

'I know, but that's not an answer to my question.'

'Truthfully, I'd be amazed if he didn't. In some ways she's like you were when he first met you. I think that's why I like her too.'

'And are you hoping to introduce her to your world?'

'Grace, that's none of your business.'

'It is if David's going to be involved.'

'No,' he said quietly, 'it isn't. You don't own him, and you can't hope to control him. He loves you in a way that he's never loved anyone else before, but he still has other needs. Surely you of all people can understand that?'

She wondered then if Andrew had been the second man at the Club two nights ago. 'Yes, but I only want to do things if David's there too. I don't know if he feels the same about always having me with him.'

'David isn't the same as you, Grace, and I think that very soon you're going to have to decide whether or not that's something you can handle.'

'Has he asked you about Suki?'

'Yes, and that's all I'm saying. I'm sorry, Grace, but you and David have to sort this out between you.' And with that he hung up.

Before she could think about what he'd said she heard the sound of David's key in the front door. 'Oh good, you are in,' he said cheerfully. 'We're going to Oxfordshire. I want to show you a place I looked at yesterday.'

'I didn't know you wanted to leave London.'

'I don't want to leave London. I want to sell this place and buy one at Primrose Hill, plus a country retreat.

Oxfordshire has some beautiful properties, and I'm really taken with this one. I think you'll like it too. I told you my plans when we had our holiday.'

'But what about my hotel?'

'We can talk about that later. Do you want to come or not?'

'Of course,' said Grace, but she was shocked to think that he'd been making plans for such big changes in his life without telling her. On the drive down she was silent, unable to think of anything she could say that wouldn't sound resentful or accusing. David didn't appear to notice, and when they finally reached a small village he slowed, and drove carefully round a winding bend in the road.

'There it is,' he said, stopping the car at a pair of opened iron gates that were at the end of a long drive leading up to a stunning Georgian-style building, with lawns on either side of the drive. 'It's called The Hall,' David continued, turning into the drive and taking them up to the front door. 'The estate agent will be here in a minute to show us round. I've seen it all, but I wanted to be sure you liked it.'

'Does that matter?' she asked.

He looked astonished. 'Of course it matters. I don't

want to spend long weekends in the country without you! I thought you'd love it. It was built in the nineteen twenties, but it's been tastefully modernised and there's planning consent for a new indoor pool complex. That should provide lots of fun, don't you think?' Before she could answer the estate agent arrived, and it took nearly an hour for them to be shown everything. There were two master bedroom suites with dressing rooms, five further bedroom suites, plus two bedrooms and two bathrooms upstairs.

Going from room to room, trying to take in the size of the place and wondering how many staff David would need to keep it running, Grace suddenly realised that until now she'd never fully grasped the extent of David's fortune.

'Do you want to see the cellars?' asked the agent at the end of the tour, but David shook his head.

'I think we know what cellars look like. I like the cinema/playroom; it will be very useful.'

The agent looked at Grace. 'Ah, are we perhaps ...?'

'Useful for when we have parties,' David said smoothly. 'I plan on doing all my entertaining here, both business and pleasure. Presumably there are already staff working here?'

The agent nodded. 'Some of them are a little old, but ...'

'It doesn't matter. I think I'd prefer to have all my own staff, in any case. There are two cottages that come as a separate lot, I believe?' The agent nodded. 'Again, very useful.'

'Then perhaps I should leave you two to talk about it?'

'We'll talk about it on the way home. Grace, do you have any questions you want to ask before we go?' She shook her head. 'I'll phone your head office tomorrow,' said David briskly. 'Thank you for your time.' With that he hurried the bemused Grace to the car, then got behind the wheel again. 'We'll stop at a pub not far from here and get something to eat before we go back to London,' he said. 'You can tell me what you think during the meal.'

She felt as though she was being rushed along, rather like Alice in Wonderland trying to keep up with the White Rabbit. When they finally sat down to eat in the small back room of a beautiful country pub, she let out a sigh of relief.

'Tired?' asked David.

'In a way, tired and confused. We've never really discussed moving out of London before; and I do work there.'

'I told you, this is a country retreat, if the deal on the house in Primrose Hill goes through all right you can look round that. I think you'll like it. My place was only ever meant to be a bachelor pad. It's no longer suitable.'

She felt like pointing out that he was still a bachelor, but she didn't. Clearly he was including her in all his plans, even if he was making them himself.

'Don't you understand?' he said softly. 'The Hall is the perfect place for us. We can tailor it to meet all our very specific needs, and then have carefully vetted friends to stay for long and hopefully deeply satisfying weekends. I'm selling my share of The Dining Club to Louise. She deserves a stake in it – she's been running it without any help from me for the past few months, and doing a very good job as well.'

'And the hotel?' asked Grace.

David looked slightly uncomfortable. 'Yes, I was coming to that. I think the hotel was a brilliant idea, and clearly it's going to make money, but I'm not sure you should be involved in it any more. I'm often abroad and you're too vulnerable running it without a man in the background.'

'But Andrew's always there.'

'Perhaps I don't want Andrew always there for you.'

'But I love the hotel. It's all my own work. I created it, and everyone who's visited it has said how amazing it is. I don't want to give it up.'

'Then you'll have to buy it from me, because I'm putting it up for sale,' said David.

Grace looked at him in stunned disbelief. 'You can't do that!'

'I'm afraid I can. The deeds are in my name. I bought it and I can sell it. Grace, this is for your own good. What would have happened if I hadn't been around when Lucien kidnapped you? I know you don't want to think about it but he and Amber didn't care how much they hurt you in order to get what they wanted.'

'You've dealt with them now. They won't – can't – ever come back here, and who else would do such a thing?'

'Grace, you don't get to where I am in business without making a lot of enemies,' he said patiently. 'Until I met you, I didn't have a weak spot they could use against me, but now I do, and in time some of them will try. The way you and I choose to live our lives leaves us open to the kind of thing that's already happened, and I need to know that you're always safe.'

'And my directing work?'

'I keep telling you we're not going to live in Oxfordshire, we're staying in London. I assume you can manage the journey from Primrose Hill to The Globe?'

'Of course I can. There's no need to be sarcastic.'

'Then I fail to see what the problem is.'

'The problem,' said Grace, taking her courage in both hands, 'is that I don't know what the future holds for us. You've never spoken about it, and even today you didn't introduce me as your partner when talking to the estate agent. You're planning a whole new life, and an exciting one, which includes me at the moment, but for how long? And what happens to me if you meet someone more interesting, or exciting and want them to move into your house at Primrose Hill? Suppose you find initiating Suki into your world develops into something deeper? What happens to me then?'

David frowned. 'I don't think—'

'You never have,' said Grace, her voice gentle now. 'It's not your fault, it's the way you've always lived your life, but I need to know because I already love you too much, and all these changes are designed to make me love you more. I'm not saying you did that deliberately, but I know it will happen. I'm not like you, David. I'm beginning to think I need more than you can give me emotionally.'

'Grace, that's not fair. I've never loved anyone as much as I love you.'

'I believe you, but you may well love someone more than me one day, because you don't love me enough to commit yourself to me even verbally. I don't want a big white wedding, or a huge engagement ring, but I need to know that at this moment you believe that you're going to love me and stay with me for the rest of your life, and you can't say that, can you? You simply can't make yourself speak the words I need to hear.'

'And because of that you're willing to walk away from everything I had planned for us?' he asked incredulously.

'I have to walk away now, or you'll destroy me,' she said. 'Please, can we get back to London? I'll stay at the hotel tonight.'

David's face was ashen, but he nodded, pushed back his chair and while he paid the bill she got into the passenger seat of his car and wept hot tears of despair because clearly, despite what she'd said, he was still unable to offer her the security that she needed. 'I can't bear it,' she whispered to herself. 'How will I ever manage to live without him, and all he's brought into my life?'

Even though he must have realised she'd been crying, David didn't comment on it. When they reached the hotel he leant across and opened the passenger door for her. 'Goodnight, Gracie,' he said quickly and then he was gone.

Chapter Three

Late the following morning, David arrived at the bungalow he'd bought for his parents in Surrey five years earlier. He'd never been there, and hadn't seen them for so many years that he could scarcely remember what they looked like. Climbing out of the car he felt physically sick, and the palms of his hands were damp. Leaving the car in the lane outside, he walked up the short, gravelled drive and rang the doorbell.

The man who eventually opened it was a stranger to him, a frail stooped man, who looked far older than the late sixties David knew him to be. 'Hello, Dad,' said David.

His father looked at him in disbelief. 'David?'

'Yes, I was in the area so I thought I'd call in – if that's all right,' he added when his father continued to stand in the doorway blocking his entrance.

'Yes, yes of course. It's just a shock after all this time. Of course we've had your postcards, and you arranged for us to have this lovely bungalow but ... '

'But you didn't expect me to turn up like this.'

'No,' said his father awkwardly. 'I confess I didn't. Come in now, come through. It's all a bit of a mess, I'm afraid. I'll put the kettle on.'

David wasn't sure which of the two of them was the most uncomfortable, and he sat in a chair in the bungalow's living room looking out at a view of the South Downs and let his father potter around in the kitchen making them tea. Something stronger would have been more helpful, he thought to himself.

When his father returned with a tray holding two cups of tea and some chocolate biscuits, David tried hard to reconcile this prematurely old man with the father he remembered. 'Where's Mother?' he asked, taking one of the cups and a biscuit. 'In bed as usual?'

'She's in a home,' said his father, his voice expressionless.

David stared at him. 'A care home?'

'Yes, in a way.'

'Well, either it is or it isn't.'

'She has problems, David. She's always had problems, only now they're too much for me to cope with. I did my best, but she needs specialist care, and it's a very nice home. You could come with me to visit her later if you want.'

David's mouth tightened. 'No thanks, that's something I definitely don't want to do.'

His father sighed. 'So, why have you come here after all these years? Not out of love, that's obvious. You've done well for yourself. Your mother and I have kept track of you through the newspapers when we could, and we were very proud.'

'I'm quite sure Mother wasn't,' said David, trying not to sound bitter.

'Always hard to tell with her,' admitted his father.

'Yes.'

There was an awkward silence. 'So, nice as it is to see you, why have you come?' his father persisted. His mind was clearly sharper than his appearance suggested.

'I needed to see you both again, to try to learn something, but if Mother isn't here, that won't be possible.'

'I told you, you can come and visit her with me.'

'No! I needed to see you together. I wanted to try to understand what happened to make you the way you were.'

His father frowned. 'Make me the way I was?'

'Not just you, the two of you. You gave up everything for her. She manipulated you all the time, keeping your friends away, pretending to be too ill to do anything and making you stay at home with her when you weren't at work. Even then she did nothing but make scenes and complain. She took your life away from you, and you went along with it. Why? Is that what love does? Did you love her so much that you let her change you into some kind of ghost person, a shadow of the man she must have fallen in love with?'

'Why do you need to know? Why dig all that up after such a long time?'

'Because it's made me who I am. That's been good up to a point, but now I need to be different, to allow myself to trust that loving someone won't ruin me in the way it ruined you, and I can't take that step.'

'You were such an observant little boy,' mused his father, 'always watching how people behaved, and later a very judgemental child. I used to worry about you, and it seems I was right, but I didn't know what to do.'

'You could have stood up to her. Or were you afraid that then she'd stop loving you, if she ever did in the first place?' he added sharply.

'She didn't,' said his father quietly. 'That was the whole point, David. Your mother didn't love me. She loved someone else, someone who scared her and let her down very badly, but I was there in the background to help her pick up the pieces when her life fell apart. I wanted to do that, because I loved her so much, and until then she'd barely acknowledged my existence.'

'So you helped her and she punished you for it?'

'She was never the same after what happened to her.'

'What did happen?'

His father hesitated. 'It's not my story to tell, but you must remember that things were different when she and I were young. It was a more innocent time. Some of the things that are apparently totally acceptable these days weren't even known about by most people back then. If bad things happened, they were hidden away, and you had to pretend they hadn't happened and get on with your life, but she couldn't do it. She'd lost her ability to trust, you see, and became frightened of life.'

'Too frightened of it even to be a decent mother?'

'She tried, and when you were tiny I think she was

happier than I'd seen her for a long time, but as you grew older she couldn't cope with you. You weren't an easy child.'

'So it was my fault?' he interrupted sharply.

'Of course not. All I'm saying is that she became frightened again, scared that she'd do something wrong. She wanted to be a good mother but she realised she wasn't. She couldn't control you, and that's why we sent you away to boarding school when you were quite young. It was for your sake, not for hers.'

'And you went along with that?'

'I loved her,' said his father simply, 'and when you love someone you do all you can to protect them and make their lives happy.'

'She mattered more to you than I did, then?'

'It wasn't that simple. I thought that what we did was best for you both, and when you consider what you've achieved in your life, I don't think it was such a bad decision.'

David shook his head. 'You have absolutely no idea what you're talking about. You spent the whole of your married life caring for your wife's emotional needs but never caring for your child's.'

His father nodded. 'I can see that. In fact, I suppose

I knew it long before you'd even finished your education. I'm sorry.'

'Sorry? You should be bloody ashamed of yourself. And why didn't you get Mother some kind of psychiatric help earlier if you knew she was so damaged? Why did you let what had happened to her damage me too?'

'I only wanted . . .'

And suddenly David knew exactly why his father hadn't protected him. 'You liked her needing you, didn't you? You didn't care about me, or anyone else. You enjoyed keeping her dependent on you, being the only person who could calm her down and by the sound of it making sure she remained sane. You needed to be sure the woman you loved wouldn't ever leave you, so you chose someone needy and then made sure they didn't have the opportunity to learn to be independent. You were an enabler, keeping her imprisoned in some kind of mental hell that almost certainly could have been helped if she'd seen the right professionals.'

'So now that's my fault?'

'Yes!' exclaimed David. 'I never realised it before, but it's the truth. She was broken, and you made sure she never had the chance to be mended. You were the one who was sick, not her. And now that she's had to go into a home, you're a shadow of your old self, because you don't have her here, depending on you, needing you, making you feel good about yourself.'

His father stood up. 'Well, you drove here because you wanted answers, and you think you've accomplished that. Will it help you with your dilemma? I doubt it.'

'You're wrong,' said David. 'I always thought that by marrying Mother you gave up everything, and let her change you. I felt sorry for you because it seemed that love had taken everything away from you, but you chose her because originally she rejected you. Then, when she did turn to you she was so damaged that you were able to make quite sure she would never be well enough to choose to leave you.'

'And that doesn't worry you? That someone you love deeply – if indeed you're capable of the kind of love I felt for your mother – might one day choose to walk away from you?'

David shook his head. 'No, that's a risk everyone takes by committing to a relationship. What I feared was something that actually never even happened, and I don't need to worry because I'm nothing like you at all.'

Without another word, David walked out of the bungalow and back to his car.

The ageing man watched him drive away with relief. He'd always hated David; had never got over the thought of another man's seed forcing its way into what was his, delivering him a child he didn't even want. With any luck he would never have to see the boy again. Unable to hold back, he shouted after him, 'Of course you're nothing like me at all. There's no reason why you should be. And if you're like your father, I pity any woman stupid enough to fall for your charms.'

Then, with keen anticipation, he went to get ready to visit his wife, sitting waiting helplessly in her small room on the top floor of her decidedly utilitarian care home, the home that David had thankfully decided not to visit, waiting for the man she'd never loved to come and visit her.

By six o'clock that evening, Grace still hadn't heard a word from David. She'd kept herself busy by making phone calls to work colleagues, going over the list of bookings for the following month for the hotel – which only reminded her that David intended to sell it – and going in to The Globe to talk to some of their practitioners, but nothing could distract her from what was really on her mind. The prospect of a future without David.

She couldn't even remember what her world had been like before she'd started going out with him. He'd become so much a part of the fabric of her life that by leaving him she knew she would destroy something unique, something that she would never find with any other man. Yet she had no choice, because the more he drew her into his world, the more he allowed her to get close to him by including her in everything he did, the greater the pain would be when he finally tired of her.

She loved him, and wanted the security of knowing that he loved her enough to plan not just a few years but a life together, and the previous day she'd seen from the look in his eyes that this wasn't going to happen. For him, the commitment of the house in the country and a shared home in Primrose Hill were enough. Either he didn't understand why she needed more or – and she suspected this was the truth – he was unable to give her more.

She was standing in the hallway, wondering what to do about dinner that evening, when he walked into her beloved hotel, the hotel he'd so casually decided to sell.

'I hoped I'd find you here,' he said, giving her a hug and then stroking the side of her face while looking intently into her eyes. 'I hope you haven't been overdoing it.'

'No,' she said shortly.

'I've booked a table for the two of us for dinner tonight at eight thirty. It's a small restaurant, but the food's excellent.'

Grace didn't know what to say. He was behaving as though nothing had happened the previous day. 'I'm not sure,' she confessed. 'I'm still upset after yesterday.'

'That's why I want us to go out. We need to talk. Is it all right if I go up and shower? I seem to have spent half of the day driving and I need to get washed and changed.'

'You can do what you like. As you pointed out to me, you own the hotel,' Grace retorted. David gave her a quick sideways glance but didn't answer. Instead, he hurried up the stairs, taking them two at a time, and leaving her even more confused than before.

The table he'd booked was in a secluded corner of the restaurant, and Grace couldn't help noticing how hand-some he was compared to the other men in the room. His blue eyes seemed extra bright tonight, and when he smiled at her across the table her stomach turned over with excitement. Shamefully, all she could think about was how much she wanted him to make love to her later on.

David cleared his throat and took a sip of his wine. 'I went to see my parents today,' he said casually.

'You did what?' she exclaimed.

'I went to see my parents,' he repeated with unusual patience. 'Only my father was there, though. My mother's in some kind of home. She's apparently always suffered from her nerves.'

Grace didn't dare speak. He never discussed his parents, and she was afraid that if she said anything he'd stop now, although she sensed that whatever he was leading up to was important to him.

He shifted uneasily in his seat. 'I need to tell you this, because all my life I've been worried that I'd end up like them. Their marriage wasn't, shall we say, a good advert for the institution. I watched my mother destroy my father, or so I thought, and I vowed I would never let it happen to me. This morning, I learnt that things aren't always what they seem. She didn't destroy him. He was happy.'

The waiter put their meals in front of them and David waited until he'd gone before continuing. 'It's complicated,' he said after the pause. 'In some ways, it's quite frightening.'

'Why?' asked Grace softly.

'To realise that I got everything so wrong.'

'I don't think any of us can ever hope to understand how other people's relationships work, least of all our parents' relationship,' said Grace. 'It's difficult enough coping with our own, and most of us just accept our parents as being normal.'

'Quite, and I vowed that if what I saw was normal then I didn't ever want it,' replied David.

Grace saw how tightly he was gripping his knife and fork. 'That was their life. You can live yours any way you want to live it,' she said gently.

'I hope so, Grace, I really do, because otherwise I'm going to lose you and I don't think I could cope with that.' Grace sat quite still, unable to believe what she was hearing. 'That's why I had to go to see them, because after last night I realised that unless I changed, you were going to leave me and all my plans, everything that had seemed so exciting ... well, none of it was going to mean anything without you. It would be pointless.'

There was a long silence after he'd finished speaking.

'I've been as unhappy as you today,' she confessed at

last. 'I love you, David, and I know that I always will. No matter what happens, no one will ever make me as happy as you've made me.'

Leaning across the table he put a hand over hers. 'Don't talk about us as though it's all in the past. Surely you understand what I'm telling you. I want you to marry me, Grace.'

She was so shocked that she couldn't think of anything to say. She simply stared at him in disbelief. 'You don't need to do this,' she said at last. 'I wasn't asking for marriage, just a commitment of some kind.'

'It's the biggest commitment I can think of,' he said with a half-smile. 'Gracie, it's what I want. Together we can have a wonderful life. You've seen The Hall, and I'll show you the house in Primrose Hill. We can entertain like-minded friends at both places, but The Hall will be perfect for carefully planned entertainment. And as my wife, you'll be safe. I don't ever want to see you hurt again.'

'And my work?'

'You know how much I travel, how busy I am. I don't want you to change. All I want is to give you what you quite rightly told me you needed: the proof that I love you, and that I want you to be part of my future.'

'I don't know what to say,' Grace admitted.

'I'm no good at this, am I?' asked David. 'I should probably be reciting poetry, or talking about a future full of beautiful children, but I'm not. That's not me, and neither is it how I want to live my life, but you know that. If you do want something different I'll understand, but if not then let's get married and move on to the next stage of our lives together.'

Grace didn't know whether to laugh or cry. 'I don't need poetry, or a future full of beautiful children, all I need is you, David. You're all I want and all I'll ever want, so yes, I'll marry you.'

Pushing his chair away from the table, David stood up and caught hold of her by the wrist. 'Let's go,' he said, ignoring the uneaten food and the surprised expression on the faces of the waiters. He whisked her out of the restaurant and into the back of the car where the chauffeur was already waiting behind the wheel, and within seconds they were on their way back to the hotel.

They went straight to the bedroom and for over an hour he kept her on the verge of a climax, repeatedly taking her right to the very edge, then stopping and waiting until her body calmed down before beginning again. She heard herself scream with frustration and sob with frantic need, but still he refused her the ultimate pleasure until he finally pulled her trembling, sweat-soaked body onto his naked thighs, with her back to him so that his long, knowing fingers could continue to caress her clitoris while he was inside her.

Her shout of delight as her body convulsed with ecstasy was followed within seconds by his groan of relief as he spilled himself inside her, before wrapping his arms around her and pulling her down onto the bed with him.

Grace fell asleep immediately, but in the early hours of the morning he woke her and as she sleepily opened her eyes he tied her hands and ankles to the corners of the bed, so that she lay spread-eagled, her body still warm from sleep. Then he proceeded to kiss and caress every inch of her using only his lips and tongue, until she was straining against her bonds, thrusting her hips upwards as every nerve ending in her body clamoured for release from the constant stimulation.

'You still have a lot to learn,' he murmured, as she tried to push her lower body up against his teasing tongue. 'The more you try to make yourself come quicker, the longer I'm going to make you wait.'

Grace felt the familiar rush of mingled excitement,

aching need and desire for satisfaction from this incredibly complex man she was now committing herself to for life. 'I need to come,' she beseeched him, as the ache in her engorged pelvis grew ever greater. 'It's painful now. Please, David, don't make me wait any longer.'

He ran the tip of one finger over her tense nipples and she drew in her breath sharply. 'How I love to hear you beg,' he murmured. 'You've come so far, but I can take you much further in the future. It will be wonderful. Just imagine the pleasure that lies ahead for you, my darling.'

When he pressed the heel of his hand deeply into the soft flesh above her pubic bone she gasped as she felt her orgasm flickering deep behind her clitoris. 'I'm going to come!' she whispered. 'I can't stop it if you keep doing that.'

His blue eyes darkened with excitement. 'Then that's something we can work on during our honeymoon,' he murmured, keeping the pressure up, and just as she'd known would happen, Grace's body was swept by a hot, searing climax that spread throughout her entire body and the restraints dug tightly into her ankles and wrists as her body twisted and arched, so that despite the pleasure there was the pain of her bound flesh.

'I love you so much,' she whispered as he untied her. 'What would I do without you?'

'You'll never be without me,' he promised, holding her sweat-soaked body close to him. 'Sleep now. Tomorrow we have a lot to organise.'

Chapter Four

'Is everything ready?' asked David, adjusting his tie as he glanced out of the drawing room at the front of The Hall in Oxfordshire, watching for the first of their guests to arrive.

'Everything,' said Grace, her backless, halter-neck dress just brushing the carpet as she crossed the room to join him.

He stroked her exposed flesh, tanned from their three-week honeymoon staying at the Cipriani in Venice, set on an island in the Venetian lagoon, that had followed their quiet register office wedding attended only by two of David's employees as witnesses. He'd been adamant that he didn't want any fuss, and it hadn't mattered to Grace either, as both her parents were dead, and now that she and Fran had drifted apart she didn't have any really close friends. In any case, all she wanted was to be his wife, and she was well aware that David's decision to keep it low-key was mainly based on his continuing concern for her safety.

'Such well-disguised decadence,' he murmured as his fingers continued to linger, straying into the cleft at the base of her spine until she shivered with delight. 'And the staff are all satisfactory?'

Grace nodded, remembering the long hours she'd spent tutoring the young men and women who would help make their first weekend party a success, as well as ensuring that they would always know what they had to do during the future parties she and David planned to hold in their country retreat. 'I wish you'd been able to be here more,' she added. 'You would have enjoyed it.'

'I've already enjoyed watching the film of you and Andrew training them,' he replied.

She looked at him in surprise. 'What film?'

'I had a recorder in the playroom, so that I didn't miss anything. Kirsten fascinates me. So much talent but at the moment far too much attitude.'

'I thought you'd enjoy subduing that,' said Grace.

'Clever girl,' he murmured, pressing himself against her back, moulding their bodies together until she could feel his hardness.

'I hope Suki won't panic,' continued Grace. 'Andrew believes she's ready but ...'

'I trust his judgement, although no doubt we'll have some interesting moments over the weekend. You're sure you don't mind Louise and her partner coming?'

'Quite sure,' said Grace, who might once have worried, but now that they were married felt far more secure than she had before.

'What are you thinking?' he asked.

'About the weekend. I just hope it all goes well.'

'I'm sure it will. Here's Andrew's car now,' he said. 'I'll let them in, darling.'

When the six of them sat down to dinner that evening, Andrew looked across the table at Grace. 'I can't believe all that's happened in such a short space of time,' he said with a laugh. 'Who would have thought that David would get married, sell the Club and the hotel, buy a house in the country and move to Primrose Hill in only six months? Don't you miss the hotel, Grace?'

'Not really. It was all getting a little too much on top

of my directing work. And as it was sold to a friend of David's all the care I lavished on it won't be wasted! Incidentally, I hope no one minds having a light evening meal, only tonight's entertainment is quite energetic.'

'I don't mind,' said Suki, smiling at David. 'I'm on a fitness regime, so it suits me.'

'Are you indeed? And what are you getting fit for – a marathon?'

She shook her head. 'I just thought I needed to get more supple, and as Andrew runs a gym and seems to spend half his life there, it's one way of spending time with him.'

David glanced at Louise. 'And how fit do you think you are, Louise?'

The honey-coloured blonde pushed her hair behind her ears and pulled a face. 'Not very,' she said regretfully. 'I hate exercising. It's so boring.'

'We have a games room here,' said Grace. 'I've really enjoyed fitting it out, so hopefully you'll find something you do enjoy doing there.'

'I'm sure I will,' she agreed, and her partner James laughed.

'You don't agree?' asked David, his eyes bright at the prospect of what this might mean.

'Not if it's very physical,' replied James, and then the talk turned to the renovating of The Hall, and Grace and David's honeymoon and the subject was dropped.

It was nearly ten o'clock before they all went to the playroom, and when Suki saw the array of large balls, wall bars and bikes with high saddles, she gave a big smile. 'It's a gym, not a playroom!' she exclaimed.

David closed the heavy doors behind them all. 'No, Suki, it's a playroom,' he said gently and as two young men moved towards the small, dark-haired young woman and Kirsten appeared from out of the shadows, Suki's eyes widened and she caught hold of Andrew's arm. 'What's happening? I enjoy what we do together, but I don't think I want ...'

Grace watched David cross the room, take her gently by the hand and lead her towards one of the large rubber balls. 'Come along, you'll be fine. We're all going to have a lot of fun. Andrew will be here, and I'll help you too. Kirsten will take off your clothes and then you can bend over the ball until the back of your head is nearly touching the ground. Louise will show you how, won't you, Louise?'

As his former PA took off her clothes and draped herself naked over the ball, so that her perfect breasts were pointing towards the ceiling, Suki started to back away and Kirsten hesitated, glancing at Grace for guidance.

Grace was also unexpectedly unsure what was expected of her, feeling a pang of pity for Suki, but then she saw David watching her and remembered that her role in these games was different from her role when she'd first met him. It was up to her to make their weekend dinner parties enjoyable, because she was the hostess, and that was partly why David had chosen her. She knew that it was important not to spoil things for him, especially this first time, and she wanted it all to go well too.

'It's all right, Suki,' she said, 'you'll enjoy yourself, I promise you. Just do as you're told, watch and listen to Louise, and then it will be your turn to have fun. Isn't that right, Andrew?'

Andrew nodded, but his attention seemed to be on Louise, who was already being stroked and massaged by one of the young men Grace had trained so assiduously.

'I'm not letting them touch me,' said Suki, backing away from Andrew, but David blocked her path.

'Try not to spoil the party, or you won't be able to come here with Andrew again,' he said softly. 'Come

391

along, let me get you started.' And with that he was
taking off her short summer dress and bikini pants
before bending her backwards over the second ball.

As Louise started to moan with pleasure, Grace set
the hands of the large wall clock moving. 'You both
have to wait fifteen minutes to climax,' she said, and
then turned her gaze back to where Suki's slender form
was being caressed and aroused by David.

Soon she too was gasping with excitement, and
although Grace saw David wipe a stray tear gently from
the young, dark-haired girl's face, she never spoke the
safe word all the women had been given before the
games began. She could tell that Suki, probably because
of the mixture of fear and excitement, was very close to
an orgasm and sure enough before the fifteen minutes
was up she gave a tiny moan and her small frame
shook.

David's hands kept her pinned to the large ball. 'I'm
afraid you'll have to be punished,' he said regretfully,
and at a signal from Grace, Kirsten quickly stepped forward with a slender whip in her hand, which she used
to strike Suki's unprotected pale breasts, causing the girl
to cry out in protest. 'Do you want to stop?' asked
David gently, but Suki shook her head. 'In that case,

watch how Grace controls herself, and then you may try again. Andrew has assured us you're a quick learner. Let's hope for your sake he's right.'

Suki's cheeks were flushed, and every time she looked at David she blushed even more, so Grace knew that she found him attractive. All the same, it was Andrew who put an arm round her, idly playing with her breasts as Grace slipped out of her dress and lowered herself backwards in an arch until the middle of her back was over the ball. 'I think you need rather more stimulation than a beginner,' murmured David, and to Grace's dismay he moved her legs even wider apart and then began to use his tongue between her outspread thighs, and now the second clock was started and her own delicious torment began.

To her relief she survived the fifteen minutes, and as she was helped to her feet by James, Andrew glanced at the wall bars. 'I hope we're going to use those,' he said, and David nodded.

'Of course, if that's what you'd like to do. We'll get the three girls up there and the one who asks to be taken down last is the winner.'

'Brilliant!' said Andrew, putting his arms round Suki's waist and lifting her up with her back against the wall bars before fastening her there with one of the leather belts hanging waiting for just such a game. Within seconds he'd had fastened her wrists and ankles to the bars as well, while David did the same for Louise.

It was left to James to secure Grace firmly, putting her in the middle of the two other young women. 'I wish I could take a photo!' he exclaimed, and Grace knew that David was almost certainly filming the scene, although James would never get to watch it.

'Can we put blindfolds on them?' he continued. 'That will make it more difficult for them, because they won't know what's going to happen so can't start controlling their bodies until the moment they're touched.'

'Great idea!' agreed Andrew, opening cupboard doors to find some black velvet masks.

To her surprise, Grace felt her whole body break out in a cold sweat. She didn't think she could bear to be masked again, despite what she'd done at David's club. All she could think about was her ordeal at the hands of Lucien and Amber, and she bit on her bottom lip to stop herself from crying out. She saw David watching her from the other side of the room, a look of concern on his face. 'If the girls agree,' he said at last.

'They have to agree,' Andrew pointed out. 'They're our playthings this evening, isn't that right?'

Now Grace was in a total panic. If she refused, then the whole evening would be ruined and it would be her fault.

'True, but I think we should each be allowed to work on our own partners,' said David. 'After all, we know them best, so we should be the ones able to make it the most difficult for them to outlast the other two.'

'And we can punish them if they fail,' said James.

'Of course,' agreed David. 'Andrew, pass me a blind-fold.

'I'm so sorry, Grace, I was worried your recovery was too quick,' whispered David as he slowly moved the velvet mask over her eyes while she struggled to supress a cry of terror. 'Remember, it's only me touching you, just as it was last time, and it will all be pleasurable, but if you can't cope then ask to be freed.'

'Time to begin,' said Andrew, and as Grace shook with terror, David's hands moved slowly over her neck and shoulders, stroking and soothing her as though she were a frightened animal until her trembling eased and her breathing began to return to normal.

All the same, the moment he attempted to arouse her by squeezing her breasts before using his tongue on her nipples, she knew that she couldn't do it. 'I want to get down,' she whimpered.

'Just say it loud enough for the others to hear, and you'll be free in seconds,' murmured David.

'I want to be untied,' she said loudly, and even before he unfastened her wrists and ankles, David removed the mask and kissed her softly on the mouth. She saw Andrew, who was pleasuring Suki with a long feather, while her swollen, engorged breasts were circled in leather rings with nipple clamps on both of them, glance across at her in sympathy.

James, who had one hand between Louise's thighs and the other behind her as he stimulated the thin walls of her rectum, was too busy enjoying Louise's moans to take any notice, but all the same Grace felt ashamed at her failure.

Unsurprisingly it was Louise who won, and as James kissed and hugged her, Andrew had no sooner taken Suki off the wall bars than he positioned her with the palms of her hands flat on the floor, her head hanging back as he lifted her beneath her hips and pushed himself into her. The rush of blood to Suki's head added to the thrill of what was happening to her and her shout of pleasure suggested it wasn't an entirely unenjoyable punishment, despite the fact that they were being watched.

From the moment he'd taken her off the wall bars, David kept Grace close to him. He caressed and kissed her body, fondled her between her thighs until despite what had happened she felt herself growing moist, and every now and then he would squeeze her nipples firmly, using two fingers like scissors, and twice she shook with pleasure as tiny orgasms rippled through her now partially relaxed body.

It was gone midnight before everyone grew tired and they all went to their rooms. 'I'm sorry about tonight, Grace,' Andrew said quietly as he kissed her goodnight. 'That bloody Lucien has a lot to answer for.'

'I'm afraid it was my fault,' said David, well aware of how sensitive Grace was about her ordeal. 'I think I wore her out before any of you arrived. I forget we're not on our honeymoon any more!'

Andrew smiled. 'In that case, lucky you! Goodnight, then, can't wait for tomorrow.'

Once upstairs in their bedroom, Grace immediately ran herself a bath and let the warm water wash over her body, hoping it would eventually wash away all the bad memories as well. Eventually, David came through to join her.

'I was afraid you'd drowned!' he joked, but his eyes weren't laughing. 'Grace, you need to come to bed. I'm sorry about tonight, and I'll make sure it never happens again.'

'But I don't want bad memories to spoil things for us,' she cried. 'I used to be nervous of being blindfolded, not knowing where I'd next be touched and aroused, but I grew to love it. And now it won't be the same for us, if you have to keep being careful of what trials you choose, or what we do alone together.'

David perched on the side of the bath. 'It's early days, Grace, and you won't always feel like this. If you like we can work on getting you back to where you were. You can start by keeping your eyes closed sometimes, and then I'll put a white mask on you that lets in a little light, until you're finally comfortable with being masked again. You were taken by surprise this evening, that's all, and I should never have put any masks in the drawers. It was stupid of me. There are so many things we can do, and games we can play. So many exciting things lie ahead for us, and you're adapting to your new role very well.

'I'm your husband, I'm not going to let what happened to you ruin things you enjoy, but it's also my job to protect you, and tonight I failed. I'm sorry about that, and it won't happen again.'

'I didn't know it would happen,' she said quietly. 'It was a big shock to me, so don't blame yourself. You're right, with your help I'll soon stop being afraid, and in time I'll forget it ever happened.'

David raised his eyebrows. 'Really? Well, even if you do, I can assure you that I'll never forget and neither will I ever forgive. Wherever those two go, I always have someone watching them, and they know this now, so unlike you they'll never stop being afraid. Now, come out of that bath and let me dry you. We need to get some sleep before tomorrow.'

As Grace drifted off to sleep, she kept remembering the way David had said 'I'm your husband', and she gave a sigh of pure happiness.

The next days they all spent a lot of time in the pool, and Suki cried out and struggled when David held her up in the water, playing with her body while Andrew entered her, and he punished her when she protested that she didn't want James touching her. However, by the end of the weekend she was learning fast, and every time David praised her she would smile her open smile, the delight plain on her face.

On Sunday night, when the maids were helping the guests to pack ready to leave, Grace found herself alone with Andrew in the walled garden at the back of the house.

'So, are you finally happy?' he asked her. 'Has marrying David made you feel secure, convinced that he's committed to you for life?'

'Yes, of course,' she said with total confidence.

He nodded. 'I'm sure you're right. We were all amazed, but he does love you, Grace, as much as he's capable of loving anyone, which is all that can really be asked of any of us.'

She sat down on a stone bench. 'I love this house and I love my husband,' she assured him.

'But ... ?'

'Does there have to be a "but"?'

'I think that except in fairy stories there's always a "but",' he said with a sigh.

'Perhaps. Possibly I underestimated my own capacity for jealousy,' she admitted.

'You must never let him know that,' exclaimed Andrew. 'For his sake and your own.'

'I know,' said Grace quietly, 'and I never will. I just never expected to feel that way again, especially as I know there's no need.'

Later, when she and David had waved their guests off, he sank into one of the deep armchairs and gave a sigh of contentment. 'Brandy, darling?'

'Lovely,' she agreed.

'You know, I think we're going to have a very interesting time educating Suki, don't you? You and Kirsten will get even better at punishing her failures as we progress, and that will add to the excitement.'

'And what happens when her education is over?' asked Grace.

'Hopefully Andrew will benefit and of course we'll move on to new guests. Andrew will always be our friend, and I'm sure he'll bring interesting new people to meet us from time to time. Who knows, perhaps one day he'll even win your friend Fran back and bring her here. That would be really interesting. In any case, I have a wide circle of acquaintances who'll provide entertainment whenever we feel the need. Apart from the incident with the mask, did you enjoy it?'

'Of course I did, although . . . ' She hesitated.

'Go on,' he urged her. 'We have to be honest with each other.'

'Sometimes, watching you with Suki as she struggled to obey orders, I wished that I could swap places with her,' she said. 'I suddenly wanted to be as innocent as her again, and have our early days together back once more.'

'But then I wouldn't love you,' he said gently. 'There are many, many young women like Suki, darling. They come and go and after a time they're forgotten. Someone like you appears once in a lifetime, and I was very lucky to meet you.'

'But what if you get bored with all this?' she asked. 'How long will erotic weekends on a country estate hold your interest?'

He shrugged. 'Who knows? At the moment it seems a good life, but if I should get bored then I'll buy a place abroad, Italy perhaps. We'll hold decadent masked balls and throw lavish parties three or four times a year when we're not working. There's no limit to the human imagination, Grace, and you have nothing to fear. You're my wife and I love you deeply. Let's go to bed. You were a brilliant hostess, and I was very proud of you, so I think you should be allowed to choose your own reward.'

As he smiled at her Grace finally knew with absolute certainty that everything was going to be all right, and at the thought of choosing her own reward she felt her skin tingle with excitement. 'I love you too,' she whispered, and together they went up the wide staircase to bed, where she claimed her reward before they fell into an exhausted sleep with David's arms wound tightly round his beautiful, sensual and deeply loved wife.

Epilogue

'It's agreed then,' said Lucien, shaking hands with an older, distinguished-looking Englishman, whose brown hair was flecked with grey at the temples. 'Amber and I will keep your Club going while you're away, and you're happy with our plans for expanding it too, at our own expense, of course.' The man nodded.

'Why are you leaving Morocco?' Amber asked the gentleman. 'You've got a beautiful home and an incredible and flourishing nightclub here.'

'I'm bored,' he said curtly, 'and I need to try to track someone down in England. It will take me a long time, and unfortunately it's highly doubtful that I'll succeed, in which case our preliminary discussions about plans for you to buy me out will come into operation.'

'His loss is our gain,' said Lucien, the moment the owner was out of earshot. 'We've really fallen on our feet here, Amber. We can make this place the most exotic in the whole of Morocco. It's going to be incredibly exciting. I can't wait to make a start on retraining the staff, and I'm sure you can't either.'

'I bet he was very good-looking once,' said Amber, who'd been watching the man make his way towards a waiting car. 'Very cold, of course, but then I've always found that strangely attractive. Did you notice his eyes? He looks so like David ...'

Lucien turned to catch another glimpse of the man, but he was too late. The stranger who he was certain was going to be their salvation, had already been driven away.

The
Dining
Club

THE
COMPLETE
NOVEL

Heat things up this winter!

MARINA
ANDERSON
THE SUNDAY TIMES BESTSELLER

You are invited to the Dining Club.
If you pass the challenges we set,
a world of pleasure awaits you.

He is everything she never wanted: brooding, secretive,
rich – and far-removed from her carefree artistic
lifestyle. Yet David has a power over Grace that
she cannot resist, a power that comes from
his darker, passionate side.

And now he is ready to truly reveal himself. Inviting
Grace to a weekend at the Dining Club, David offers her
the opportunity to discover his deepest desires and to find
pleasures far beyond her wildest imagination – but only
if she is willing to play a series of sensual games.

Grace faces a choice: give in to her doubts and retreat to
her quiet life, or truly embrace happiness with David
and win over her mesmerising lover for ever.

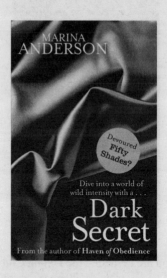

MARINA
ANDERSON

Devoured
Fifty
Shades?

Dive into a world of
wild intensity with a . . .

Dark
Secret

From the author of Haven *of* Obedience

Harriet Radcliffe is bored with her life. At twenty-three,
her steady job and safe engagement seem very dull.
If she is to inject a little excitement into her life,
she realises, now is the time to do it.

But the excitement lying in wait for Harriet is
beyond even her wildest ambitions. Answering a job
advertisement to assist a world-famous actress, Harriet
finds herself plunged into an intense and secret world of
sexual obsession – playing an unwitting part in a very
private drama, but discovering in the process more about
her own desires than she had ever dreamed possible . . .

MARINA
ANDERSON

Devoured
Fifty
Shades?

Experience a place like no
other in the . . .
House *of*
Decadence
From the author of **Haven** *of* **Obedience**

Megan Stewart feels that there should be more to
life than working in a library in her twenties, so she
answers an advert for a post in a country house –
and discovers what she has been missing.

Handsome Fabrizio Balocchi is far from his Tuscan home
and feeling bored. But he instinctively knows that Megan
will be a natural player in his games of domination
and step by step, he leads her into a darker world,
a world where pleasure is mixed with pain. Now
Megan must decide how far she is willing to go in
order to stay in Fabrizio's house of decadence . . .

MARINA
ANDERSON

Irresistible passions will be
awakened in . . .
Legacy *of*
Desire

From the author of **Haven** *of* **Obedience**

Davina Fletcher had a comfortable life and a comfortable
boyfriend until the death of her uncle changed all that.
As her home and artist's studio were in the grounds of
his house, it was always assumed she would inherit
everything. Instead she finds she has a new landlord
in the shape of tall, dark and handsome Jay Prescott,
an American lawyer with a taste for Davina's
paintings – and soon for Davina herself.

If she is to continue living at the house, Davina must
be obliging towards Jay, but she soon realises he has
an unconventional way of collecting the rent. In order
to keep her home she must be a player in his games,
but the power he wields over her is far stronger
than just that of landlord . . .